Black Diamonds

Vogue

Crown Jewelz Publishing

No One Is Invincible.

Black Diamonds
Part IV of The Diamond Collection

ISBN-13: 978-0-9888004-4-1
ISBN-10: 0988800446

Cover Design by Vogue

Website: www.simplyvogue.net
Email: blaq_pearls@yahoo.com; crownjewelzpub@gmail.com
Facebook: www.thefacebook.com/SimplyVogue (April Blanding)
Twitter: @SimplyVogue_B
Instagram: marilyn_monRHO1922

1

Trapped

Copperton City, Georgia

It could have been the swift movements of the car or even the light hum of the radio, which caused Kristian to stir. A thick aroma of vanilla and clove hung in the air; her nose sniffing the scent as she started to come to. Although her eyes were still firmly closed, she heard and felt enough to let her know she was in a moving vehicle. Now, she was listening to see if she and the driver were alone.

No one was talking or even moving. Her position told her there could possibly be three people in the vehicle—her, the driver, and another individual who was keeping watch. She was laid out flat on her stomach, the left side of her head faced downward. Her legs didn't hang off the seat, which meant she was probably in a limousine. She also knew no one was sitting beside her. When she heard a small exhale, she had the evidence she needed. The sound was familiar, which she instantly connected with the scent she smelled. A little more pleasurable than a cigarette, she attributed the smell to that of a cigar. When the person exhaled again, her eyes blinked several times before becoming wide open.

Darkness completely entrapped her until her eyes focused on her surroundings. The sky was murky, which told her it was nearing or slightly past midnight. In addition, they were passing barely lit streets. If it was indeed midnight then she had been gone from campus for a little over three hours.

That wasn't the mystery, though. The mystery started with her. She had to find out where she was and who she was with. She looked away from the window until she found herself staring at the bottom of a pair of black Mauri shoes. The person was wearing dress socks of the same color, and she quickly learned the other passenger was male. When she gazed upward, she noticed his hands were light in complexion and his wrist bore an Audemars Piguet watch, a clear sign of his wealth.

A slight exhale escaped the man's lips once more, prompting her attention. She turned to face him, meeting eyes with none other than Shawn Blumington or Blu for short. He was a known drug dealer who once claimed to be a part of the Santiago cartel. Months ago, on a previous encounter, Blu had expressed his displeasure of getting the boot. His pink slip had come from the hands of her mother's boyfriend, Jay Santiago, the cartel's boss. Blu had exhibited his revenge by sending a slew of his goons after Jay. Since he failed to kill him, she assumed Blu's new plan was to throw her in the mix. She had a biological connection to Jay's biggest and only love, Carmen Davenport, and Blu knew Jay would do anything to keep her mother in his arms.

"You're not far from home," he said, pulling the cigar from between his lips.

Kristian stared in horror as he spoke. His words flowed out in such a calm manner she wondered if he thought he had rescued her. Certain that wasn't the case, Kristian moved frantically to both sides of the limousine, trying the locks on both doors. Blu stayed put, not moving an inch because he knew the child safety locks were on. He also didn't speak when she made several pleas for help. A limo partition separated her from the driver who also ignored every word she uttered.

As a result, Kristian looked for anything she could use as a weapon. She came up short, wrapping her arms around herself as her anxiety increased. *This isn't happening, this isn't happening*, she repeated to herself. She rocked back and forth, pinching her arms, yet she didn't wake from the nightmare. In fact, it became more real. No longer moving, the limo was now parked in front of Soulshock, a soul food restaurant about eight minutes away from Copperfield University where she was currently enrolled. Kristian wasn't quite sure what was about to happen when she noticed the restaurant was pitch black on the inside. Her fear of the unknown forced her to gaze at Blu who now had a pistol resting in his lap.

"No problems, right?" he said right above a whisper. "You're going to cooperate?"

There was no longer an absence of tears as Kristian began to think the worse. With a gun in his hand, Blu now had complete control. Whatever he wanted, he could get. Kristian looked at him through her tears, the pistol now pointed directly at her. His left hand held it while the right one reached for the door handle. At that moment, she heard the child safety locks coming off. While her first thought was to exit out the other side, the image of the pistol reminded her she couldn't. The bullet would catch her before she made it to safety.

Blu waved the pistol in her direction, encouraging her to follow him. She did as he asked, noticing how deserted the area was. Not a single car passed them as they walked inside the dark restaurant.

Nonetheless, Blu seemed to know Soulshock like the back of his hand. He led them to the kitchen without error. "Did you miss me?" he asked, taking a quick look at her. "It's been awhile, Miss Kane. I guess you thought I had forgotten about you."

Kristian swallowed, the only reaction she gave. In their previous encounters, Blu had expressed his attraction, or better yet obsession with her. She had always made it known she wasn't interested yet he was a predator who would never break the pursuit.

"This is all business," he told her as they approached double doors. "Don't take it personal." He pushed open the door with his right hand while the left one pointed the pistol inside the room. Though it wasn't verbalized, the expression on his face said, *After you.*

Kristian hesitated for a few seconds only because the room he was leading her into was completely black. Her body stood there frozen until Blu waved the pistol in her face. Unable to see anything, she walked inside, listening carefully to Blu's movements. So far, the only thing she heard was the sound of the door closing behind him.

It was followed by a burst of light, stemming from a lit match. With light in the room, Kristian could see they were in a short corridor which was filled with boxes. A strong odor was in the area, prompting her to cover her nose. Since his hands were full, Blu couldn't do the same, proceeding to lead her down the corridor until they were at the far end of the hall. Now standing in front of another door, Kristian watched as he slid the pistol underneath his right armpit before retrieving a key. He unlocked the door in front of them, revealing a long set of steps, which led to the basement.

"Go ahead," he ordered, holding the match at eye level.

Kristian glared at the steps as she realized Blu's intent. He was holding her for ransom. He wanted her in the basement because he knew if she went down there, no one would find her until he was ready for them to. She would be solely in his possession until he got whatever he wanted from Jay. For all she knew, she could be down there for days, weeks, or even months.

The fear of being trapped made a series of thoughts form in her mind. One idea came into play. She latched her arm onto Blu's as she swung the match down onto his suit jacket. The flame lit quicker than she imagined, garnering an instant reaction. He shoved her into the open doorway and with a final thrust, pushed her down the flight of steps.

"You fuckin' bitch," he yelled as she tumbled down each one.

By the time she was at the bottom, her whole body had fallen numb. She closed her eyes tightly, moaning at the pain, barely hearing the footsteps that were coming towards her. Her eyes opened for only a quick second before closing back. Several seconds later, her eyes fully reopened. With the match and flames out, all she saw was darkness.

Then, she felt a gust of cold air on her skin from where Blu was standing directly over her. Moments later, the room became lit, revealing an empty space. Yet, it was the least of her concerns. A sharp pain was now shooting through her back, forcing her eyes shut. She started to see black again just as Blu grabbed her by her shirt, pulling her towards him. The scent of burning cotton filled her nostrils even more than the smell of cigar on his breath.

It was followed by the cold hard slap of Blu's hand across her face. She thought for sure he would kill her, but he didn't. Instead, he released her from his grasp before pulling on a shoestring, which was attached to the light fixture. He gave it a hard tug until it broke loose, sending her into complete darkness.

Kristian knew the task was complete. He had her right where he wanted her and now he was making his retreat. "Wa-wa-wait," she mumbled, trying to crawl towards him. She grabbed for his legs, but he only kicked her off him. "Plea-plea-please," she whimpered. She tried to follow his footsteps, but for some reason she never reached the stairwell. Seconds later, she heard the sound of the door as it locked. She didn't give up, continuing to weep bitterly as she looked for a way out.

2

Telephone

Brookstone, New York

A heavy vibration sounded from the bedside dresser, prompting Carmen's eyelids to flutter. Still very much asleep, her eyes never opened, allowing the buzzing to disappear back in the night. A few moments later, the sound became repetitive. Her eyes finally opened as Jay's body draped over hers. "It's your phone," he whispered, still somewhat dazed. His words went in one ear and out the other as Carmen's eyes slowly closed. She dozed off as the sound ceased until it returned for a third time. It was then she became fully awake and pushed Jay onto the opposite side of the bed.

Carmen reached her arm out from underneath the sheets, grabbing her cell off the bedside dresser. She blinked her eyes several times before she was able to decipher the word *Unknown* that was flashing on the home screen. Unsure of who was calling, Carmen answered the phone. "Hello," she muttered, trying to wipe the sleep from her eyes.

"I'm trying to reach a Carmen Davenport," the male voice said on the opposite end.

Carmen raised her brow before looking at the alarm clock. It was a little past twelve, which meant she had been sleep for only three hours or so. Somehow, in between that time, something had happened to prompt a phone call. Instead of instantly thinking the worst, she told the man she was indeed Carmen.

"Mrs. Davenport, I hate to disturb you at this hour, but I am Detective Morris from the Copperton City Police Department. I'm calling because your vehicle was located at the corner of Middleton Avenue. For some reason, no one was in it. Now, the number I'm calling is a New York number. Did you recently move to Copperton City from New York?"

"No, no," Carmen repeated as she continued to wipe her face. "I'm not in Georgia. I have two daughters who are. The car is a Lexus, right? You said you located it where?"

"Mrs. Davenport, the car is a Lexus, and it's in your name. We located it at the corner of Middleton Avenue and Parrish. No one was in it, but the front windshield has been shattered as well as the driver's side window. The car is badly damaged, but no one took anything. There was even a purse and cell phone located in the car. A wallet was also there with money, debit cards, and credit cards still inside. The driver's license we found was for a Kristian Kane. Do you know her?"

"That's my daughter," Carmen yelped, now fully awake. She pushed the bed sheets away from her just as Jay's arm latched onto hers.

"Who is it?" Jay asked, sitting up as well.

Carmen shook her head at him, pulling her arm away from his. To put even more space in between them, she stood from the bed, heading towards the balcony.

"Ma'am, most of the time in these situations, we find a victim and their property is gone. Since there wasn't a victim found, we are ruling this as a kidnapping. We would like for you to come down to the station in the morning. That will give us enough time to piece together the details. Will you be able to make it by let's say ten o'clock?"

While her face once held an expression of concern, it now became enraged at the detective's words. She tried to contain her anger, feeling a slew of expletives about to fly from her mouth. She turned to look at Jay who was making his way towards her. She heard him ask who is it for a second time, but she didn't respond. However, when he tried to pull the phone from her ear, she smacked his arm away.

"Are you trying to tell me my daughter has been kidnapped?"

The detective cleared his throat as he started to repeat himself. "Mrs. Davenport, from what we're seeing here, that seems to be the only explanation. No one took the car or the money she had in her purse. Now, if you are able to come down to the station, we can go through her personal items together and see if there are some clues. We are still running tests on the car for fingerprints so I won't be able to relinquish the vehicle to you until later today."

"Okay, okay," Carmen repeated. "I'll be there. I'll start looking at flights now."

"Thank you, Mrs. Davenport. We're going to try and do everything we can on our end. Have a safe trip and I'll see you in a few hours."

Carmen didn't respond to the detective's words, as she hung up the phone. Though the outside air was cool on her skin, her body temperature was rising traumatically. It seemed to escalate when she heard Jay's voice coming from the bedroom. He was pulling a pair of sweatpants over his boxers as he walked onto the balcony.

"I heard what you said, Peaches. What happened to Kristian?"

Carmen shook her head as she started to think the inevitable. She didn't want to point the finger, but she knew Kristian's kidnapping was a direct effect of the ongoing war between her fiancé and Blu. She hadn't known of her daughter to have problems with anyone for something like this to happen. She couldn't even come up with an explanation of how Blu had found his way to Georgia to even get close to her. "This motherfucker," she whimpered. "He keeps coming. Now he has gone and touched my child? Fuck no," Carmen screamed, pushing her way past Jay.

She felt his hands as he tried to grab her, but she moved too fast. Carmen headed inside their walk-in closet, grabbed the first piece of luggage she saw, and threw it in the bedroom. "You can't kill him," she screamed, picking up another suitcase. "King sure as hell can't kill him because he's on probation." Carmen threw the suitcase in the room missing Jay by a few inches. "I've already paid my debt to society. I can do what y'all can't."

"Peaches, this thing is much deeper than what you think. If he took Kristian, then that means he wants something. If he left evidence then he wants us to know he has her. He's not trying to kill her. He wants to use her for ransom."

"I don't give a fuck what he wants," Carmen blurted, turning to face him. She walked up to Jay, her finger pointed directly in his face. "You know why? Because whatever it is, you're going to give it to him. You better pray my daughter is alive when I find her. If this motherfucker even touches a hair on her head, I promise you, Jay, I'm spraying bullets in all directions."

Jay rolled his eyes, but he didn't do it while Carmen was looking at him. He waited until she had gone in the closet. If she had seen him, it would've only tripled her anger. "You need to calm down. Nothing can be done until we get to Georgia. There aren't any flights going out in the middle of the night. I can't even get my pilot right now. These things take time."

"Time," Carmen questioned. She walked in the room where Jay was standing. "We don't have fuckin' time. Every second I stand here and listen to your bitch ass, my daughter is one step closer to being murdered. What you need to be doing is picking up the horn. You need to find out where this motherfucker has her and do something about it. You're the reason for this shit."

Jay knew to keep his cool. Carmen was already being aggressive and if he matched it, the entire house would be woken up. "Listen to me, Peaches. We can't move right now. All we can do is pray and go to sleep. In the morning, I'll call King and let him know what happened. Then, we'll make our way to Georgia. That was the original plan, anyway. You can go to the police station while we start the hunt for Blu. Trust me on this one."

Carmen stared at him in disbelief. "Trust you? You want me to trust you? This motherfucker has my daughter. He took her because he couldn't get you. You're the reason for this shit." Her right hand balled into a fist and she immediately went to strike him. Jay appeared to have seen it coming because he grabbed her arm, using it to push her away. When she went to hit him with the other one, he grabbed it as well before pushing her down on the bed. He used his body weight to restrain her, pinning her down.

"Right now," Jay said, sternly. "You're going to shut the fuck up and listen. I know what I did and I know how this came to be. I don't need the reminder. Fussing and trying to throw blows is not going to get Kristian back. Tonight, you're not worth a damn to anyone. You need to calm down before you take one step out this house. Operating on emotions is not going to get you far because you're not using your head."

Carmen didn't respond, crying even harder than before. To add to her fury, a door was opening down the hall. Without a doubt, Carmen knew it was her mother. She figured she heard the arguing and was coming to see what was going on. Jay heard her as well because he loosened his grip, standing on his feet.

Since the sound of her mother's footsteps was drawing closer to them, Carmen didn't budge. Jay didn't move either, which worked to their benefit when her mother's shadow appeared underneath their doorway. Patricia stayed there for only a few seconds before disappearing into her room. It wasn't until they heard her door close that Jay spoke.

"You may see otherwise," he said, "but we're in this together. You can't move without me. I promise you, if you let me lead this thing, I will make sure we get Kristian back."

Carmen covered her face as her emotions became riled once again. Deep down, she knew Jay was bothered by the news like she was. She was simply more open with her feelings while he was being nonchalant. Though she knew she wasn't overreacting, she told herself to calm down. Jay was right when he said there wasn't anything she could do. Even if she did make it to Georgia, she would have to wait for the detectives to finish examining the evidence before she could do anything. The only thing she could do at the moment was break the news to Kane. He was a detective in his own right and to top it off, he was her soon-to-be ex-husband and Kristian's father.

Carmen sat up, nodding her head to let him know she agreed. "I'm sorry," she told him, softly. "That's my baby, you know? This shit would be hard for anybody." Carmen sniffled as she wiped both sides of her face. "You're right, though. We can't do anything right now. Until then, all we can do is call Kane and pray. We're all in this together."

To show her he agreed, Jay picked up her cell phone and handed it to her. "Go ahead and make the call. I'm going to check up on the kids to make sure I didn't wake them. Are you okay by yourself?"

Carmen mouthed the word yes as she started to dial Kane's number. He didn't answer right off, but she knew he was probably asleep. When the phone continued to ring, she hoped it woke him. He didn't answer and when his voicemail came on, she hung up the phone only to call him again. When he didn't answer the second time, she found herself growing upset. Instead of giving up, she called him again. *Third time is supposed to be the charm*, she thought. From the way things were going, it appeared that the saying didn't apply to her situation. Kane still didn't pick up so she simply left him a message.

Since Jay hadn't returned to the room, she called Akaila, her adopted daughter, who was in Copperton City with Kristian. The moment she said hello, Carmen quickly updated her on what was going on. Akaila was unaware of the situation and stated she thought Kristian was still out due to the bitterness she had about their parents' pending divorce. Carmen had filed for divorce only a couple of days ago while she informed the family of it only yesterday. Worried about her safety as well, Carmen advised her to get a one-way ticket to Brookstone. Their conversation didn't last long and shortly after she hung up, Jay returned to the room. He got in the bed without a word. Despite her growing resentment, Carmen joined him and even allowed him to hold her. While he instantly went to sleep, Carmen prayed silently to God until her eyes were forced into a peaceful slumber.

***

Kane's left hand trembled ever so slightly as he watched Carmen's name disappear off his phone. She had called him repeatedly, but the pain of the divorce filing wouldn't allow him to answer. In fact, she was the reason he was sitting at the Blue Lagoon, holding his fifth glass of Jack Daniels. He was less than a second away from downing it, when his phone lit up, displaying her name. Now that the calls had stopped, he downed the drink, setting his phone on the bar counter. He then held up his glass to signal to the bartender, Ms. Rita, that he was ready for another one. In return, she gave him a suspicious look before coming to his aid.

"This'll make your sixth, you know. You got a way home?"

Kane didn't bother to answer the question as he handed her the empty glass.

"This ain't the way to do it, Agent. Jack Daniels isn't your friend. He can't speak one word of advice to you. You need to deal with your problems head on," she told him as she fixed his drink. "I say we let this be your last one. I'll even go ahead and close out your tab."

Ms. Rita sat the glass in front of him right when a woman joined the bar. Kane ignored the lady who sat next to him, choosing to focus on the drink that had been placed in front of him. In the meantime, Ms. Rita kept her eyes planted on him as he took it down, giving him the chance to study her appearance. An older woman in her mid-fifties, she had a short crop of dyed blonde hair, which shaped her pudgy face to a T. She reminded him somewhat of the comedian, Luenell. Not the least bit attracted to her, he turned towards his right.

He could only see the woman's side profile, but he instantly mistook her for his wife. They both bore the same chocolate complexion, and their hair fell across their shoulders in the same direction. However, they differed at the bust line. Smaller than his wife's, the woman's cleavage was barely enough to catch his eye. She also had a perfect set of shapely legs that he knew his wife didn't possess. When they met eyes, Kane became mesmerized. Her lips had been painted a light pink while her almond-shaped eyes had a shimmer of mystery and sex appeal. Suddenly captivated by her, it went to the extreme when she gave him a warm smile. Automatically, Kane snapped his fingers, signaling for Ms. Rita. "Get the lady a drink, whatever she wants," he ordered.

"Wait a minute, Agent, I don't do the snapping. If you want my attention, you raise your glass or you call me by name. You want to snap, you take that down to Spoken Word Thursdays over there on 34th Street. We don't do that here."

The woman beside him let out a small chuckle before ordering a French 75. Not having heard of the drink, Kane looked at Ms. Rita who instantly went to work. When he saw she was aware of the ingredients, he looked at the woman beside him. "Michael Kane," he told her, introducing himself, "but you can call me Kane. You are?"

"Hmm," the woman moaned, giving him a questionable expression. "Who am I?" She looked at the ceiling before placing her eyes on Kane's. "You tell me."

Kane was about to answer, but Ms. Rita set the woman's drink on the counter. When she went to grab it, he did the same, snatching it up before her hands could touch it. "No, baby, you tell me." He gave her another smile as she parted her lips to respond.

"Jean Monet," she said, quietly. "I moved here from Miami."

"Jean," he repeated. "I like. What brings you here from Florida?"

Jean held out her hand for her drink, not answering the question until Kane gave it to her. "Work," she told him. "There were some openings here so I decided to take a chance, withdraw my savings, and come up North. I have an interview lined up for tomorrow and if all goes well, I'll leave with the job."

"I wish you the best," Kane replied. He started to say more until he saw the rim of the glass slide in between Jean's lips. For those six seconds she sipped, he pictured himself as the glass. While he had been moping around over his failed marriage, he was now seeing some light at the end of the tunnel. In a few short minutes, Jean had made him forget about all things Carmen. She may have slightly favored his wife, but there was still something about her that intrigued him. Then again, he also knew he was horny. The last time he had felt a woman was when Carmen was about five months' pregnant with Nyla, her third child with Jay. Since then, he had been pleasuring himself. With a possible opportunity in his face, Kane became adamant about staying on the train.

"Shot of tequila," he yelled in Ms. Rita's direction. "Give me one for the lady, too."

"You better make sure she sees you home," Ms. Rita fussed. "I'm not responsible for you, Agent. I'm telling you that now. You better catch a cab or have the Miss drive you." She fixed the two shots and placed them both on the counter. Jean took hers while Kane let his stay in its spot. Not yet ready for it, he watched in awe as Jean took hers down.

"Agent?" Jean questioned, once she had swallowed. "Let me find out you have a badge."

Kane shook his head, not ready to disclose his employment. His mind was already in the gutter and the last thing he wanted was for Jean to be fearful because of his occupation. If things worked in his favor, Ms. Rita wouldn't utter agent out her mouth anymore.

In an attempt to thwart the subject, he ran two of his fingers along Jean's upper thigh. "You're not dressed for this scene," he told her, admiring her lace peplum dress. "Where were you before you came here?"

Jean picked up his hand, placing it on the counter. "Home," she told him, plainly. "I told you I was new here. I don't have a tour guide. I thought I was dressed for the occasion until I walked in. If you ask me, this doesn't look like your scene either…Agent."

Kane looked at his clothes, knowing Jean was telling the truth. He was dressed rather ruggedly, which was not quite the look for someone who was trying to seduce a woman. Instead of agreeing with her, he decided to use her words to his advantage. "Doesn't look like the scene for either one of us. Maybe, we should take this party elsewhere."

Jean laughed loudly, as if she was going to turn him down. If she was, Kane wasn't going to give her the chance. He took out a hundred dollar bill, resting it on the counter. Ms. Rita was still in earshot and noticed it as soon as he placed it there. He met eyes with her, giving her a wink as a sign she could keep the change. He then picked up the shot of tequila, taking it down in one gulp. The entire time, he could feel Jean's eyes burning on his skin. Her gaze told him he had her hooked. She was intrigued by him like he was her.

About to find out for sure, he slammed the shot glass down on the counter. He stood up only to almost trip over his own feet. It was then he realized how wasted he was. Jean grabbed his right arm, hopping off her stool. In the meantime, he heard Ms. Rita's laughter as her prediction came to light.

"See, look at you. You aren't worth shit now." Ms. Rita chuckled. "You better not let him drive, Miss. He has money. Get him a cab, or take him home. He ain't fit to be walking around this city by himself."

Kane stuck his middle finger up at Ms. Rita as he tried to pull himself together. After a few seconds, he was able to get out of Jean's grasp. He even walked to the exit in one piece. Jean followed behind him until they were standing in an alleyway in the back of the bar. Kane rested against a brick wall, far from the entrance of the Blue Lagoon. For what he had in mind, he needed to be away from watchful eyes.

"You're really something, Agent," Jean told him, leaning against the brick wall opposite of him. "I'm not going to chase you anymore. Where did you park?"

"Right here," he whispered, pointing at himself. "Do you need a ride?"

Jean let out another round of laughter before walking towards him. "What kind of agent are you?" she asked him, now chest to chest. "I think what you're implying is a little illegal. Maybe it's the tequila talking."

"Maybe," Kane replied, leaning in closer to her. He rubbed his lips across hers to see what she would do. When she didn't back away, he parted his lips as she did the same. In less than two seconds, they were engrossed in a full blown kiss. Since Jean had fallen into his trap, Kane immediately started to rush things. Both of his hands found their way onto his belt buckle as he started to undo his pants.

"This is new for me," he heard Jean mutter. "I've never done this before."

Kane knew he should've said the same. Instead, his hands were too busy pulling down his boxers to say anything. When his hands did become free, both of them went to the edges of Jean's dress, pulling it up towards her thigh while she pulled down her underwear. In less than two seconds, Kane was pushing his way inside of her walls. In that exact moment, everything that was weighing on his shoulders vanished. It was like he could feel the bouts of jealousy, the torment of betrayal and rejection, all flooding out his pores. In a way, sex with Jean was almost like a cleansing.

He felt it even when he reached his peak, spilling his seed inside of a woman he had barely known for eight minutes. Jean didn't seem to mind, which he could tell from the orgasmic pants erupting in his ear. While their connection seemed to be greatly needed, it was cut short when the sound of voices interrupted them. Two people were leaving out of the Blue Lagoon and seemed to be headed in their direction. Unaware if they had the same idea as them, Kane grabbed his pants, which had fallen at his ankles. Jean immediately pulled up her underwear, straightening her clothes until she was presentable. By that time, the voices had disappeared.

"That was nice." Jean giggled, pressing her chest up against his. "Was that my Welcome to New York gift?"

"Maybe," Kane responded, wrapping his arm around her waist. "Why don't we go to my place for round two?"

Jean gave him a smile as a sign she accepted before digging into his pants' pocket for his keys. Once she had them in her hand, she allowed Kane to direct her to his car. His Jeep was parallel parked outside the Blue Lagoon and they got inside, making small talk until they reached his condo. Round two started immediately when they were inside the house and lasted longer than the first. This time, they made their way to his bed, ending their connection with Jean falling asleep next to him. Kane, on the other hand, remained awake as he tried to piece together the evening. Though they shared a one night stand, something told him it was the start of something more. While he couldn't quite express his feelings at the moment, he knew when Jean awoke, he would.

He eventually fell asleep and when his eyes reopened, he woke to find Jean standing beside him, putting on her clothes. The time read 4:12, a whole lot later than he imagined.

"You can stay for breakfast, you know. Homemade biscuits are my specialty."

Jean flashed a quick smile in his direction as she zipped the back of her dress. "I can't. I have an interview in a few hours that I need to prepare for. I've already called a cab."

Kane sighed out of frustration as he continued to watch her dress.

"I really need this job," she started to explain. "Most of the money in my savings is gone and if I don't get this job, I don't know what I'm going to do next month."

Kane sat up as she grabbed one of her shoes, putting it on her left foot. He started to offer his place to her until he noticed the label. She had mentioned she had blown through her savings yet she was putting on a pair of Gucci pumps that he knew totaled a little over two grand. Thanks to his soon to be ex-wife and her lavish requests for Christmas, he knew the prices of lots of designer shoes. He just didn't expect to run into the same thing with Jean.

"So, is there anything I need to know about you before we take this further?" Jean asked.

Kane's head shook ever so slightly at the sudden change in topics. It took him a few seconds to digest her question and once he did, he began to wipe his face nervously. There were a slew of things he needed to tell Jean. For one, he needed to tell her he was going through a divorce. He also needed to tell her he had kids. Since she had never gotten a proper tour of his condo, she had never seen the family portraits. Therefore, he had to spill his life story. "My wife filed for divorce," he revealed. "Um…Carmen Davenport, she owns Flame."

Jean stared blankly at him for a second or two before her agitation showed. "Wow," she said, sarcastically, "that's some kind of luck, eh? Move to New York and the first guy you fuck is married to one of the richest women in the country. I guess that's what you get when you have a one night stand. Oh, I forgot, y'all are getting a divorce. Well, that explains why you were drinking yourself to death." Jean grabbed her purse, heading for the door, which instantly made Kane jump from the bed. He didn't even bother to grab his clothes as he followed her. Jean was moving double time out his condo as if she wasn't giving him another second of her time.

"Can you stop for a moment?" he yelled, nearing the bottom step. Jean's hand was firmly around the doorknob and she was getting ready to open it despite his nakedness. "Wait a second." Kane walked towards her and pressed his hand up against the door to hold it closed. "I'm getting a divorce. We're legally separated. She's already moved on."

"I know who your wife is, Michael. The whole city does. I also know she's dating Jay Santiago. What I didn't know was that you were her husband. Now I do."

"Well, let me—" the sound of a car horn interrupted him. Kane knew it was the taxicab so he started talking a mile a minute. "Let me get a number, an email address, give me something," he said, quickly, knowing she was getting ready to leave.

Jean exhaled before looking around the living room for anything she could write on. She spotted an Allstate envelope on the coffee table as well as an ink pen and picked it up. She quickly scribbled her cell number, handed it to him, and left. Normally, she would've said goodbye, but it wasn't necessary with the news he shared.

Kane felt differently, but he couldn't voice his opinion. Without any clothes on, he had no choice but to remain behind closed doors. While he did understand her frustration, he wished she understood his marriage was over. In his mind, he was as single as a dollar bill.

A curse word sounded out his mouth as he went up the steps. Even without being there, Carmen had somehow found a way to ruin his evening. In fact, she had ruined it way before Jean had come in the picture. It had all started with her calling him back to back when he was on his fifth glass of Jack Daniels. He had never found out what she wanted and at this point, he didn't care. Whatever Carmen wanted could wait. She was no longer a priority in his life like he wasn't in hers.

3
Dilemma

With the amount of anxiety she was feeling, Carmen was surprised to learn she was able to sleep until daybreak. While she expected to wake on her own, the sound of her alarm caught her attention. She opened her eyes to find her bedroom empty and the house awkwardly quiet. Unsure of where Jay was, she listened for any sound of movement. So far, the only thing she heard was the air conditioner. Well aware he was around somewhere, she immediately got up and headed for the bathroom. She quickly showered and dressed before starting to pack for the trip to Georgia. By the time Jay returned to the room, she had already secured two tickets to Copperton City for an eight-thirty flight.

"Rakim is up, but Nyla is still asleep," he announced, coming in the room. "I tried talking to your mother about keeping them for us, but I'm not getting a word out of her."

"She ignored you?" Carmen asked, starting to make their bed. When Jay didn't answer, she glanced over at him only to see the, *you know she did* face, he was giving her. She cracked a smile, knowing her mother most definitely had. "Don't worry about it. Fiona is here so I can pay her extra to stay the night or we can see what Tiara and Malik are doing."

"Fiona left. She said she had a family emergency. As for Malik, he's going to be in Georgia with me and King. We could get Tiara to keep 'em, but that's three babies on her hands—our two and her own daughter. You don't think that's a little much?"

"Yeah, but my mama isn't in the mental state to keep them," Carmen replied. "She's still grieving over my dad. I'll see what Tiara says. I'm pretty sure she's out all this week. She and Malik were supposed to take a vacation then all of this stuff popped off with Blu and my father." Carmen looked at Jay as she started to put the pillows on the bed. "Did you want me to pack your things?"

Jay bit his lip, shaking his head. In such a short amount of time, his plans for the morning had changed. Originally, he was supposed to be leaving at six to head to Georgia so he could handle Blu. The plan became null and void when he received the news of Kristian's kidnapping. He got the idea of sending the others to Georgia without him so he could stay with Carmen until he got another surprise. About five o'clock that morning, he received a phone call from his business partner in Africa who kindly informed him a package was on its way.

At first, Jay was unsure about the contents until his friend told him one word—carbonado. When Jay heard those four syllables, he knew he had to take every precaution. Any package containing only black diamonds had to be handled delicately. The second it arrived on Flame's premises, he needed to have it in his hands.

"I went ahead and got us two plane tickets," Carmen was saying, finishing up the bed. "The flight leaves at eight-thirty so you got some time to get ready. Have you spoken to King?"

Jay reached across the bed, pulling the accent pillow out of Carmen's hand. He placed it on his side of the bed as he started to reveal his plans. "We might have to push the flight back."

"Huh? What are you—?"

Jay interrupted her before she could finish. "My friend in Africa sent me a package this morning. It's on its way to Flame and I need to get to it as soon as it gets there. I actually need to take it to San Juan."

"Whoa, whoa, whoa," Carmen yelled, coming around the bed. "Are you saying this package of yours is more important than me finding my daughter?"

"No, what I'm saying is that we have to make another stop on the way. This package is–"

"I don't give a flying fuck about your damn package. You got men all over this damn country that answer to your beck and call. Get one of those motherfuckers to get it. Isn't that what you pay them for? Where are Cesar and Linx? I know their asses are around here somewhere. They're always peeking in and out. Don't you pay them to watch us? Have them go to Flame."

"Carmen, this package is delicate. I need to get it out the states as soon as possible. If you let me make this stop, we can be in Georgia in no time. There's even a tracker on the package. I'll know in less than two seconds when it's at Flame."

Carmen stared in shock as Jay spoke. It was like the severity of her situation didn't even matter to him. He was so focused on his material possessions he couldn't see her daughter's life was on the line. Once again, his nonchalant attitude was triggering her anger.

"The package should be here soon. I'll pick it up, we'll fly to San Juan, I'll secure it in my safe, and then we'll be on our way to Georgia.

Puerto Rico isn't far from that area, anyway. If we're lucky, we'll get to the station by eleven at the latest."

"Do you feel this way because Kristian isn't your daughter?"

Jay's eyes became outstretched. "What kind of question is that? When I marry you, she will be my daughter. Are you trying to insinuate that I'm stalling because Kane is her father?"

"That's what I'm starting to believe," Carmen shouted. "If it was Nyla, we would've been in Copperton City the second I got the phone call. In fact, the situation would've never happened. She probably already has her own bodyguard. Admit it."

Jay believed wholeheartedly that the accusation placed in front of him was wrong and out of order. His relationship with Kristian might not have been where he wanted it, but he was willing to do anything to get her home safely. "I would never admit that because I don't feel that way. All I'm asking is that you…" Jay stopped speaking when he noticed Carmen had picked up her cell phone and was now dialing numbers.

"Kane, I don't know where you are or what you're doing, but you need to call me ASAP. For some reason, you keep sending me straight to voicemail. Something happened with Kristian and we need to get to Georgia. I've already purchased two plane tickets for us. Call me so I can give you the details."

Jay watched as Carmen hung up the phone. His mouth wasn't wide open, but his lips had parted from disbelief. "Did you really do that shit?"

"I'm going to call Tiara to see if she can watch the kids. Then, I'm going to get them ready. You can do whatever you want. I'm not on your time anymore."

Carmen attempted to walk out the room, but Jay grabbed her arm, pulling her towards him. His fury could easily be read on his face and he hoped she saw it. "You can run down to Georgia all you fuckin' want, but you're not going to get far without me. I know what I'm doing. If you go down there with Kane, you're putting strain on not only our relationship, but you're risking getting Kristian back."

"I'll take my chances," she murmured, pushing him away.

Carmen didn't hesitate to leave the room, giving Jay time and space to figure out a plan. One foot needed to be on the plane with her while the other needed to be in San Juan securing the package in his safe. It was a feat that wasn't physically possible. Jay was forced to believe he had no choice but to allow Kane to take his seat on the plane. The only downfall was he ran the risk of him trying to reconcile his marriage.

Under normal circumstances, Jay knew Carmen wouldn't be vulnerable. Due to the situation at hand, Jay could easily see Kane trying to play the blame game. Her soon-to-be ex would convince Carmen that he was the reason Kristian was kidnapped and then try to lay his sweet talk on her. In no time, he could have Carmen eating out the palm of his hand.

On the flip side, Jay knew if he continued to believe that Carmen was still the same woman who dropped him left and right whenever she was angry than their relationship would fail. He had to remind himself Carmen was only devoted to him. That didn't mean Kane wouldn't try anything, but he had to trust his fiancée wouldn't fall victim to his advances.

Since he would be thousands of miles away, Kane had all the free range he wanted. All Jay could do on his end was let him know what was coming to him if he tried anything. *Not a bad idea*, he thought. He picked up Carmen's phone and redialed Kane's number. As expected, it went to voicemail. His words flowed out sternly so Kane could get a clear visual of the repercussions. Whether he heard the message in the next five or ten minutes, the delivery would be the same. All that mattered was that the message was given.

***

After a wild night of alcohol and sex, Kane woke up to a headache and the sound of a dog barking from his neighbor's backyard. A large part of him wanted to stay in bed, but he knew he couldn't. His cell phone was still in his Jeep and at this hour, his partner, Sanders, was probably calling every five minutes. Although he and Sanders were very thorough detectives, lately they had been coming up short. Now, Kane felt it was time for them to step up their game.

Before he could, he had to get out of bed. It took a few minutes, but eventually he was in the shower and out the door. When he finally reached his phone, he saw he had even more missed calls than the night before. Four were from Carmen while the rest were from Sanders. He also had three voicemails, which he knew he needed to listen to. All from Carmen, she had been calling like crazy since he was at the Blue Lagoon. He knew he needed to return her call yet he didn't want to. To keep from doing so, he started up his car and backed out the driveway.

If there was anyone he wanted to call, it was Jean. He wanted to apologize to her again for not telling her he was married. Though it was impossible when they were two seconds away from having sex, he knew he should have. Not one to have one night stands, he wasn't quite sure how much he was supposed to reveal. The whole experience was new to him. Now, he was concerned about the next step.

Nevertheless, Kane knew he couldn't focus on Jean at the moment. Regardless of his animosity towards Carmen, she was still the mother of his kids and he needed to return her call. Anything could've happened and with him not answering, he was not only ignoring her, but also the situation.

With a guilty feeling in his stomach, Kane was glad when he reached a turn that would take him to downtown Brookstone. Only minutes away from the offices of Flame, he got the idea to make a stop at her job. If Carmen was in, he could ask her in person why she was blowing up his phone. If she wasn't then he would have to call her. He took a chance, pulling into the company's parking lot. He parked near the back so he could be close to the exit and turned off the car. About to head out, he was distracted by the sound of something hitting his window.

Automatically, his face scrunched up until he noticed Sanders standing next to him. He was holding a black thermos, which he had obviously used to bang on the glass. Kane gave him a weird expression before he rolled down his window. "Are you stalking me now?"

"You didn't hear me blowing at you back there? I was behind you the whole time. I guess you got a lot on your mind. What are you doing outside of Flame? Are you about to meet with the ex?"

Kane looked in his left rearview mirror to glance at the building behind him. "Yes and no," he told him. "She's been blowing up my phone. If I didn't have kids by her, I would ignore her all together. She got the man she wants."

"Sounds like you're finally accepting it."

Kane looked at Sanders yet he didn't utter a single word. Instead, he got out his Jeep and faced Flame. There was a FedEx truck in front of the building that hadn't been there when he first turned in. He figured it had passed him when he was talking to Sanders. Unimportant to him, he turned towards his partner. "I did accept it. Jack Daniels and I had a real long conversation last night. He allowed me to see my marriage the way it really is… Over."

"Great, so now we can get back on the vault. We still have to find a million dollars' worth of coke that we let Jay steal. You still want to go inside?"

Kane shrugged his shoulders, taking another glance at Flame. This time, there was a black car directly behind the FedEx truck. He didn't think anything of it until he noticed the silver rims on the car. Automatically, his mind went to the parking lot of Blue Magic, the restaurant his wife co-owned with Jay. A shootout had occurred at the eatery only a short while ago in which his wife's boyfriend was involved in a fierce gun battle with men who were driving black Mercedes Benzes. The car in front of him was almost identical to the ones at the restaurant. Certain of it, he told Sanders to get in his Jeep.

"Uh oh, what do you see?"

"Get inside," Kane told him, moving his cell phone from the passenger's seat. He set it in his lap, starting up the car. He kept his eyes on the Benz as he backed out in case he needed to follow it. The car hadn't moved, which allowed him to get directly behind it. "Does this look familiar to you?" he asked Sanders, keeping his eye on the vehicle. "This car looks like the ones at Blue Magic."

"Too much like 'em," Sanders agreed. He took out an ink pen and scribbled down the license plate so he could run the tag. "What does it want with this FedEx truck? The driver appears to still be in the car. It's actually hard to tell because the windows are tinted."

"I didn't see anyone get out," Kane added. "I also didn't notice anyone in the FedEx truck. I guess the mailman is inside."

"Maybe it has a package that the person in the black car is waiting to get."

Kane looked over at Sanders, just in time to see the deliveryman returning to the truck. He paid close attention to him, even taking a picture with his cell phone. The man had an olive skin complexion with jet black, wavy hair that made Kane believe he was of Hispanic descent. In fact, Jay was known to employ Latinos to help him do his dirty work. Whatever the driver was delivering, the person in the Benz desperately wanted. "Our focus was always on what Jay did," Kane admitted. "We never questioned why someone was shooting at him." Kane stared at the FedEx truck as it started to move. The black car moved as well, but he didn't follow it.

"No one cared to know," Sanders replied. "I guess that leads to my next question. Do you care?"

"We'll see," Kane answered, picking up his cell phone. He called his voicemail and started to listen to the messages. The first one was from Carmen and he knew instantly something was wrong. She was crying, which made it hard for him to make out her words. When the second message came on, he could hear her clearly. Something happened to Kristian and they had a flight leaving out at eight-thirty. It was only a little after seven which meant he had enough time to pack and get to the airport.

"We're gonna have to split up," he told Sanders. "Something happened with Kristian and I have to go to Georgia." He continued listening to his messages as he drove to Sanders' car. "You…" Kane paused when he heard the verbal threat left by Jay. "I know this motherfucker didn't," he mumbled. "Must I remind him that Carmen is still my wife? You're threatening to put me in a garbage disposal if I try anything with the woman I've been married to for twenty years? I dare this motherfucker to lay a hand on me. I'll slice his neck from ear to ear."

"Leave it alone, Kane. Find out what's going on so we can get to the vault. We still have to make a million dollars' worth of coke reappear. It wouldn't be a concern if we hadn't cut that deal with Jay."

"We'll get to it. Right now, I need you to run that tag. I want to know who that car belongs to. Call me with the details and leave a message if I don't answer."

"Done," Sanders replied. He opened the door so he could get out, but he didn't leave the vehicle. Though Kane didn't always want to hear it, he had to give him a few wise words. "Don't fall into Jay's bullshit, Kane. Stay focused on what's going on. You get wrapped up in his mess then it'll be another long set of months away from the force. I know you don't want that."

Kane gave Sanders a facial expression that read, *save it.* His partner took it for what it was worth before getting inside his own car. In the meantime, Kane made a quick phone call to his wife. Carmen answered on the first ring with a mouth full of expletives.

"What the fuck is your problem? You don't know how to answer a fuckin' phone?" she shouted, not even saying hello.

"What the fuck is yours?" Kane replied with as much thunder. "I'm not your number one priority so you sure as hell aren't mine. This isn't even about you. What happened to Kristian?" Kane put the call on speaker and threw the phone in the passenger seat.

"Her car was found on a road in Copperton City. Her purse and cell were still in it so they're ruling it as a possible kidnapping. We need to go down there, claim the car, and find out who took her. Once we find 'em, we'll kill 'em, and it'll be a done deal."

Kane's eyes became outstretched at the news. "Who's behind this, Carmen?" he barked. "I know you know. You're not going to sit up here and say my daughter has been kidnapped and not give me a suspect. I bet…" Kane paused. "Forget it, I'll find out when I get to Georgia." Kane looked in his rearview mirror. When he saw the way was clear, he moved to the left lane so he could make a turn. "I'm on my way home. If you hear anything from the detective, let me know. Have you heard from Akaila?"

"Yeah, she should be here in an hour. Her flight left early this morning. I haven't talked to King yet. Jay said he was going to call him so we'll see."

"Well, sit tight. Where do you want me to meet you?"

Kane waited until Carmen said Tiara's house before he hung up the phone. Still downtown, he stopped at a red light, wondering where the quickest shortcut was to his house. He thought to turn on 47th until a figure crossing the street caught his eye. Even from where he was sitting, he could make out Jean's legs. He stared at her as she walked, noticing the black pencil skirt she wore and the crisp white button-up that hugged her chest. She had paired it with a red clutch and black Christian Louboutin platforms. "Something is up with this chick," he muttered, thinking about the price. Well over nine hundred dollars, Kane knew her job in Miami had to pay well for her lifestyle to follow her to NY. Though he was itching to talk to her, he knew he couldn't. With his daughter missing and an unclear amount of evidence on the table, finding his flesh and blood was now his main goal. Anything other than that was miniscule.

4

Resentment

While Kane was on his way to his condo, Jay and Carmen were piled in a limousine with their kids on their way to Tiara and Malik's house. For the last two minutes, a tracking notification had been displayed on Jay's phone, announcing his package's arrival at Flame. Aware he needed to be headed in the opposite direction, Jay turned his phone over so he wouldn't anger himself. A part of him wanted to defy Carmen and order Linx to turn the limo around, but when he thought to do it, he would catch a side eye from Carmen.

"Did you call King?"

Jay had to blink twice to make sure it was Carmen's voice he was hearing. She had barely spoken to him after she had left their bedroom and it surprised him to hear her voice. In fact, the only thing she said to him since leaving the bedroom was that she was going to the car. Every other piece of information had come from either Cesar or Linx. Unsure of when she would talk to him again, he quickly told her no.

"So do you want me to? Why is it so hard for you to make a simple phone call?"

About to give a response that was filled with as much anger as her question, he looked over at Rakim and Nyla who were still asleep. Their peaceful faces were all he needed to see to convince him to change his tone. "Cesar has already made the necessary arrangements. King knows where to be and what time to be there. I'll call him when I'm in route to San Juan."

"What kind of answer is that?" Carmen barked. "Is that your way of telling me to mind my fuckin' business? I know you're on some bullshit now."

Jay pointed towards their kids who were sitting in car seats opposite of them. It was a clear reminder to Carmen that she needed to watch her language. If she woke them, they both would have two screaming babies on their hands. "Chill," he said, softly. "In due time."

Carmen made a gargling sound yet she didn't ask any more questions. She remained quiet until they pulled up in front of Tiara's house. Though Jay was well prepared to help her with the kids, she asked Linx to get Rakim out the car.

Two seconds from straightening her out, Jay listened as Cesar told him from the front passenger seat to stay put. An obvious ploy to keep him out of a heated argument, Jay followed his advice. It worked to his benefit because in no time Carmen was in the house with Linx following in behind her.

"This thing is going to get ugly, you know," Cesar told him once they were alone.

"She'll be fine once we're both in Georgia."

"I'm not talking about that," Cesar shot back. "I'm talking about the secrets you're keeping from her. The secrets that are keeping you from making that phone call to your son, King. See, Carmen doesn't know that Blu is from Copperton City. She also doesn't know King asked you to find a bodyguard for his sisters. Add that to the fact that you didn't do it and here comes the start of World War III. King's anger is one thing, but your fiancée's is another."

Jay sucked his teeth as he realized where Cesar was leading the conversation. He knew King would find out about Kristian's kidnapping, but he didn't think about Carmen finding out about Blu's place of residence.

"Tell her now and you'll save yourself some grief. If you have King tell her, you might as well be prepared to get that two million dollar ring off her hand. I promise you, Carmen is going to look at this like you practically offered her daughter to Blu. Trust me."

Jay didn't give a response. He knew Cesar was right, but he figured he would cross that bridge when he got there. He just didn't expect for it to be so soon. When he turned his gaze towards the front of the car, his eyes saw something move in the rearview mirror. A silver Mercedes Benz was behind him, which only said one thing. Kristian's kidnapping had reached King's ears. For some reason, his son chose to drive his girlfriend's car instead of his own.

"Here we go," Cesar bellowed, seeing King getting out the vehicle.

Jay watched his son carefully as he walked towards the limo. Everything about King's swagger screamed battle. His sweatpants were ripped at the knees and his white wife beater was dingy and torn at the edges. He was dressed for the occasion, one that didn't require him to be presentable.

"He can't see us through the tints," Cesar noticed when King walked past the car.

"He'll be back."

Cesar looked over his shoulder to see if he could catch an expression from Jay that wasn't as relaxed as his tone. "You know what's about to happen, right?" he asked, noticing how cool and collected his boss was.

"You warned me before his car pulled up."

Cesar shook his head back and forth as Malik answered the front door. King showed his true emotions when he pushed his way inside, clearly expecting for Jay to be in the house. Malik closed the door, but Cesar knew it was only a matter of seconds before it would reopen. He could already see King storming out the house and demanding for Jay to get out the car. The vision was so clear he almost missed it happening live in front of him.

"Get your bitch ass out the car," King barked, banging his fists down hard onto the back window. "You don't need to hide. What the fuck are you hiding for?"

"Don't get out this car, Jay," Cesar said, calmly. He looked over his shoulder to see that Jay had taken off his suit jacket and was unbuttoning his shirt. "Please don't get out this car," he begged. "Malik is right there," he continued, seeing Jay's best friend running out the house. "Let him calm King down first. Maybe you two can talk over breakfast. I know Tiara whipped something up in there."

Jay shook his head. He knew there wasn't going to be any talking involved. King wanted to fight him and he had to give his son the ass whooping he had missed on several past occasions. Not to mention, he noticed the imprint of a weapon in King's waistband. It was never Jay's intent to become trigger happy, but he wasn't going to take a bullet from his son. He would kill him dead before he allowed him to be the first person to pop a bullet in him.

As for Cesar, he continued to watch Jay for a few more seconds before taking matters into his own hands. He unlocked the doors and stepped out, pushing King away from the car. "Not here," he roared, pushing King hard in the chest. He tried to direct him towards the house, but King wasn't having it. After the third push, King had pulled the pistol from his sweatpants, which Cesar knew he was ready to use. In defense, he drew his own weapon.

With two guns being waved, Malik was quick to get in between the two men. "Don't you know where I live? Put the heat away," Malik begged, trying to reach for King's gun. "We can sit down and talk about this like men. This fighting, this bickering, it's going to get us nowhere."

"I don't want to hear voices of reason, Malik," King shot back. "I want to hear that motherfucker in there. I want an answer from the one sitting behind that protective glass." King walked in circles around Cesar and Malik as they continued to try and block his path.

"We don't need this right now, King. Calm down and we can talk about this," Cesar encouraged, continuing to try and diffuse the situation.

"I will kill you both right now if you don't get the fuck out my way. I promise you."

"You're not shooting up a damn thing," Malik yelled, reaching for King's gun. Malik realized he made a mistake when he and King started battling for it. It was enough to make Jay emerge from the car, which then prompted King to pull the trigger. He fired into the air; the sound of the bullet spreading like wildfire throughout the neighborhood. It was a wrong move that could send any one of Malik's neighbors to their nearest telephone to call the police.

While Cesar and Malik struggled to get the gun out of King's hand, Jay did the one thing he knew to do. He took his own 9mm and pretended to pistol whip his son. A flash of fear appeared in his son's eyes, which naturally made him loosen his grip on the gun. Those two seconds was enough time for Malik to pull the pistol from his hand, leaving King weaponless. "Now we can talk as men," Jay muttered. "You want to come up here all big and bad, but you don't know what the hell you're about to walk into."

"Give me back my gun."

"You fired your gun," Jay shot back. "You fired your gun in one of the richest neighborhoods in Brookstone. Do you know what that means? It means, motherfuckin' blue and white. Malik and Tiara got millionaires on both sides of them. All it takes is one gunshot for the whole fuckin' Triad to come busting through here. You don't care though. You just want to come out here and fuck somebody up. You don't care you're about to send us all to jail. Who's going to find Kristian then? You can't have a fuckin' gun, King. You wanna know what else? You for damn sure can't shoot it."

"I'll fuckin' shoot whenever I need to."

"You hardheaded son of a…" Jay's voice trailed off when he was interrupted by the sound of a motor behind him. Though he knew Kane was going to show, he didn't expect to see him at that moment. He was already dealing with King and having to manhandle his fiancée's husband wasn't something he wanted to add to his task list.

"I don't give a fuck," King yelled in his ear. "You're lucky Akaila is already on her way home. Not to mention, I had to get Coco out of Copperton City, too. If Blu had of gotten all three of them, I would've fucked you up for real."

Jay stuck up his middle finger as he headed inside the limousine. He refused to continue to entertain his son or give Kane the pleasure of seeing them in a disagreement. King had been fighting this war with him for a while and it was becoming second nature. Instead of arguing with him, he was starting to think it was best to simply ignore him all together. It seemed to work because King eventually calmed down and their argument appeared non-existent when Carmen exited the house.

Linx was behind her while Tiara stood in the doorway with Rakim at her legs. Well aware they heard the commotion, neither of them stepped foot outside the house until now. Jay figured Malik had ordered them to stay put while he and Cesar rectified the situation. If that was the case, it explained why Carmen didn't say anything to him. She got her carry-on bag out the trunk while Linx carried the rest of her luggage to Kane's Jeep. Jay watched her through the rearview mirror, wondering if she was going to say anything to him before she left.

In the meantime, Jay had the pleasure of listening to King explain how he found out about Kristian's kidnapping. Apparently, Akaila had called her brother, Malachi, the night before to tell him she was coming home. In true sibling fashion, Malachi had spread the news to King. His son simply chose to wait to confront him and place the blame.

At times, Jay wanted to step out the car, but he kept his composure. He didn't move an inch, not even when the back door of the limousine opened and someone sat beside him. He didn't turn to see who it was until he felt a hand on top of his. Only then did he shift his eyes downward and he was forced to see the engagement ring he had placed on Carmen's hand. She was still wearing it, which told him their relationship had survived the morning.

"You won't look at me," she began, "but that's okay. You don't have to." She paused for a few seconds before clearing her throat. "I'm tired, Jay. I'm tired of going back and forth, trying to figure this out, trying to figure that out. I refuse to do it anymore. We're going to make this work. I don't know how, but we're going to do it. Lord knows, I want to choke you right now, but I promised myself that you're it for me. This ring stays on my finger until you replace it on December 25th. Do you understand?"

Jay understood completely. Carmen was determined not to let him go despite what had occurred in the last twenty-four hours. "I love you," he whispered. "I know I fucked up. I'm going to get Kristian back. I promise." Jay lifted his head slowly as his eyes found their way onto hers. Instantly, he felt her right hand as it grabbed his face, pulling him closer to her. They shared a kiss, which was cut short by the loud blare of a car horn. Jay thought for a split second to verbalize his threat to Kane again. If he had the time, he would have, but he knew it was best for him to stay in the car. He didn't have time to deal with Carmen's husband when he had a large number of black diamonds that needed to be in his possession.

"Call me as soon as you land," Carmen told him, getting out the limousine. "Okay?"

Jay nodded his head, watching her as she walked to Kane's Jeep. The back door to the limousine was still open, which allowed King to sit inside. Jay rolled his eyes at his son's presence only because he knew their argument wasn't over. Thankfully, King's gun was still in Malik's hands. If any battle was set to go down, it would be a war of fists.

"I know you got one for me so give me the order," King barked.

Jay ignored him and started to fix his clothes back. At the moment, he didn't have anything for King. His plan was to simply head to Flame, get his diamonds, and fly to San Juan. Somewhere in the mix of all that, King and his men were supposed to get to Georgia. How? He didn't quite know. The private plane he had, he needed, which meant they would possibly be getting their own private aircraft or riding first class and weaponless to Copperton City.

"Oh, so you can't talk now?" King yelled. "Fine then, motherfucker, fuck you." King opened the back door and stepped out the limousine, slamming it closed in the process. He had tried to give Jay a second chance, but his father had shown him once again what a selfish prick he had become. In King's mind, he was now responsible for ensuring his sister made it home. Although he didn't have the same connections as his father, he could still get the job done.

Unaware of his son's thoughts, Jay waited impatiently as Cesar and Linx got inside the car. Neither of them spoke until the car was backing out the driveway.

"Malik isn't going to Georgia," Linx announced. "He's going to stay here with Tiara. I don't know where King or Nicholas is headed. I figured we'll go to Flame, get on the plane to San Juan, and then catch up with them later. What do you say?"

"Ditto," Jay responded. "I don't care what they do. I got this covered."

His response garnered a look from Cesar. His right-hand wanted him to show more compassion towards his son while Jay believed King's antics prevented him from doing so. Now, the wedge between them had grown even deeper. Everyone wanted them to fix it yet it wasn't something that could be done overnight. Years of pain were built up inside both of them that a bulldozer couldn't even break through. Eventually, it would be worked through, but Jay didn't see it happening anytime soon.

5

Trust and Believe

Carmen set her purse down in her lap as Kane started the drive to the airport. She hadn't said much to him though she knew the tension between them wasn't as thick as it once was. In fact, it was best if they were cordial to each other since they would be glued at the hip until Kristian was home.

"So do you want to tell me what happened?"

Carmen shrugged her shoulders only because she didn't know what he was referring to. Too much had happened in the last twenty-four hours for her to read his mind. He could've been speaking of Kristian's kidnapping or the fight between King and Jay. She didn't catch much of it although she did hear the gunshot. If Nyla wasn't in her arms and Rakim wasn't demanding her attention, she would've been right outside with Malik and Cesar, trying to get the argument under control.

"So you want me to accept the fact that my daughter has been kidnapped?"

Carmen looked over at Kane and shook her head. "I don't even want to accept that. I most definitely wouldn't tell you, too. All I know is what I've told you already. I guess we're going to have to wait and see what the detective says. He probably knows more since they've been running tests." Carmen bit her lip out of fear only because she knew she was withholding information from Kane. She was wrong in not telling him that Kristian's kidnapping was a result of the beef between Jay and Blu, but she knew if she did, Kane would demand they return to Malik's house. *Shit, he would shoot Jay dead*, Carmen thought. *Humph, like I don't want to do the same. The only thing stopping me is the fact that I'm in love with him.*

"Kristian never mentioned anything to me about having a problem with someone. She didn't say…" Kane paused as he made a right turn, starting to remember a conversation he shared with his daughter. Shortly after Carmen announced she wanted to separate, he had come home to remove his items from their bedroom. Kristian had tried to talk to him about someone who was bothering her, but he had pushed her away. Now, she was gone and the only thing he had left was her cell phone and purse, which were miles away in Georgia.

"She didn't say what?" Carmen probed, turning to look at him. Kane had stopped in mid-sentence, which made her believe he was holding something back as well. She was about to urge him to continue when he abruptly changed the subject.

"Nothing," he said, quickly, as if he didn't want to discuss the matter. "So much is going on. It seems to me like Jay and King have a little tiff, too. What is that about?"

"The same ol', same ol'," Carmen replied. "It's nothing new."

Kane had placed his eyes on the road, but now he was looking at Carmen. He was harboring a secret, and he could tell she was, too. Jay and King weren't arguing over the same ol', same 'ol. Something new had happened, which had Malik and one of Jay's workers trying to separate the two. He had heard King fussing about something when he pulled up. However, his stepson's words were sometimes inaudible when everything he said was always followed by the words fuck, shit, motherfucker, and bitch ass. To top it off, Carmen had come out the house right in the middle of it and his focus had gone to their impromptu trip to Georgia.

"When all of this is over with, I want them both to sit down with a therapist."

Kane rolled his eyes before taking another glance at his wife. This time, he noticed the huge rock she was wearing on her left hand. He hadn't noticed it earlier, which meant Jay had proposed in the last twenty-four hours. The ring contained only white diamonds and was far more exquisite than anything he could ever afford.

"That's not going to happen," he told her, speaking of the engagement.

"What do you mean it's not going to happen?" she questioned, turning to look at him. "They don't have a choice in the matter. I'm sitting them down with a therapist or even Minister Harrison so they can hash out their problems. If it calls for it, I will force King to break ties to Jay's businesses so he can concentrate on their personal relationship rather than this business one. Shit, it's not like King is going to go broke because he's not working at Sapphire."

"I'm not talking about that," Kane snapped, turning on the road where the airport was located. "I'm talking about that million-dollar mansion you're wearing on your hand. That shit isn't going down. Every year, you and Jay try to start up an engagement and the shit never happens. That ring is a joke."

"No, you're the joke," Carmen muttered. "We are getting married. It's about damn time I give him what he deserves. We've been playing this game for far too long. Way longer than what we've been playing. My father wanted this, anyway. He wanted me to be with Jay."

"Shit, your father was the one praising me for making an honest woman out of you. I slipped up, had an affair, and now I'm the worst husband ever. You were the one cheating first. You were fuckin' Jay the whole time I was undercover in LA. You even got pregnant by him."

Carmen narrowed her eyes as Kane started the walk down memory lane. He always did it whenever they had a disagreement. It was like he was determined to show her how terrible of a wife she had been. Carmen was well aware of her past sins and had already accepted the fact she was the one who ruined their marriage. It was the main reason she was so adamant about correcting her mistakes. While her relationship with Kane was completely tarnished, she was determined to be faithful to Jay and be the wife she was supposed to be in her first marriage.

Normally, she would've voiced this to Kane, but he kept talking a mile a minute. He went from reprimanding her for continuing a relationship with a man who once assaulted her to mumbling she had gotten engaged when the ink wasn't dry on their divorce. Deep down, Carmen knew Kane simply wanted to argue. He wanted her to give him the same fire he was spitting at her. She wouldn't do it, though, because she knew it was pointless. Nothing he said was going to make her stop the divorce. If anything, he was merely wasting his breath.

In Kane's defense, it wasn't his intention to voice their problems publicly. His emotions had simply overcome him. Carmen, on the other hand, wasn't responding to anything he said. Even when they picked up their tickets at check-in, she had remained silent. Nevertheless, he knew that would soon change. Lucky for him, his prediction came true once they boarded the plane and he was holding the latest issue of *Girlfriend Magazine*. Though she wasn't on the cover, there was a feature on her recent arrest.

"Well, look, uh, here," he bragged, seeing the headline. "Santiago and Davenport-Kane arrested in connection to restaurant shootout. I remember that incident. I wonder if they mention the drug allegations. Do you know who got them out that charge?"

Almost instantly, Carmen's eyes landed on the page he was reading. Not only did it have her name bolded at the top of the page, but there was also a copy of her most recent mug shot. To add on to her fury, Kane was now reading the article word for word for everyone on the plane to hear. He had officially gone too far. With one hand, she snatched the magazine, pulling it out his grasp while the other tore the page out the issue. She then threw it in his lap though she knew he should've gotten decked in the face.

"This magazine didn't belong to me." He chuckled. "I got it from the lady beside me. I will not be paying for this."

"Go to hell," she retorted as she tore the page up in tiny pieces. She threw the remains in his lap before standing up. "You throw around all this shade like you're a righteous man of God. You for damn sure aren't perfect. Don't forget about the crackhead you were fuckin' when you were trying to make amends with me." Carmen spoke of Akaila and Malachi's birth mother, Tricia. After learning of her affair with Jay, Kane made an attempt to reconcile their marriage only to cheat on her with Tricia. She died of an overdose, allowing them to officially adopt her kids.

"Oh, the crackhead who died and gave you the two kids you can't live without?" Kane shot back as he picked up the paper from his lap.

Carmen lowered her head, whispering her words directly in his ear. "You know, you wouldn't be like this if you would go stick your dick in something. Get laid and leave me the fuck alone."

Kane laughed even harder as he thought about Jean. "I have stuck my dick in something," he revealed with a smile. "What? You thought I was going to stay celibate because we're not divorced? Hell no, I did that shit when you were pregnant. I got mine, Carmen. I am so good in that area."

Carmen growled in anger as a flight attendant walked past their row. At the sight of the young woman, she decided to take full advantage of her. "I need to change seats," she ordered. "I refuse to sit next to him. I want a new seat now."

"Um, ma'am, that's not possible. We're about to take off, I need you in your seat."

"I'm not sitting here," Carmen stressed. "I need a new seat."

The flight attendant looked dazed for a few seconds as if she was unsure of what to say. It also didn't help that she recognized Carmen as one of the many celebrities she usually saw in first class. "Ma'am, I'm sorry, but I really need you to sit down and fasten your seatbelt. We're less than a minute away from takeoff."

Carmen sighed out of frustration, not bothering to sit down. When she realized she was stuck with Kane, she plopped down in her seat, folding her arms across her chest.

As for Kane, he was still flipping through the magazine like nothing had happened. With Carmen forced to sit next to him, he declared himself the winner of their argument. "Oh, I love it," he taunted. "Life can't get any better than this."

Carmen turned towards the window, spewing curse words left and right in her head. *Let this motherfucker say one more thing to me. I swear I will knock his head off. He will be real lucky if he makes it to Georgia in one piece. Shit, fuck luck, he'll be blessed. The last thing I ever should've done was brought him along. I should've done this shit on my own.* Carmen gave Kane a side eye, which only irritated her more. He was still reading the magazine like he cared about the latest celebrity tea. Carmen knew Kane couldn't care less about what was going on in the entertainment business. However, as long as he was reading, he wouldn't be bothering her. Therefore, the magazine being in his hands was a plus. She only had to find something to take her attention away from him. Her brainstorm didn't last long before she settled on taking a quick catnap. With her eyes closed and her head tilted towards the window, Carmen drowned out everything around her including her ex.

***

The time was drawing closer to nine o'clock, which told Jay that Carmen and Kane were now well on their way to Copperton City. Currently, he was walking out the doors of Flame with his package secured inside of a black briefcase. Cesar and Linx were both outside the limousine as if they had been waiting impatiently. He had only been inside for about eight minutes or so, but it could've been a minute too long since they were on a bounty hunt.

"Erase those long faces," he joked. "I didn't take that long."

He let out a slight chuckle as he stopped in front of them, waiting for the doors to be unlocked. When they didn't budge, he knew something had happened. It read on both of their faces and explained why they were standing outside the car. "Who did it?" he asked, clutching the briefcase even tighter in his hand. "What happened?"

"King called to say he took your plane to Georgia. His friend, Nicholas, went with him. He must've told your pilot he had your permission. You know your plane is decked out in a lot of heat. He's trying to do this shit without you," Cesar summed up. "I already knew where your head was going to be so I put in a call for three tickets to San Juan. We've got about thirty minutes to get to the airport before the plane starts boarding. Security is going to be tight so I suggest you leave all things of steel in the consoles."

"I'm going to fuck his ass up," Jay muttered, quickly looking around him. His guard was always up, but it went to another level when he realized that every weapon he had on him had to stay inside the limousine. He wouldn't have a pistol, knife, or anything on him until he was able to link up with someone in Georgia. If he was lucky, he would find his plane and rid King of all his burners. "You know, he tried it at Malik's house, but he's really trying it this time."

"Well, he's going to keep trying it," Linx added. "We gotta deal with it and keep pushing. One monkey doesn't stop a show. We get to the airport, we get to San Juan, and then we get to King. You might have enough time to give your son the ass whooping we all want to give him right now."

Jay cracked a smile before motioning to Cesar to unlock the doors. The second he heard the locks turn, he got inside, placing the briefcase in his lap. His right-hands got inside as well and before long they found themselves on a first class flight to San Juan. Once they arrived in the city, he called one of his security guards at his house there to pick them up from the airport. Cesar and Linx both had families in San Juan so he gave them a small window of time to handle their personal business while he tended to his diamonds.

When he first walked in the house, the only thing he heard was silence. With his butler, Silvas, being the only person that stayed there, it wasn't abnormal. He simply made his way to the basement, secured his diamonds in the safe, and then made his way to the kitchen. Upon entering, he could smell the scent of salmon and lime, which told him Silvas had finished cooking. Dishes were in the sink and two wine glasses sat on the island. One of them even had a bright red lipstick stain. At the sight of it, Jay picked it up, carrying it in his hand as he retreated to the patio. It was there he found Silvas cleaning off the picnic table.

"So, you're bringing your dates to my house?" Jay joked, holding up the glass.

Silvas stumbled a bit, somewhat surprised that Jay was at home. Most of the time, he would tell him when he was coming. This visit, however, was a surprise. "No date, Mr. Santiago. I'm a little too old for that," he told him with a smile. "She was a visitor from America. She was sent by your psychiatrist, Dr. Stuart. Matter of fact, she came yesterday. I was too lazy to clean up so now I'm spending my afternoon straightening up the patio."

Jay peered down at the glass oddly, wondering who his psychiatrist had sent to San Juan. Dr. Stuart knew he spent most of his time in Brookstone. If she wanted to reach him, the last place she would've looked was Puerto Rico. "Who was she?"

Silvas didn't speak right off, continuing to wipe down the table. Once he was finished, he motioned for Jay to take a seat. He did the same before giving him a quick run-through of the visit. "Dr. Stuart saw all of that nonsense on the TV. She knows you're in trouble. She wants to help, but she knows your sessions aren't court-ordered anymore. Apparently, there is another lady in her office who wants to help you as well. Her name is Monifah Harris. According to her, y'all were acquaintances a long time ago.

She also said she used to be one of Carmen's best friends. She figured she could take you on as a client and help you make sense of your madness."

"Monifah is back in town? What the hell?" Jay set the glass down on the table. "This shit doesn't make sense, Silvas. This isn't Dr. Stuart's work. She broke every confidentiality agreement I've ever signed."

"All I know is what the lady said. I didn't speak to Dr. Stuart. Besides, your men checked her before she took one step in the house. She didn't come with anything besides the necessities: a license, keys, some credit cards, cash, and a bottle of laxatives." Silvas chuckled at the last item he had named before grabbing the empty wine glass. "She thought she could find you here and set up a one on one consultation. She also wants to get in touch with Carmen. She figured you could help. I said I would pass the message along as well as her business card. So," Silvas said, reaching into his pocket, "here you go."

Jay took the business card out of Silvas' hand to see that Monifah was now a psychiatrist, working at the same practice as Dr. Stuart. Never a person he paid much attention to, it shocked him that Monifah had sought him out. Not to mention, she wanted him to help her get in Carmen's good graces. "I don't know about this, Silvas. If Monifah wants to reach out to Carmen, I'm the wrong person to go through. She should've gone through Tiara. Shit, she should've gone through Malik. Monifah dated his brother."

"Maybe so," Silvas agreed, standing up. "What are you going to do?"

Jay shrugged his shoulders. "I don't know. I can't deal with this right now. I'm actually on my way to Georgia."

"Georgia?" Silvas questioned.

Jay knew he had only told him minimal information about Blu so he had no idea what was in the Peach State. "I'm going on a hunt for Blu," Jay explained. "It's not national news, but he kidnapped Kristian last night. So as you can see, the clock is ticking."

Silvas shook his head at how badly the war had gotten. It was bad enough when Blu had attacked Carmen. Now, he put an innocent girl in the mix. He knew for a fact Kristian's disappearance was wreaking havoc on Jay's fiancée. "How is Carmen?"

At the sound of her name, Jay began to replay their last conversation. Carmen told him she was determined to make their relationship work, but he knew her attitude could change. In a way, it would become the deciding factor in the future of their relationship. "She blames me," he began, knowing how Carmen truly felt. "She's sticking by my side, though. She's actually on her way to Georgia. She and Kane went down this morning."

Silvas nodded his head understandingly as he continued to stare at Jay. He could see the concern in his face and it bothered him to know Jay was dealing with so much in such a short amount of time. While he longed to help him figure out his problems, Jay needed to get moving. "You need to go. I got things covered. If I hear anything else from Monifah, I'll let you know."

"Do that," Jay responded, pulling out his cell phone. He called Cesar first who was quick to inform him that he and Linx were on their way. The words Jay needed to hear. He hung up the phone only so he could text Carmen. Certain she was in Copperton City, he expected to get a quick response. When his text went ignored, Jay became concerned. He told himself to give her some time since she was dealing with so much. Nevertheless, if he didn't hear anything soon, he would contact her again.

6

Politics as Usual

Copperton City, Georgia

Unbeknownst to Carmen, she had missed more than Jay's text message. Emails from Flame went ignored as well as texts from Akaila who was now safely at home in Brookstone. The messages were easy to forget when all of the necessary tasks of the trip had been put in her hands. Upon arriving in Copperton City, she had been the one responsible for securing a rental car as well as locating directions to the police department. Carmen made a mental note as they waited on Detective Morris to talk about the issue once their meeting with the detective was over.

"He's taking longer than I thought," Carmen muttered, taking a peek at her watch. "We've been here, for what, ten minutes or so?" She looked at Kane who appeared to be in deep thought. They hadn't spoken much since their argument on the plane so she was unsure of what was on his mind. "What are you thinking?"

Kane didn't answer right off, using the silence to his advantage. For the past few minutes or so, he had been having a tug of war about whether or not to tell Carmen about the conversation he shared with Kristian. Unsure of Detective Morris' findings, he knew if he revealed his daughter was having problems it could be crucial to the investigation. He also knew if he kept it a secret he would have a leg up on the case.

"Say something," Carmen urged.

Kane swallowed before disclosing the secret. "Someone was bothering Kristian," he whispered. "She mentioned it to me before she left for college. I brushed it off because it was right after our paternity trial. My mind wasn't in the right place to deal with anyone's issues, but my own." Kane shook his head in disbelief as he thought to that night. "I was selfish and I pushed her away. She did say it was a guy though. I just don't know who."

Carmen bit her lip as she saw an image of Blu in her mind. She didn't have any recollection of him having met Kristian, but she figured it happened somehow. If it wasn't Blu then it had to be a guy she didn't know. She suspected something happened between her and Nicholas Powers, but she didn't have any solid proof. However, judging from Nicholas' presence at her father's funeral, the only thing he was concerned about was getting in King's inner circle. "What else did she tell—" Carmen was interrupted when she saw someone move in front of her. A rather tall gentleman with a stocky build, she took him to be Detective Morris. "Hi," she said. "I'm Carmen Davenport. I believe we spoke on the phone."

"Detective Morris," the man replied. He held out his hand, which they each shook. "I hope I didn't keep you waiting long. I know you didn't want to come on these terms. I've been trying to piece together as much as I can. Follow me and I'll let you know what I've found."

The detective took a few steps forward, prompting them to follow him to his office. He opened the door to reveal a cluttered desk where two large plastic bags had been set. The bags were clear, allowing Carmen to see the items collected from Kristian's car.

"Right now," Detective Morris began, sitting in a chair opposite of them. "The most valuable thing we found is her cell phone. She hasn't erased her messages in a while. There were some text exchanges between her and a boy named Dijuan. From what I've read, he was having some difficulty with the distance in their relationship. Some of the conversations had gotten—"

Kane cleared his throat loudly as he prepared himself to clear Dijuan's name. "He definitely isn't a suspect," he told him, firmly. "He's Kristian's high school sweetheart and the son of our minister. Dijuan is in college at Duke University on a basketball scholarship. The distance may have been a factor and possibly caused some tension between them, but he isn't behind this. What other suspects do you have? Did you look at the fingerprints?"

Detective Morris paused before setting Kristian's cell phone on the table. "We need to get rid of the elephant in the room. I know who you are. With all due respect, Agent, as we go through what we've collected, I believe we'll have the understanding that this case belongs to the Copperton City Police Department. We don't need any Triad involvement."

Carmen raised her brow before looking at Kane. His face was suddenly becoming tense so she patted his leg as a reminder he needed to keep his anger at bay. "Kane is no longer employed with the Triad," she disclosed. "He's here because he's Kristian's father. He knows this is your case. He won't get involved at all."

"Well, as long as we have that understanding," the detective shot back. He picked up the cell phone, continuing where he left off. He also didn't bother to answer Kane's question regarding the fingerprints. "Now, the last call made to her phone was late last night. In actuality, it was a missed phone call. When we traced the number, which was local, we learned it was recently disconnected. The service was through Verizon and the previous owner was Jerome McFadden. The odd thing about all of this is that the number wasn't disconnected until this morning. We missed getting in contact with him by about an hour."

Carmen's face tightened. Jerome was one of King's best friends. His other best friend, Rico, was Jerome's cousin, and one of many men who were killed by her fiancé. Whether or not Jerome had ties to Blu, she didn't know, but she knew he had a motive for revenge.

"I know him," Kane spoke up. "He's a known drug dealer. I don't understand why his number is local, though. He lives in New York. Do you have an address for him?"

Detective Morris gave Kane a stern look to let him know he was going into a barred arena. The question wasn't one he was ready to answer because he didn't want Kane gathering too much information. If he did, he could potentially ruin their investigation. To keep him from doing so, he decided to steer him in a different direction. "Do you think he may be a suspect?"

"What reason does he have to be in Copperton City?" Kane asked, not answering the question. "The last time I saw him, he was standing outside of Blue Magic, wearing a business suit. He works for Jay Santiago."

Carmen cut her eyes at Kane's words. Detective Morris didn't need to know that Jerome had a link to Jay when her fiancé was already under the microscope with every law enforcement agency in the world. The last thing he needed was to be attached to a potential kidnapper.

"Okay, so let me ask you again, do you think he could be a suspect?"

Carmen and Kane both said yes and no simultaneously. It confused the detective who gave them both a closer look. "You said yes, Ms. Davenport. However, Kane, said no."

"Jerome is my stepson's best friend," Kane cleared up. "He has known Kristian all his life. He wouldn't hurt her. I know that for a fact. He probably looks at Kristian like she's his little sister. He didn't do this."

"Why is he here then?" Carmen shot back. "He has a local number."

Kane's eyes flickered over to Carmen. He knew the answer he wanted to give yet he had already felt her eyes burning on him when he dropped Jay's name only seconds before. He wanted to tell her Jerome was probably in the area, trying to sell whatever dope he still had from his days in the Santiago cartel. Nevertheless, he had to steer the conversation in a different direction. "I don't know why he's here. Obviously, he planned on staying a while because his number is local."

"I agree," Carmen added. "I think he's a suspect. If we find him, we find some answers."

"I think he's worth looking into since Kane said he's a drug dealer. I say we try and locate him. Hopefully, he's still in the area." The detective paused for a few seconds before showing them the rest of the items in the bag, which were miniscule. "An officer was able to get over to the university where Kristian was staying. Her roommate, Akaila, seemed to have already left. According to two girls, Angi and Chantel, who stay in the same dorm, Akaila was her sister. I'm guessing she is your daughter, too?"

"Yes," Carmen assured. "We adopted her and her little brother, Malachi, a couple of years ago. I sent for her when I found out Kristian had been kidnapped. She should be home in Brookstone now."

"I'm guessing you two are no longer together, right?"

Carmen nodded her head. "I recently filed for divorce. We've been legally separated for several months now. As you can see, I've been using my maiden name."

"It explains the statement we got from those two girls back at campus. They said the last time they saw Kristian, she was very upset. They wanted her to go out to eat with them, but she decided to drive around the city. They said she was rather distraught because her parents were going through a second divorce. Is this information correct?"

Carmen became confused at his question. "Does it matter? We know Kristian is hurt over our divorce. That isn't a secret. All our kids probably are."

"It matters because another theory is that your daughter is perfectly safe and sound and possibly staged all of this for attention. So, once again, is that information correct?"

"It will be our second," Kane replied. "This isn't Kristian's work. The evidence supports that. She wouldn't leave her wallet, her cell phone, none of that stuff in a brand new Lexus for some damn attention. She was upset, she wanted some fresh air, and that was it. Someone took advantage of her being alone and kidnapped her. My guess is that it is a person who wanted her and nothing else. Wouldn't you agree? They didn't take her money or her car."

"We have to look at all options, Mr. Kane."

Kane grabbed the two plastic bags and started to stuff Kristian's belongings into them. The detective had told him enough for him to move forward. He was no longer of value besides telling them they could get the car out of impound. "I think we're done here," Kane told him, standing up. "You have Carmen's contact information, stay in touch if there are any developments."

"Mr. Kane, I have a feeling—" the detective was interrupted when Kane started to stress even more that the conversation was over.

"Detective Morris, the only thing we need to know is if the car is available for us to get out of impound. Anything regarding our divorce is not up for discussion."

Carmen swallowed at Kane's tone while the detective replied that the car was available before rattling off the name of the impound lot as well as quick directions on how to get there. Unsure of what to do, Carmen stayed in her seat until Kane motioned for her to come forward.

"Look, I know this situation is sensitive for both of you," Detective Morris said, standing up, "and I apologize for my questions. I'm looking for any information that can help. There isn't a lot to go on here. Right now, our only lead is Jerome McFadden. He called Kristian for a reason last night. Now, if you can contact your son and see if he knows anything, that information could potentially help us find your daughter."

"We understand," Carmen replied. "We know you only want to do your job."

Carmen gave the detective a warm smile as the door opened to the interrogation room. When she turned to look behind her, she saw Kane walking out. Not wanting to conform to his behavior, she gave the detective a quick wave and whispered thank you. The detective probably took the words to be somewhat meaningless because of Kane's behavior, but Carmen was appreciative for the things he told her. She only needed to get her hands on King or Jay so she could inquire about Jerome. From the way things were looking, he was the missing link.

"Well, that went well," Carmen said sarcastically once she was in the car. She looked over at Kane who was busy pressing buttons on the GPS. She could see the screen, which displayed the address for the impound lot where Kristian's car was located. "I guess we're going there next, right? Or did you want to try and find Jerome?"

"Both," Kane replied, starting up the car. "Actually, we need to be multitasking. I got the directions already pulled up for the impound lot. Can you locate a hotel and book two rooms?"

Carmen raised her right brow at the words hotel and book. So far, she had been the bank for the whole trip. The flight, the rental car, as well as the gas, had all come from her pockets. "So you can't pay for the hotel?" Carmen asked with an attitude. "Don't even worry about it, I got it. By now I should know which role I play… ATM." Carmen pulled out her phone finally noticing the email and text message alerts. When she saw Jay had texted her, she breathed a sigh of relief. With him on his way to Georgia, he could finally help her put together some pieces. It would mean more tension, but it was a risk she was ready to take.

***

While Carmen was thinking of Jay, she was on his radar as well. More than an hour had passed since he had sent his text message and Carmen still hadn't responded. Highly concerned, he checked his phone for the umpteenth time. When he saw he didn't have any new messages or missed phone calls, he mumbled a few choice words under his breath. He told himself she would call as soon as she could, which seemed to lessen his fury.

In the meantime, he was still weaponless, searching his private plane for any piece of steel he could find. Just his luck, his pilot called after he landed in Georgia to talk about King's surprise trip. If it wasn't for the phone call, he wouldn't have known that his private plane was at the same airport he'd flown into. The only downfall was that all of his weapons had been removed from it. Even the ones he hid in various compartments were coming up missing.

"They did a thorough search of this thing," Cesar voiced, coming from the cockpit. "He made sure you weren't left with any heat."

Jay's eyes peered upward as he gave up. "I'm going to do a thorough search of kicking his ass, too. I don't know what game King is trying to play." Jay pulled out his cell phone once again as Linx came on the plane. He had been busy trying to locate King and it seemed he didn't have any luck. Not waiting for him to say it, Jay decided to use his last lifeline.

Living in the outskirts of Atlanta was a man by the name of Guillermo Perez. The product of two parents who were full-blooded Puerto Rican, he was Jay's first cousin on his father's side. Nicknamed Gully, his cousin used his mother's maiden name in place of Santiago to disassociate himself from the family. While they had gotten along as kids, Gully held a grudge against him ever since their late teens.

For more than thirty years, Jay had given Gully his space. He always kept a contact number for him for situations like this though he never had to use it. With charges attached to his name as well as his history with the law, the last thing he could do was buy weapons from an actual dealer. Since Gully was rumored to be working as a bounty hunter, Jay was certain his house was well stocked with everything he needed.

"Gully," he said quickly, once he heard his cousin answer. He motioned for Linx and Cesar to be quiet since they were making too much noise trying to search the plane. Once they were settled, he listened for any signs of movement coming from Gully's end. His cousin didn't respond yet he knew he was still on the line from the sound of his breathing. "It's Jay," he told him, "Hector and Lady's son." He gave him a second to respond yet Gully was being hardheaded. He was obviously still upset with him and hesitant to say anything. "Come on, Gully, I need you right now."

"Bitch, what do you want?" Gully shouted in the phone. "These motherfuckers got your ass all over the TV and newspapers and you're going to call me? I'm not getting caught up in your bullshit, Jay. Ya hear me?"

The phone went dead, leaving Jay with a disconnected call. He somewhat expected it yet at the same time he hoped Gully had matured. Not letting it stop him, he called the number back. He knew Gully wasn't going to answer, which was proven when his voicemail came on. Jay had no intention of trying him for a third time so he left his request on the machine. "Look, man, you know you never gave me a fair chance of clearing up the issue you have with me. I'm willing to give you time and space to discuss it. After that, I need you to help me. I need some heat and I know you're the go to guy in Georgia for it. I got some trouble on my end. My fiancée's daughter got kidnapped. Call me back with an address and I'll get you squared away. Money isn't an issue."

His last four words rang truth as Jay stuffed the phone in his pocket. "He's going to do what he's going to do," he explained to his right-hands. "I prefer to go through him because I know everything will be clean. The last thing we want is to buy guns off the street that the police are looking for. Gully, right now, is our only option."

Jay scratched his head as he tried to determine his next move. Since Carmen hadn't returned his call, he couldn't meet up with her. Obviously still wrapped up in whatever she was doing, he figured he would continue the search for King.

"Alright, let's head…" Jay paused when his phone started ringing. He pulled it out his pocket only to see the word Gully on the screen. "We might have some luck," he whispered. He answered the call only to hear his cousin's thunderous voice once again.

"Come through in the morning," he bellowed. "Ten o'clock, no sooner, no later. Oh, and before I forget, if you want to find your bitch, her ass is up at the Ritz Carlton with that baldheaded scumbag who got you in this shit in the first place. I saw their asses when I was on my way downtown. They're driving a four-door black Cadillac Coupe."

"Thank–" Jay was cut off once again when the phone hung up. He smiled as he realized just how much Gully had kept up with him. While he didn't favor him calling Carmen a bitch, he was glad Gully had looked out for him. He now knew where to find Carmen, which meant the Ritz Carlton was the next place he was headed. He quickly shared the news with Linx and Cesar before telling them to abandon the plane. They may have been weaponless, but in less than twenty four hours, they would have as much heat as the US Army.

7

Passion, Pain, and Pleasure

Carmen pulled a light pink tee out her suitcase, the last of several to put in the hotel's dresser. Normally, she would've kept her things packed, but something told her she would be in Georgia for more than a few days. Therefore, she unpacked all her belongings and even arranged her personals to her liking on the bathroom counter.

Although Jay hadn't reached the hotel, Carmen estimated he had been in the city for about an hour. She had texted him her room number yet she hadn't received a response. The lack of communication made her nervous while her anger with Kane made her want to unleash. Unlike Jay, Kane was only across the hall and would be the perfect person to feel her wrath.

Nevertheless, she was stuck with him until everything blew over. *Who am I kidding?* Carmen asked herself. *I'm always going to be stuck with him. Kristian, Akaila, and Malachi are the main reasons why.* Carmen wrinkled her face at the thought until she heard a loud knock at her door. Certain Kane was coming to ask for a credit card, she hesitated in answering. However, when the knocks continued, she headed to the door. The last person she expected to see on the other side was her fiancé. He was standing in front of her with a duffle bag in his left hand and a suitcase in his right. Carmen's lips trembled for a few seconds before she grabbed him into a hug. "You got my message," she screamed, her voice somewhat muffled from her mouth being buried in his shoulder. She pulled away from him to give him a chance to come in the room.

"Took you long enough to tell me where you were," he fussed. "I guess King forgot to tell you he took my plane and guns." Jay threw his duffle bag on the floor right before setting his suitcase in the middle of the living room.

"So King is here?" Carmen asked, somewhat surprised. She knew he was supposed to come yet she didn't think he had followed through with his plans since his girlfriend, Coco, had returned to Brookstone. She assumed he stayed in New York to be with her.

"King is walking around with a lot of heat on him. I got both my men looking for him."

"And how do you know where they should look?"

Jay had ventured in the bedroom, sitting on the bed, which had been covered in cream sheets and a gold comforter. The neatness of the bed told him Carmen hadn't been to sleep. Somewhat tired, he wiped his face as he debated his answer. He knew it was time to come clean since she had recently visited Detective Morris. He didn't know what she was told, which meant they could potentially be withholding information from each other. "You want to sit down?"

He pulled her near-empty suitcase off the bed and placed it on the floor. Not quite sure how she was going to react, he said each of his words slowly as she sat next to him. "I never told you this, but Blu is from Copperton City. He owns three businesses here. Two clubs, one named The Sphinx Club and the other is called The Kingdom. He also has a restaurant called Soulshock. I didn't tell King at first either. It's part of the reason why he's mad at me. When I did tell him, I made the agreement to hire someone to watch the girls. I didn't do it and…" Jay paused right before he dropped the bombshell. "Now Blu has Kristian."

The room went silent for a few short seconds. He wasn't quite sure what Carmen was thinking because the expression on her face was rather blank.

"The guilt is killing you, isn't it?" she whispered.

They met eyes, which only made Jay wish he hadn't been looking in her direction. The look of hurt on Carmen's face was one he could barely stomach. Most things he could be nonchalant about, but when it came to hurting her, it bothered him to his core. "All I want to do is protect you. I thought the less you knew the better off you'd be. I didn't expect for any of this to happen. I didn't even know he had crossed paths with Kristian."

Carmen bit her lip hard to keep her tears in. She even closed her eyes yet the waterworks still came. "You knew when I got that phone call he had taken her. Blu is the man Kristian told Kane about. He was stalking her, and she tried to ask her father for help. He ignored her and now she is somewhere scared out her mind." Carmen rose from the bed, heading towards the living room. She immediately started to pace the floor as she soaked in the news. Her right hand constantly went over her left, pulling at her two million-dollar engagement ring. It would come halfway up her finger yet she didn't take it off.

Carmen looked in the bedroom where Jay was sitting. She thought of Kristian's cell phone and the call from Jerome McFadden her daughter had missed. Since he was in the mood to unleash secrets, she decided to ask him about one of his former workers. "Jerome," she yelled, walking in the room. "He called Kristian right before she was kidnapped. His phone number was local. Did you know he was here?"

Jay nodded his head. "I found out yesterday. Nicholas told King who then told me. I didn't know before then, though. My relationship with Jerome went sour when I murdered his cousin, Rico. It doesn't surprise me he's here. What does surprise me is that he called Kristian. It sounds to me like he may be involved in the kidnapping, too."

"Kane is supposed to be getting an address on him. We find him, we find some answers."

Carmen folded her arms across her chest as she stood in the doorway. Her eyes were still planted on Jay though his image was somewhat blurred from the tears that were running down both sides of her face. The more she stared at him, the more she felt her anger intensifying. If she didn't turn away soon, she knew she would charge at him. "I need to drink this off."

"I'm sorry, Peaches."

About to turn on her heel, Carmen looked at him. "I know you are. I also know the guilt is going to continue to eat at you until we find her. That's something you're going to have to deal with. I don't have any intention of telling Kane about this. We both know how the afternoon will be if I did. So, I'm going to the lobby bar and I don't want to see you until I'm ready. Find something productive to do."

Carmen grabbed her key card and cell phone, leaving the room. She walked at a fast pace, ignoring the sound of doors opening around her.

Little did she know, Kane was one of the people who opened his door. Somewhat famished, his plan was to treat her to lunch since she had paid for most of the trip. When he saw her walking on the elevator, he wondered where she was headed. The keys to the Cadillac were in his possession, which meant she couldn't have been going far. Instead of following her, he allowed the elevator doors to close while he ventured in his suite. Certain she would be back soon, he decided to start the search for Jerome's address.

Right when he started to make a call to an old colleague at the Triad, Sanders beeped in. Perfect timing. He clicked over to see what his partner had discovered about the Benz at Flame. "Talk to me," he greeted, sitting at a conference-styled table.

"We got a lot of shit on our hands, Kane. I hope you're ready for it."

"Talk to me," he repeated, taking out an ink pen. A notepad was already on the table, which was where he had written his colleague's cell phone number. He simply tore off the page so he could start writing on a new sheet.

"I guess I'll tell the good news first," Sanders said, speaking excitedly. "The lieutenant got another warrant to search Blue Magic. I didn't find out about it until I came to the station. The general manager met with one of the detectives here who found a tape that hadn't been confiscated. It's from a camera that actually faces the section of the parking lot where the shooting occurred. Someone tried to destroy it, but didn't do a very good job. Only half of the tape was ruined while the other half was damn near perfect. We have picture-perfect footage of Jay Santiago shooting up the entire parking lot. We needed evidence to place him at the scene, well, we got it. The lieutenant is already in front of the courthouse about to tell the world we're issuing a warrant for his arrest."

Kane's hands shook to the point that he dropped the ink pen. "Are you serious?"

"The broadcast is about to go live. If you're with Carmen, you better tell her now. If she knows where Jay is, she needs to get word to him. Every cop, every agent, every detective is about to be on his ass. We have proof he's responsible for those deaths at Blue Magic. Put that tape in front of a jury and he will be spending the rest of his life behind bars."

Kane stood up from the table, grabbing the keys to the rental. He knew Carmen couldn't have gone far so the first place he checked was the hotel lobby. Still on the line, Sanders was making small talk about the warrant, but Kane ignored him. However, Kane heard him when he said the black car was owned by BNYC Media, a company focused on entertainment news. Since the black car at Flame was just a bunch of paps, Kane's attention became more focused on finding his wife. Eventually, he located her at the lobby bar. A glass of wine was in her hand, which he grabbed once he reached her. "Where's Jay?" he asked, hanging up on Sanders. He grabbed her shoulders to pull her towards him until he realized she was crying.

"I'm trying," she cried out to him. "I really am. I don't know what else to do. I don't. I made the decision to be with him, but it's like, every day, something happens, and I question myself. I love him, God knows I do, but it gets so…things get so difficult. Why can't…" Carmen covered her mouth. "Why do I have to deal with this? Why can't I be happy and have normal problems? Why can't I just be mad about him leaving the seat up? Why can't I just be mad because he ate the last bit of cinnamon ice cream in the fridge?" Carmen threw her hands up in the air to further illustrate her thought. Although Kane had taken the wine out her hand, she grabbed the glass once more, taking a large gulp. "I guess I have to work through it."

The words *what happened* were on the tip of Kane's tongue because he knew Carmen wasn't upset over the warrant. He wanted to ask the question, while at the same time he debated about whether or not he needed to break his own news. Already crying and drinking her problems away, he knew what the news could do to her. He had seen her break down before and he didn't want to witness it again.

"You don't want to hear this," she was saying. "Why would you? I'm divorcing you to be with him." Carmen let out a slight chuckle only to down the rest of her drink. "Fuck it, Kane. You hear me? Fuck it. Forget I even said anything."

Carmen hopped off the chair before signaling to the bartender she wanted to close out her tab. It wasn't until she was stuffing her debit card in her wallet she realized she hadn't answered his question. All of their paths were set to cross so she went ahead and told him Jay was upstairs in her suite. She even told him she was headed to the room, but to give her an hour or two before he bothered them. Carmen figured that once things calmed down between her and Jay, they would walk across the hall to Kane's room to discuss whatever was on his mind.

On that note, the conversation ended and Carmen returned to her suite. Jay was inside unpacking and didn't speak when she entered. Glad he hadn't, Carmen grabbed the remote, turning on the television. It had been set to ESPN, but she quickly scrolled through the channels to keep her fingers busy until she reached CNN.

She had been on the channel for only a second, but she was certain her eyes weren't playing tricks on her. Frozen on the screen was Jay's mug shot. The picture had been taken only a few short weeks ago. She could spot it in a crowd of hundreds. At first she was unsure about why he was the topic of discussion until the newscaster introduced a clip of the shootout at Blue Magic. When the tape played, Carmen watched as Jay's six foot five frame appeared. A gun was clearly in his hands and he was firing in several different directions, shells flying all across the parking lot.

Out the corner of her eye, Carmen saw her fiancé as he dropped to his knees. A news ticker was starting to come across the screen, telling citizens everywhere that a warrant had been issued for his arrest. Every law enforcement agency in America and Puerto Rico were being instructed to be on the lookout for him. The headline alone explained why Kane had asked her where he was. He knew the Brookstone PD was looking for him. That told Carmen only one thing, she and Jay both needed to get out the Ritz Carlton.

She looked at him as a round of knocks sounded at the door. Jay moved quick, getting off his knees and running to the bathroom. It left Carmen somewhat stuck between a rock and a hard place. If police were on the other side, she could tell them Jay wasn't there yet they would still demand to search the suite. Either way she went, she could be walking into a dead end. Well aware she had to take that chance; she opened the door to see Cesar with a face full of sweat.

"I fucked up," he rattled, coming inside. He walked quickly around the suite as if he was looking for Jay. "I was supposed to get rid of the tape. I was supposed to get rid of all of 'em."

"He's in the bathroom," Carmen told him, closing the door. "He probably thought you were a cop. Shoot, I thought you were a cop." She walked in the bedroom and knocked on the bathroom door. Jay didn't answer so she told him Cesar was in the room so he would come out.

"I fucked up," Cesar repeated once he saw him. "I was in a hurry. I left your apartment, I went back there, and I tried to get everything I could. I thought I destroyed all the tapes, but I guess I didn't. I—"

Jay cut him off, starting to display the aggression Cesar initially expected. "I got every fuckin' cop in this damn city and across the US looking for my ass. You think I want to sit up here and listen to you whine? I don't have time for that shit. You want to help, get me a fuckin' limousine. Figure out how I'm going to get out of this damn hotel."

Jay sat on the bed, shaking his head back and forth. "King landed my plane at the airport, which means the police have probably already confiscated it. The good thing, though, is that they won't find any weapons. All that's on there is some cigars and booze." Jay spoke as an image of his private plane surrounded by blue lights formed in his mind. To him, it was a prophecy of what was to come. "I gotta see my kids," he mumbled. "Someone has to call Malik. He's going to have to meet us somewhere. We'll be lucky if we get out of this state before they find me."

"We need to leave in the middle of the night," Carmen suggested. "If we go now, anyone can see us. It doesn't even matter if we take the back way. Cops will be everywhere."

"Cops are everywhere right now," Jay yelled. "They are going to search for you because they know you're probably with me. You paid for your flight with your debit card, right?" Jay didn't even allow her to answer. "They track that and then they find you right here in the city until they're standing outside our hotel room. We don't have time to do anything." His hands were now covering his face as he tried to wipe the sweat beads off his forehead. "Kane is right across the hall, too. He's probably waiting for the right moment to break the fuckin' door down."

"Do you want me to take care of him?" Cesar asked.

"You don't have a fuckin' gun," Jay yelled. "What are you going to do, strangle him, leave some fingerprints this time? Get the limo and find Linx. Tell him to come to the hotel. I don't give a fuck about King anymore. We'll deal with his ass later."

Jay jumped from the bed, grabbing his cell phone. He went in the bathroom, closed the door, and locked it. Carmen could hear him talking, but she couldn't make out his words. Cesar didn't know what he was saying either because he was too busy heading out the suite.

"I'm sorry, Carmen," he told her once his hand was on the doorknob. "You know how that day was. I tried my best to handle everything. Sometimes, even the best fail. I love Jay like he's my own brother. I didn't do that shit intentionally. I made a mistake."

"I know," Carmen replied. She stared at Cesar, hoping he understood she didn't blame him. He had done the work of ten men in a short amount of time. If it wasn't for him, Jay wouldn't have been able to get away from the restaurant. In her opinion, Jay was indebted to him. She sighed at the thought as Cesar opened the door. He stepped out and she followed behind him, locking it. Jay was still inside the bathroom, but she knew his conversation had come to an end when she heard the locks turn. He came out, headed straight towards the windows, and closed the curtains. From there, he grabbed his suitcase and duffle bag, starting to pack his things. She was about to ask him what his plan was until he asked her a question of his own.

"Are you still going to marry me?"

The question was one Carmen had been contemplating ever since Jay had broken his silence about Blu. She had debated it even when she was downstairs at the lobby bar. Still, she had returned to the suite with the understanding she was there for the long haul. If she continued to fault Jay for everything he did wrong, she would never be there for when he did things right. He would never be perfect, but neither would she.

"Are you still going to marry me?" he shouted.

Carmen swallowed when she realized she went too long without answering. She quickly told him yes. "I am going to marry you. This situation is going from bad to worse, but if we suffer the bad times now, it'll be like taking candy from a baby when we're actually married."

Jay looked away as he felt a sense of relief. A large part of him honestly believed Carmen was going to turn on him. Not only because he revealed Blu's birthplace, but also because his life was now in the hands of the country's law enforcement. "I don't want to lose you," he told her, turning to look at her. "I don't want to lose my kids. I already did that shit for seventeen years. I refuse to do it again."

Carmen felt a rock sit in her stomach at how helpless Jay looked. The expression was the same one he wore when he was given a life sentence twenty years ago. They weren't necessarily on speaking terms then, but Carmen could imagine how he must've felt. Then, a blessing came from God when a judge overturned his sentence. It made her wonder if the same could happen now. Jay had changed for the better, but his past always found a way to corrupt him.

Carmen grabbed him in her arms, allowing him to rest against her. As each minute passed, she thought more and more about how this could be the last time she ever held him close. The idea frightened her yet at the same time it made her want to explore every inch of him. Her hands wanted to cradle his face, her lips wanted to be shoved against his, and her tongue longed to taste his skin. While the moment was too sensitive for her to be thinking of intimacy, Carmen longed for the connection.

She moved slowly, placing her hand on his upper left thigh as her lips found their way on his. He didn't flinch or push her away, kissing her softly while his arms wrapped tighter around hers. As they connected, the noises around them seemed to disappear.

Naturally, Jay's body moved in sync with hers as they pulled away each other's clothes. His body was warm as they met chest to chest, his shaft slowly starting to penetrate her inner walls. The first stroke she received almost made Carmen's heart stop. Gentle yet firm, there was something noticeably different about the way he was catering to her. He moved at an even pace like every thrust was timed to perfection to send the right amount of shock through her body. His hands were entangled in her hair yet he wasn't pulling with as much force as she was used to. If Carmen had to describe it, it was like his fingers were merely gliding.

Her hands, however, were situated along his upper back right at his shoulders. One on each side, she grabbed at his butterscotch skin as the weight of their lovemaking intensified. His name sat at the edge of her tongue, longing to be let out. The deeper he plunged, the further it was pushed over the edge. She tried to contain herself for several minutes yet he made the task difficult. He was giving her everything she wanted without her even asking.

Almost on the brink, Jay's hands framed her face as he pulled his lips off hers. His eyes, which had been closed throughout most of their connection, were now wide open. It was the start of a perfect ending as she climaxed. Her eyes were forced closed as his hands went right in her hair, tightening around her jet black locks. Unable to control the urge, he grunted loudly as he came inside of her. Enthralled in a state of orgasmic bliss, Carmen exhaled as Jay's body fell complacent on hers. Heavy on her chest, Carmen wouldn't dare tell him to move. The closeness merely sealed their connection, relaxing her to the point that she fell into a peaceful slumber.

8

Long Gone Missin'

Quiet was the only word Kane could use to describe the sound coming from Carmen's room. She told him to give her an hour or two before he came up, but he couldn't wait. With the state's local Triad agency on the hunt for Jay, he needed to make sure he kept his eyes on him. Carmen claimed he was in her room, but Kane needed to make certain of it. He needed to assure Sanders and Lieutenant Harris that he knew of Jay's whereabouts. If he was viewed as the one who brought Jay in, the feat alone could secure him another position at the Triad.

Therefore, he raised his hand to knock on the door. Before he could, his phone ranged, causing him to drop his arm at his side. Kane grunted at the interruption as he pulled his phone from his pocket. He would've ignored the call, but Harris was on the other end. That only meant one thing—Sanders had gotten in contact with him. Kane knew he had to answer so he decided to take the call in his suite.

"We're on the verge of cracking the biggest case this year and you're about to ruin that for us. Do you think I'm going to let that happen?" the lieutenant barked. "Don't even bother to answer. Shut up and listen. Sanders said you and Carmen are together. Is Jay there?"

"You want me to answer or shut up?"

"Don't give me the slick talk, Kane. Answer the damn question."

"I'm waiting to put eyes on him. I can't guarantee he's in the city until I do."

"What the fuck are you doing in Georgia? You know what, I don't care. Go get Carmen."

That's what I was trying to do, motherfucker. He didn't voice his thought, opting to return to Carmen's suite. This time when he raised his hand to knock, he became fearful of what he would find. The lack of noise only told him two things. Carmen and Jay weren't on speaking terms or they were in bed together asleep. Believing it might have been the latter, Kane took a step from the door. He didn't want to knock yet Harris was waiting for an update. He decided to buy himself some time.

"I didn't tell Sanders," he said, returning to his room, "but my daughter was kidnapped last night. That's why I'm in Georgia. You know she was going to Copperfield."

"She was kidnapped? Kane, what the fuck is going on? Is Jay there or not?"

"Did you hear what I said to you? My daughter was kidnapped. Carmen and I are in Georgia together. She said Jay is with her. If you give me some time, I'll bring him to you."

"So, you're trying to tell me you're going to withhold information about Jay's whereabouts until you find your daughter?"

Kane swallowed at how Harris was taking his words. "No, what I'm saying is that I want to bring Santiago in. I want to take him down. Let me place eyes on him first. I need to make him believe he's safe. Matter of fact, call everything off. Let me do this, Harris."

"You're out of your fuckin' mind!" the lieutenant screamed. "Nah, nah, I'm going to get another officer down there. You concentrate on your daughter and I'll have someone else come and get Jay. Where are you at right now?"

"Now I am going to withhold information," Kane fired back. "Give me until morning, Harris. I promise you. I will secure Jay and bring him to you myself."

"Kane, your badge is on the line. Where is Jay? Don't make me do this the hard way. That would be firing you and tracing every credit transaction that you or your ex-wife has made in the last forty-eight hours."

"I dare you to fuckin' threaten me. I told you my daughter was fuckin' kidnapped last night. I need Jay right now. Do you hear me? I need him."

Lieutenant Harris let out a loud sigh. "You got until nine o'clock tomorrow morning to secure Jay. I want his ass in New York by tomorrow afternoon. If he's not, your job is gone. Are we clear?"

"Crystal," Kane replied, hanging up the phone. He threw his cell on the other side of the room, watching as it hit one of the piano legs. He stared at it for a few seconds as he tried to form a plan in his mind. He needed to find Kristian and he needed to get Jay in police custody. How he was going to do both, he didn't know. Unsure of where to turn, he walked over to the piano and picked up his phone. He needed support and he didn't want it to come from Sanders. While he knew Jean was somewhat upset with him, he decided to give her a call.

"Hello?" she answered, right after the third ring.

Her voice was soft yet inquisitive. The tone instantly calmed Kane's nerves as he remembered how she made him feel. "It's Michael," he told her, saying his first name. "We had a moment last night. Do you have a minute?"

Jean giggled at his words. "I knew who you were when you said Michael. You didn't have to say we had a moment. You can just say we fucked."

Kane chuckled as he took a seat on the piano bench. "I woke up this morning to learn my daughter was kidnapped. I'm not even in New York. I'm in Copperton City where she was going to school." The loud sigh Kane expected sounded on the phone. It was then followed by silence. "I need someone to talk to. I'm here with my wife; she has her fiancé with her and I feel kind of alone, you know. Then, I got people at my job hounding me."

"It's the Jay Santiago stuff, isn't it? I saw it on the news."

"You know it is."

"What do you need for me to do?"

"You shocked me with that one," Kane replied. "Shit, you shocked me by answering the phone. I guess I'm out the doghouse, huh?"

Jean let out another snigger. "Something kind of like that. I looked up some stuff. You know how the blogs are. Carmen has really put you through a lot. Why did you marry her? You should've known she was going to keep Jay's dick in her pants."

"Thanks for the reminder," Kane shot back.

"Oops, I guess you didn't need the visual." Jean paused for a second or two as she tried to sense how offended he was. When he didn't respond, she decided to ask her question again since he hadn't answered it. "So, what do you need for me to do?"

"Hop on this dick and relieve me of some stress," Kane suggested. He smiled at the thought, somewhat unsure if it was possible. He was stuck in Georgia until he was able to turn Jay in. Once he returned to New York, he would be in Brookstone just long enough to get Jay booked and get the praise due to him. After that, he needed to be in Georgia, trying to locate Jerome McFadden. If he was lucky, he could squeeze in a screw before his flight.

"Order up," Jean agreed, interrupting his thoughts.

"Cool," Kane replied. "I'll call you tomorrow." After Jean replied with a low okay, Kane held the phone to his ear until she hung up. Once the line disconnected, he set his cell on top of the piano. Though Jean had somewhat calmed his nerves, he was still in the same position as before—alone. Kane knew he had to take matters in his own hands. With a Cadillac Coupe at his disposal, he had the means to get his questions answered.

Copperfield University was only about ten minutes away and seemed to be a good place to start. All he needed to do was get there.

***

With everything that had transpired, Kane could be described as a piece of thread in Carmen's mind. From the lovemaking session she had shared with Jay to the three hours they had slept, Carmen awoke to only think of the man who was asleep on her bosom. The most vulnerable she had seen him. Jay refused to let her out his grasp. Even now, both of his arms were secured around her. It made it difficult to move, but she managed to free her right arm from underneath him.

She didn't want to wake him yet she smoothed the palm of her hand over the top of his head. Normally kept shaven, Carmen noticed he was allowing his hair to grow in. She was about to close her eyes when something told her to look at the clock. It was drawing closer to six, which reminded Carmen that she hadn't accomplished anything. The only thing that was a work in progress was the repairs on Kristian's Lexus. The thought sickened her as she started to feel as if she was putting a man before her child. Instead of searching the streets of Copperton City for her daughter, she was naked in bed with Jay.

The guilt ate at her soul, forcing her to move Jay away. The slight push made him stir and this time he grabbed her even harder. He was being resilient to the point she knew he had no intention of letting her go. "I need a second," she said, softly. Carmen grabbed his shoulders, trying to push him off her yet he only tightened his grip before telling her no. "Jay, please," she whispered. "Give me a second."

"No," he mumbled, his voice somewhat muffled.

He moved around until his body was once again on top of hers. Two hundred and fifty pounds of solid muscle, Carmen knew she wouldn't be able to break free of him. Then, as if he was going to make certain of it, he pushed his way inside of her for round two.

Carmen would've been lying if she said she didn't want it. She wanted it just as much as he wanted to give it. However, she didn't need it. What she needed was to be getting out from underneath him, showering, and finding her soon-to-be ex-husband who was probably doing more work in finding their daughter than her. Instead, she was stuck underneath her fiancé whose only intention was to punish every inch of her box with his nine inch pole.

Most times, she liked the roughness while on occasion, she wanted to be held and caressed. This time, however, she wanted him to stop. Too nervous to voice it, she allowed him to finish, hoping he would be easier to maneuver once he came. She assumed that was all he wanted because once he climaxed, he rolled right off her. Carmen's nerves hadn't allowed her to share the same fate so she merely laid there as whiffs of wild sex floated throughout the air.

She looked at him to see if it was safe for her to make her escape. His eyes were closed yet his mouth was wide open as he tried to catch his breath. When she pulled the covers back, he didn't move so she continued to the bathroom. She showered quickly before changing into jeans and a white tee. A copy of Kane's key card was right next to hers so she grabbed it before heading in the living room. At this point, Jay was asleep so she snuck out the suite and into the hallway. A couple was up ahead with their luggage yet she paid them no mind as she knocked on Kane's door. When he didn't answer, she slid the key card into the reader, unlocking the door.

His luggage was still in the middle of the living room as if he hadn't even bothered to unpack. From what she could see, the bed was still made. It was obvious he wasn't there, so Carmen continued to snoop until she was certain there weren't any clues regarding his whereabouts. The keys to the rental were gone so she knew he was driving around the city.

With nothing there to see or find, she left the room and retreated inside her suite. Her expectation was to find Jay as she left him yet he was missing from the bed. She didn't hear him in the bathroom nor had she seen him when she walked through the living room. "What is this shit?" she voiced. Carmen scratched her scalp as she suddenly became nervous. *I left his ass right here. Let me check the bathroom. Maybe, he's in there. Shit, he couldn't have gone far.* Carmen opened the door to find the space empty. *I'm not trippin'*, she thought, starting to pace the floor. *I know I'm not. I left his ass right here. Let me call him.*

Her cell phone had been placed on the right bedside dresser yet now it had also turned up missing. *Don't tell me he disappeared and took my damn phone.* Carmen plopped down on the bed until she remembered all the juices the sheets contained. Her clothes were fresh from the suitcase and the last thing she wanted was for Jay's seed to be *on* her rather than *in* her. The chances of there being another set of bedding were slim to none yet she pulled the sheets off.

By the time she was done and had found a flat sheet and blanket, Jay still hadn't showed. His sudden disappearance made her uncomfortable so she checked Kane's room again. The suite was exactly the same so she went to her own room to wait for whoever showed first.

Time passed slower than usual, making Carmen's fight against sleep ten times harder. The clock now read 9:08 and her eyes were much heavier than before. No longer able to stop her eyes from closing, she hoped whenever she woke, Jay would be by her side. Whether or not it would happen, she didn't know. She just prayed when he showed, he didn't come with a surprise.

9

Cocaine Waitress

Sleep had become a plague that was slowly infecting Copperton City. It had tackled Carmen and was now a threat to Kane. He had been busy trying to locate anyone who could lead him to Jerome or give him answers regarding his daughter's kidnapping. So far, nothing had been accomplished and his eyes were becoming heavy. He had taken five trips to Copperfield University with the expectation he would see someone who could help. Always coming up short, he retreated to the area where Kristian had been kidnapped to scour it for clues. The police had done their job a little too well because the street was left with nothing except road kill and litter.

Still, Kane refused to give up and made his sixth trip to Copperfield, this time parallel parking outside Potter Hall. Only three students were outside, standing on the steps without a textbook in hand. He hadn't seen them on his previous visits so this time he took a good look at them. Two of them were male while one was a female. All of their hands were in their pockets, which was a pose Kane knew too well. Automatically, he rolled down his window and waited. One of them was going to serve him and he waited to see who would be first.

The female made the first move. She approached his car slowly, allowing Kane to study her appearance. Small-framed, the girl had to be no bigger than a hundred and fifteen pounds. Her jet black hair had been pressed bone straight and hung past her shoulders. She looked much younger than he expected, but he knew she had to be at least eighteen.

"You look like you need some help," she said with a mild Jamaican accent. "It might be your lucky night. I'm the best tour guide Copperton City has to offer."

Kane watched as her eyes quickly scoured the car and then him. He knew she was looking to see if he was a cop or if she was about to get involved in a bad sale. Though his profession was what she initially suspected, Kane wasn't looking to take her or her partners down. "You're the best?" he asked, jokingly. Kane shifted his body in his seat. "It doesn't seem like you were born here, ma. I hear the accent. Where are you from?"

"I was born in Spanish Town. My family moved here when I was eight. What do you know about that? You don't look to be from around those parts."

"Not everything is on the surface, ma. You ever heard of King Kong?"

"Who hasn't heard of him? Kong was one of the dons of Kingston. I had a cousin who worked for him. He calls him the Puff of Smoke. Said he came in, did the takeover, and was out right after he made a quick couple of million. Ain't no one seen or heard from him in years."

"I bet you don't know you're staring at him."

The girl laughed in his face as she stood up straight. "Alright, alright, playtime is over. Let's cut to the chase. What do you need?"

Kane took out his wallet, hoping he had a stash of bills inside. She didn't believe for one second he was Kong, which meant it would be ten times harder getting information from her. What she didn't know was that Kong was a man born Michael Kane who was a federal agent for the International Triad Intelligence Agency. He had come to Kingston to take down the city's biggest drug lord, Luck Myers, who had an estimated wealth of almost a billion dollars. He entered the scene as his rival, set up shop, and once he had all he needed, brought the Triad in to help bring Luck down. Once everything was said and done, he got on a plane to America and went home to his wife and kids. Since that case, he hadn't stepped foot in Jamaica and of course, neither had King Kong.

"You really don't believe that I'm Kong? I guess I wouldn't believe me either," he said, counting the money in his billfold.

"Look, we don't even have to get into all that," she said, leaning into the car. "Tell me what you want and I'll let you be on your way. I got pills, mollies. My boy hooked me up with something that'll really get you right. You ever tried Nitrous?"

"Where can I find Jerome McFadden?" Kane asked, ignoring everything she said. "Do you know him?" Her eyes grew big. "You do know him, don't you?"

"What business do you have with him?"

"Where is he?" Kane asked, this time raising his voice.

"You're on my turf," the girl argued. "What do you want with him?"

Kane chuckled at how she was interrogating him. While she had heard of Kong, it was evident she didn't believe he was the famed drug dealer. She was giving him the runaround while most people would've given him a flat answer. "Jamaica did a poor job of educating you on Kong. Maybe, you need another lesson."

"Jamaica died after Kong left. He got the hell out of dodge right after Luck got indicted. If you are who you say you are then you're a coward. You put your hand a little too close to the fire, thought you were going to get burned, and pulled away. The cops bring out the biggest punks in…" her voice quivered when Kane placed his gun in the passenger seat. She had been so into her spiel she didn't see him draw his weapon.

"Where can I find Jerome McFadden?" he asked again, this time staring directly in her face. "All I'm asking for is an address. Give me that and I'll leave you alone."

"What did he do?" she asked, quietly. "I haven't seen him all day."

"Where can I find him? You obviously know him."

The girl swallowed out of nervousness and Kane watched as she turned to the guys standing behind her. They were still on the steps and didn't even acknowledge her.

"I'll take you to him," she told him, opening up the car door.

"Great answer." Kane moved the gun from the passenger seat and set it in his lap. He waited until the girl had her seatbelt on before he took the car out of park and eased slowly away from Potter Hall. He headed towards the entrance of campus where she instructed him to take a right. He drove for a minute or two before she told him to make a left at a stoplight.

"Jerome is usually our fourth," she told him. "He didn't show today so it really should be no surprise that someone is looking for him. Do you usually buy from him?"

Kane didn't answer yet he looked at her. His lack of response didn't stop her from giving him directions, which was proven when she told him to go four blocks and make a right on Central Avenue. In reply, Kane asked a question of his own without ever answering hers. "How long has Jerome been in Georgia? You haven't known him long, have you?"

"Jerome has only been here a couple of months. Blu brought him from up North. He was like an extra. I never took him too serious because I always thought he had a hidden agenda. Like, he was out here for something else besides the money."

"Blu?" Kane questioned. He looked at her again as she started to get comfortable in her seat. "He works for Jay Santiago. Why was he bringing Jerome down South to work for him?"

"Blu never worked for Santiago. He took a meeting with him, but Santiago wasn't feeling him. Blu tried to force his way inside, but he only became Santiago's enemy. That is why Blu's spots got shot up. He just rebuilt his clubs."

Kane's eyes closed for a quick second as everything started to make sense. He had never done an extensive investigation of Blu, choosing to let him run free in Brookstone. He assumed he was another one of Jay's workers who would eventually get taken down, too. From what the girl was telling him, bad blood had formed between the drug lords. That bad blood, in particular, could've been the cause of the war that took place at Blue Magic, which left over ten men dead. Somewhere within that war, Jerome had chosen Blu's side and…

Kane saw an image of his daughter being kidnapped as if he was standing there when it happened. Blu knew the kidnapping would put a strain on Jay's relationship with Carmen and also force him to give up whatever it was he wanted. The thought angered him as he made a right turn on Central Avenue. A minute later, the girl pointed at a small, white house. No cars were in the driveway, all the lights were off, which made him question if he had walked into a trap. To protect himself, he picked up his gun and held it at her temple. "You got three seconds to tell me who lives here."

"Jerome McFadden. This is what you asked for. It's the only place I can think of him to be. Like I told you, I haven't seen him all day. He's usually our fourth."

"We'll wait then," Kane told her, pulling the gun away from her head. He pulled up alongside the house and put the car in park. From the way the house looked, it seemed that Jerome liked to keep a low profile. The yard wasn't decorated with flowers neither was there anything outside that said someone lived there.

"Do you know how much money I'm losing right now? Damn, man, if you are Kong, you sure as hell don't know how to look out for the small-timers."

Kane cracked a smile as he looked over at the side-view mirror. A dark vehicle had made the same right turn he had made. The only difference was the car had upped its speed way over the 35 mph limit. It sent Kane's survival instincts into full gear and he brought the gun again to the girl's temple. "Who followed us?" he yelled as he watched the car pick up speed.

"What the fuck are you talking about? No one followed—" the girl's words were cut off as the car slammed into the passenger side of the Cadillac. The sudden impact caught Kane off guard while the bright headlights blinded him. In a flash, he went from holding the gun to firing a round of bullets in the direction of the car. The gunfire alone forced the car to retreat. Not yet far from him, Kane opened his door and ran out the car, shooting at the side of the car as it tried to turn around in the street. A dark blue Honda Civic, Kane made it in time to see the face of his attacker. Though the person was unrecognizable, the features were all too familiar.

The man had a fully groomed beard and mustache. His jet black hair wasn't cut low and appeared to be somewhat bushy. He looked to be of mixed descent and had the same rugged look Jay possessed. The similarities made Kane believe the guy had been sent to deliver a message. Unsure of what the message was, Kane watched in agony as the car turned onto another street.

With the car gone, he began to take notice of the scene in front of him. Porch lights were now turned on, dogs were barking, and he could see people peeking through their blinds. A situation much bigger than him was now on his hands. "Shit," he yelled, remembering the girl. He ran towards the Cadillac to see the passenger side of the rental badly dented in. The door was pressed in on top of the girl while a single gunshot wound was in the center of her forehead, courtesy of him. Kane instantly dropped to his knees as police sirens sounded in the distance.

The incident was now one he couldn't run from. If he attempted to leave, he would have to pull the body from his car; yet there were eye witnesses who could place him at the scene. At the moment, the best thing for him to do was to go through the motions of the system.

He needed Lieutenant Harris and Sanders. They could vouch for him and clear his name of any charges that may arise. They knew what he had come to Georgia to do. What they wouldn't understand is why he had an unknown girl in his car. He would have a lot of explaining to do, but until then, all he could do was sit there as the sirens grew closer.

10

Go

Central Avenue was minutes away from the Ritz yet Carmen opened her eyes, feeling every bit of an impact. Unbeknownst to her at first, the impact she felt was caused by her suitcase, which had been placed on the bed. The sound of tussling followed, forcing her to look over her shoulders. For the first time in the last couple of hours, she learned she was no longer alone. Jay was beside her, packing some of her belongings.

"Get your shoes on. We have to go," he ordered, zipping up her suitcase. "Put these on," he continued, throwing a pair of black sunglasses her way. "This, too," he added, tossing her a jacket. "Put the hood on. There's a camera in the hallway. Even if they know we're here, they don't need to know we left. We can get out without any problems."

"Where were you?" she barked, grabbing her sneakers off the floor. "I left you right here in the bed." Carmen watched as he grabbed her other suitcase in his hand and started to make his way towards the bedroom door. "Where were you?" she yelled again, noticing he was already dressed in a hoody and shades.

Jay didn't answer the question. He only looked in her direction to see how she was coming along. When he saw she still didn't have the shades on or the jacket, his patience dwindled. "Hurry up," he shouted, continuing towards the door. After a minute or two had passed, he ventured in the bedroom to see what was keeping her. "What the fuck are you doing?" he yelled. "Get the shit or leave it. We don't have fuckin' time for this."

Carmen rolled her eyes before grabbing her phone from the TV stand. Now that it was in her possession, she knew Jay had taken it. She didn't know why and it was obvious he wasn't about to tell her. "What's going on?" she asked him as he opened the door to their suite. "What happened? I was worried about you."

"Shut up," he whispered. "Don't say a fuckin' word." Jay looked down the hall only to make sure the way was clear. When he saw the hallway was empty, he quickly exited the suite, trying his best to get to the stairwell before anyone came out their room. He could hear Carmen struggling to keep up with him yet he didn't slow his pace until they were standing in the stairwell. It was then he noticed she had never put the jacket on. A few choice words sounded in his mind yet he didn't voice them.

"You vanished into thin air," he heard her say as they started down the steps. "I didn't know what to think. I come back from looking for…" Carmen's voice trailed off as the sound of someone coming up the steps interrupted her. Not quite sure who it was or where they were headed, Jay's hand became frozen on her chest as he held her in place until the footsteps ceased. He then quickened his pace until they both stood at the emergency exit. The door was closed, which told him when he opened it, a security alarm would sound.

Without warning, Jay pressed the crash bar, opening the door. Linx, standing outside with a limousine, rushed to him, pulling Carmen's luggage out his hands. The trunk was already open and Linx worked double time throwing the suitcases inside. By the time he and Carmen had their seatbelts on, Linx was in the car, taking the limo out of park. They were halfway out the parking lot before security even showed.

"Maintain the speed limit," Jay ordered. "Don't give the cops a reason to pull you over." He looked in the rearview mirror so he and Linx could meet eyes. When his right-hand nodded his head, Jay removed the shades from his face as well as the black hoodie he had been wearing. He threw both items on the seat opposite of him before looking at Carmen whose back was to him. "What are you looking at?" he asked, turning around as well. He didn't see anything suspicious except a black Lincoln that was merging into their lane. "You wanted to ask questions before, this is your time," he said, surly.

"There's an ambulance," Carmen answered, "and three police cars outside the hotel."

Jay took off his seatbelt, stretching his body out on the seat so his head fell directly in her lap. He tried his best to get comfortable, knowing there was a long road ahead of them. "Sometimes, we have to make hard decisions," he muttered. Jay closed his eyes yet he reopened them when he felt Carmen's hand on his chest.

"What decisions?" Carmen was persistent in her questions since she couldn't get anything out of him when they were at the hotel. Since there was now opportunity, she was using every available second. "You better do some talking because I spent hours worried out my damn mind. I am liable to punch, kick, bite, and do whatever I have to, to get some answers."

"You're not going to punch me," he told her, closing his eyes. "You definitely aren't going to kick me. Now the biting," Jay paused as his mind went in the gutter, "we can come to an agreement on that. Depends on where you want to put your mouth." A slight snigger escaped his lips until Carmen punched him hard in the chest. The jab made him sit straight up as he stared her in the face.

"I'm carrying my fuckin' life on my shoulders," he spat. "Do you know what that shit feels like? I'm trying to cross as many state lines as I can to see my kids before they lock my ass away. You think I want that for him?"

"Who?" Carmen yelled. "Who wouldn't you want that for?"

"If they saw me then you know they saw Cesar. He's better off this way."

Carmen's eyes shifted towards the rearview mirror where they met with Linx's. In a split second, they went from staring at each other to his eyes turning towards the road. It was like he was telling her he didn't want any parts of the conversation. "You didn't kill him to keep him out of prison. You killed him because he left that tape at the restaurant. It's like you forgot he saved your life and Nyla's."

Jay's head fell in her lap as if the conversation was miniscule. He even closed his eyes, which gave Carmen the impression he was going to brush the issue aside. "They have enough evidence to lock you away for the rest of your life and you go and do the one thing they're accusing you of? You drop another body? How are you going to cover up this one?"

"You'll understand in due time," Jay mumbled. "I promise."

Carmen's lips parted at Jay's nonchalant attitude. The fact he didn't care about his actions made her question why she was in the limousine. Her daughter was being held somewhere in the city against her will and she was doing absolutely nothing about it. Too busy running after her fiancé, Carmen had officially put him before her child. The idea of it disgusted her while the guilt gnawed at her to the point she could feel bites on her skin.

"I shouldn't be here," she said, sternly. "I should let you go to New York and I should stay behind. What good am I in Brookstone?"

Jay's eyes opened as he heard her questioning her actions. Carmen was on the outside looking in; therefore, she didn't know the plans he had for her. The truth was, she was no good in New York. She belonged in Georgia, which was where he planned to send her once he met up with Tiara and Malik in DC. The plan was for them to bring Nyla and Rakim to him so he could spend time with them before he turned himself in. Carmen would then return to Georgia to handle Kristian's kidnapping.

"I'm already four steps ahead of you, Peaches."

"So what are—" Carmen was cut off when her phone started to ring. Her purse was right underneath Jay's legs and she thought he was going to move so she could get to it. Not moving an inch, she was forced to pull it from underneath him. She stared at her phone, not the least bit surprise to see Kane calling her. Carmen knew what he wanted. He wanted to know Jay's whereabouts so he could make an arrest. The mistake had already been made one time before and she couldn't do it again. Kane was better off finding him on his own than going through her.

Moments passed before Jay grabbed her phone from her hands. He threw it on the seat opposite of them before telling her to never answer her phone. She was about to tell him it wasn't her intention until she saw his eyes close. A simple reminder of the long night ahead of them, Carmen made the decision to leave him alone. For now, all she could do was sit back and wait.

***

The night was starting to take a toll and in Kane's opinion, the final straw was when Carmen didn't answer his call. He knew the warrant for Jay's arrest had been splashed on every major news station yet he needed his wife to play her position. Before she covered for her fiancé, she needed to be covering for their daughter. Her focus had changed to the point Kane felt as if he was the only one concerned about finding Kristian.

He wanted to throw the towel in on the Santiago case yet something told him to keep pushing forward. Harris had already vouched for him and gotten him out of a potential murder charge though he had to stare several officers in the face and explain why there was a dead girl in his car. Not to mention, that same girl had been previously booked on a prostitution charge. *No wonder she called herself the best tour guide. She's gotten in plenty of cars.*

As a result of the murder, he revealed they were attacked and broke the news of his daughter's kidnapping. In addition, he had to file an official missing person's report. In a couple of hours, everyone in the world would know Kristian Kane was missing. Whether it would help them find her, he didn't know. He only knew it was a start.

Now with clearance, Kane debated his next move as he sat in the interrogation room. His first thought was to call Carmen, which he did, yet she didn't answer. He wasn't quite sure where to turn though there was a vehicle at his disposal, courtesy of Sanders. In terms of the vehicle he wrecked, Carmen had paid for additional insurance so the damages were covered. Enterprise would eat the cost and all he had to deal with was Carmen's anger once she learned he had been in an accident.

Instead of waiting for her to hear the news, Kane made his way to the Ritz hoping she was still in her suite. The drive was longer than he would've liked and he returned to the hotel only to see paramedics and flashing lights. There was also a black body bag being ushered towards the ambulance. Immediately, he went to it, flashing his badge for everyone to see. The carriers hesitated for a few seconds, but eventually complied. Once the bag was unzipped, he was face to face with one of Jay's workers.

"We're still trying to figure out what happened to him. He doesn't have any cuts or bullet holes. There weren't any pills near the body," one of the paramedics said. "I hope his family agrees to have an autopsy done. Otherwise, we can't explain why he's dead."

Kane's forehead furrowed as he backed away from the body. The paramedics proceeded to put the stretcher on the truck while he headed inside the Ritz. The lobby was filled with police and other concerned guests who were staring outside. Not letting their presence faze him, he hurried to Carmen's room. Now that Jay's worker had turned up dead, he knew she had to be inside. However, when he knocked, no one came to the door. He knocked louder, interrupting the sleep of the people next door. He could hear them complaining, but their remarks went on deaf ears.

To show them he didn't care, he pulled out his gun and fired at the lock. The gunshot caused screams from various rooms yet he got what he wanted. Carmen's door was open and the entire room was free range. Kane went inside, looking for any sign of her or Jay. What he found was an empty room that didn't have anything in it aside from a dirty set of sheets.

"Sir, what is going on?" a voice yelled from the hallway. "Is everyone okay?"

Kane didn't respond to the bellhop who was standing in the doorway. Instead, he headed straight for the stairwell. Something told him Jay had made a run for it and Carmen had gone with him. If Jay was on his way out of Georgia, he had to be on his tail. He had to bring him to Harris or else his job was on the line.

Automatically, he pulled his phone out his pocket as he reached the first floor. Once he made it to the front desk, he already had Sanders on the phone. "Jay made a run for it. Tell Harris I need eyes in the air, on the street, everywhere. He couldn't have gotten far. This trip ain't a quick one either. Every limo on I-85 needs to be stopped and searched until we locate Jay."

While Sanders was telling him he would handle everything, Kane was asking the lady at the front desk about Carmen's room. When she said his wife hadn't checked out, he knew for sure she had made a run for it. She knew not to leave any paperwork behind, which was why she had simply grabbed her stuff and jetted. Though he wasn't sure how long they had been gone, he knew he could catch up with them. One hundred miles per hour is what he intended on driving and he dared any cop to stop him.

11

Phone Tap

For most of the drive, the limo had kept a steady pace; however, a sudden jolt forced Jay's eyes to fly open. Although he couldn't see the traffic, he noticed Linx was turning up the volume on the radio. The limo had been dead silent until the sudden noise interrupted his sleep. Although he preferred the silence, he figured Linx needed some background noise to help him stay awake. The ride to New York was more than a quick trip around the block and he needed Linx to be able to hold out for the long haul. Nonetheless, if it called for it, he would take the wheel so Linx could get some sleep.

"Are you okay up there?" he called to him, continuing to look in his direction.

Linx turned around to look at him yet he didn't answer. He only pointed towards the radio as if he was telling him to listen. Jay quickly sat up, waking Carmen in the process so she could hear the DJ.

"King did that shit, didn't he?" he asked, hearing about the shootout at The Kingdom.

"Four men were killed," Linx replied, turning the volume down.

Jay cursed under his breath. He turned to look at Carmen who appeared to be somewhat dazed. He figured she was still waking up and hadn't caught the conversation. He knew he was going to have to tell her, but he figured he would let her get herself together first.

"No suspects," Linx added, starting to change lanes. "That's the best news of the night."

"No shit," Jay replied.

Jay closed his eyes, leaning his head into Carmen's lap. About to get himself comfortable once more, he felt his phone vibrating in his pants pocket. Without a doubt, he knew King was calling him. By this time, his son had to have learned he no longer had a way of escape. His private plane was always the first piece of property the police would confiscate. The only good thing about the plane was that it was an inheritance and the district attorney couldn't prove it had been purchased with drug money. It was the main reason he was able to get it back when he lost it the first time.

"Your phone is vibrating," Carmen said, interrupting his thoughts.

Jay shrugged his shoulders. He wanted revenge for what his son had done to him and he finally had the chance to get it. On the other hand, he knew blood had never been on King's hands. As a father, he could only imagine what was going through his son's head. Currently on probation, if his son was to get caught, he would be spending a large number of years if not life behind bars. To prevent that from happening, King was probably calling him because he needed help cleaning up his mess.

King was his firstborn and the heir to his fortune. The fear of being imprisoned while their relationship was still on the rocks disturbed Jay. His son may have betrayed him by stealing his plane, but he had to forgive him. Four men had been killed and he knew where King's head was. His anger towards his son made him want to leave him out in the cold yet his love for him made him answer his call. "Did you have fun tonight?" he asked. He said the words calmly so King could see he was serious about the question.

"Ain't no fun if the homies can't have none," King replied.

Jay was somewhat taken aback by King's response. He expected for his son to be in a different headspace. Since he appeared to have found his balls, Jay decided to treat him like such. "You should be thankful none of 'em were Blu," he told him as he glanced at Carmen. He saw she was wide awake yet her face was turned towards the window. She appeared to be in her own world, but he knew she was hanging on to every word. "Blu knows where Kristian is," he continued. "She's been gone for 24 hours and could be anywhere in the world. If one of those men were Blu, you would've lost any chance of finding her. "

"Your plane is gone," King voiced. "The Triad has it surrounded. We went to the airport after we left Blu's other club. They still haven't found those men."

Jay chuckled at his son's words. "So you dropped even more bodies than the four? You know they're going to connect the two shootings, right? They're going to know someone is after Blu. I wouldn't worry about the plane, though. Yeah, you took it, but you're not the reason they have it surrounded. If I fight this case, I'll get it back. No worries."

The phone went silent for a few seconds, leaving Jay to wonder if King knew there was a warrant for his arrest. When his son didn't speak, he looked at Carmen. Her eyes were still glued to the window and her face was wearing more concern than before. He knew it didn't sit too well with her that their son had become a murderer.

"We're on Interstate 85," he told him. There's a Waffle House at Exit 102. Meet us behind the building. We need to talk."

Instead of hearing a response from him, Jay heard shuffling. Not quite sure where King was or what his plans were, he became somewhat anxious. King had already made a stir in Copperton City and he didn't know if his son had plans to do further damage.

"We'll meet you there," King finally said.

Jay parted his lips to say more, but the phone immediately hung up. He quickly pulled it from his ear, staring at his son's name as it disappeared from the screen. Not quite sure what King was trying to prove, he set the phone on the seat. In the meantime, he heard Carmen's phone ringing from the seat opposite of them. He already knew who was calling and he figured Carmen did as well. Still, she grabbed the phone. He told her once again not to answer, which she didn't, but she still showed him the screen so he could see Kane's name.

"Is he calling about what you did or what King did?"

Jay shrugged his shoulders. "It could be either of the two. Our son is officially a murderer. Maybe Kane knows, maybe he doesn't. If you ask me, he doesn't care about King. He's not going to put him in prison. All he wants is me. I'm his payday."

"Were you behind the hit?"

Jay rolled his eyes. It was always a part of his plan to shoot up Blu's spots. However, he wanted to do it after finding Kristian. With the way King handled things, they had a bunch of dead bodies on their hands without any knowledge of where Kristian was. "Yes and no; things happened out of order." Jay turned his head to stare Carmen in the face; however, her fist flew down hard onto his chest before he could look at her. The sudden blow forced him to sit up and his left arm accidentally knocked her cell phone out her hand.

"That was number two," he said through gritted teeth. "If you don't want me to put my hands on you, don't put your hands on me."

"I know you put him up to it," Carmen shot back.

"Is that what you think?" Jay stared at Carmen for a second before continuing. "I didn't put him up to anything. We made plans to come here, but that was all we did. We made plans. I didn't give him orders and I definitely didn't tell him to shoot up Blu's clubs. Was I going to do it? Yes, but not this soon. I wanted to ask some questions first."

Carmen folded her arms over her chest. "He's still on probation. If he didn't clean up his mess well, he'll be in a cell right next to you."

Jay laid his head in her lap. "Maybe this will calm your nerves. King and Nicholas are on their way to meet us. You can ask him anything you want. He'll most definitely tell you I didn't put him up to this."

"We'll see," Carmen mumbled. She peered over Jay's shoulder to take a look at her phone. A picture of Kane was frozen on the home screen as the numbers on the timer increased. More than two minutes had passed and the image only told her one thing: Her ex-husband was listening in. She touched Jay's chest and when they met eyes, she pointed towards the floor where her phone was.

Jay looked down to see what she was pointing at. While several thoughts came to mind when he saw the phone, he didn't speak. He simply picked it up and ended the call. Kane was bound to catch up with him and as a result of his spat with Carmen, he was now coming quicker than expected.

***

Kane's foot naturally pressed harder on the accelerator after he heard Sanders' confirm Carmen's location. Although he was miles away, with advanced technology and a three-way call, his partner was able to track her down through the signal in her phone. The call only lasted a few short minutes, but it was enough time for Sanders to see she was near Blacksburg, a small town in South Carolina. Now aware of her location, Kane sped in that direction.

Intermission

Dreams and Nightmares

The sense of sight had been stripped from Kristian since Blu had sent her into a sea of blackness. Forced to use her hands as guides, she traced the walls of the room until her hands stumbled upon the stairwell and eventually the door. For hours on end, she screamed as she thrusted herself against it, yet her screams went unheard. The task left her feeling powerless until she started to hear voices flowing out the vents.

"So you mean to tell me you worked in this kitchen all day with that smell? None of the customers complained?" she heard a guy say. "I can barely stomach standing here. Someone had to say something. What about the waitresses? Maybe something went bad in the freezers."

"I, I, I don't know. I mean, may-may-maybe," a voice stuttered.

Kristian sat up straight when she realized how close the voices were. Unlike the others, their tones weren't muffled and she could understand their speech clearly. Somewhat hopeful, Kristian placed her fists on the door, beating against it for dear life.

"You hear that?" she heard the first male say. "That's what you were talking about, right? You said you've been hearing something beating all day."

"I don't know, Mr. Fontaine. It might be. I…" the second voice trailed off.

Kristian placed her ear directly on the door as the voices disappeared. Soon replaced by the sound of footsteps, she listened as one of the men drew closer to her. He had to be less than a foot away when she heard him say the banging was coming from the basement. Those words alone made Kristian beat on the door again.

When he hit hard up against it, Kristian ran down the steps, falling on her back as he forced his way inside. Her hands became planted on the floor in a puddle of her own urine. All at once, the stench hit her as she recalled the numerous times she was forced to relieve herself. With no time for embarrassment, the door flew open, sending a beam of light in the room.

A dark-skinned man was standing at the top of the steps, his face in absolute shock. His attire was pure white and the gold medallion around his neck stuck out like a sore thumb. "What the fuck?" His initial words were written on his face from the way his eyes bulged and his mouth hung open. His hand was still on the door as if he didn't know what to do. A few seconds passed before he walked down the steps. The stench of urine hit him hard and he covered his nose to shield himself from the scent. "How did you get down here?"

Kristian didn't answer him as she struggled to stand. Due to the amount of urine on the floor, she had to use both her hands to keep from slipping and sliding. The man was impatient, shouting question after question as his thumb and index finger held his nose.

"Bl-Bl-Blu," she stammered, finally answering.

His eyes bulged even more at her response. "Blu brought you here?" he questioned. He started to pace the floor as if he was trying to put the pieces together. "Look," he said, walking near her. "I don't know what Blu is thinking or what's going on, but you can't be here. I'm running a business upstairs."

He waved for her to come to him, but Kristian didn't move. He hadn't even told her his name yet he was ready for her to trust him. Though he seemed to be her only lifeline, Kristian hesitated. He could've been pretending to be a knight in shining armor while he was really bringing her one step closer to death.

"What's wrong? You want to stay here?"

Kristian shook her head, but she still didn't move. Since she hadn't, he draped his hand at his side as he realized taking her out the basement wasn't going to be an easy feat.

"I co-own this restaurant with Blu. I'm Victor Fontaine. Is that what you want to hear?" he asked her. "My chefs heard you banging, but didn't have the guts to come down here."

Kristian's face still held uncertainty despite the insight Victor gave her. She could see he noticed it because he continued his spiel to convince her to come with him.

"I'm not going to hurt you," he coaxed. "I'm not trying to get wrapped up in anything. If my name gets attached to this, not only do I lose my business, but I also lose my reputation in this city. You think I asked to come to work and find a girl in my basement? I've never been down for the shit Blu was into, but he has a lot of paper. I have to deal with him."

His words were so quick and fierce it brought out emotions Kristian had kept bottled up for hours. Tears flew down her face as she mumbled she wanted to go home. She might've been suspicious of him, but his presence was diminishing her doubts. Victor was her only ticket to Brookstone, which meant she had to put her faith in him. While she didn't know where she was headed, she did know what she was walking away from. She was stepping out a nightmare and into a dream.

***

From the first thirty minutes Kristian had spent with Victor, she had gathered enough information to deem him as a successful businessman. He may have had only one restaurant under his belt, but he had profited well. He drove a white Bentley and lived in the ritziest section of the city in a complex called Sola Estates. His lifestyle was what she was accustomed to which she saw when he directed her into his bachelor pad. He didn't give her a tour, immediately taking her into his spare bedroom. A California queen-sized bed dressed in cream and chocolate brown was in the center of the room while French décor decorated the space.

A man who appeared to have an expensive taste and an eye for design, Kristian wondered what his master bedroom looked like. A part of her wanted to see it while another part of her simply wanted to get out her wet clothes. Victor had purchased a slew of toiletries and clothes for her right after they left the restaurant, which she now had an opportunity to change into.

"The bathroom is over there," he told her, pointing towards a closed door in the upper right corner of the room. "Go ahead and get settled. I'm going to order a pizza. The food should be here by the time you're done."

Kristian watched as he headed towards the doorway. Though she had told him thank you a hundred times, she repeated the words once more. "I really do appreciate it," she told him.

"I know you do," he replied, stepping in the hallway. "Right now, we don't need to be wasting time. Go ahead and get cleaned up."

Kristian parted her lips to say something else yet Victor disappeared from her sight. Since time was of the essence, she didn't follow him. Instead, she grabbed all the bags and headed for the bathroom. All the lights were off, but when she hit the switch, she could see he had never used it before. Everything was blindingly white and not one single scratch was on any of the surfaces. The sight of cleanliness made Kristian undress. Five seconds barely passed before she was in the shower, allowing the burning hot water to run on her skin.

She didn't time herself, but by the time she was dressed, the pizza had arrived. Victor hadn't eaten, yet he was sitting at the kitchen table with a plate in front of him. "Sorry, I took so long," she told him, sitting down. She gave him a warm smile as he handed her one of the pizza boxes. Kristian took it from him and proceeded to fix her plate.

She hadn't realized how long it had been since she had eaten until she had already devoured two slices of pizza and a third was going in her mouth. Out the corner of her eye, she saw Victor get up from the table and head for the cabinets. He grabbed a glass before pulling a pitcher of iced tea from the fridge.

"I think I heard Blu talking about you once before," he said, his back still towards her. "It was a while ago." Victor turned around so he could study Kristian's face. Now that she was smelling fresh and had run a comb through her hair, he could see what Blu was talking about. Kristian was young, beautiful, and appeared to have possibly been untouched. Her innocence was an attraction in itself and at the same time, it meant hands-off. It was the main reason Victor took his eyes off her and went back to fixing her tea. Once he was finished, he brought it to her, joining her at the table.

She was still eating and Victor decided to use the time to discuss a plan of action. He knew he needed to go to the police, but at the same time, he was trying to protect his name. He was listed as the owner of Soulshock while Blu was only a silent partner. If his restaurant became tied up with a kidnapping, his livelihood would be threatened. It wasn't a risk he wanted to take so he figured he needed to secure her a one-way ticket home.

"Where are you from?" he asked her as she picked up the glass of tea.

"Brookstone," she answered before taking a sip of her drink. She took a large gulp before setting it on the table. "I can repay you for the flight."

Victor didn't care about her repaying him. He simply wanted to send her home without police involvement. As soon as she was out his apartment, he could wash his hands of the whole thing. "Whatever you want to do," he told her, finally reaching for a slice of pizza. He grabbed one as Kristian started working on her fourth. Though he was busy eating, he listened intently as Kristian told him what happened to her.

In those ten minutes, he learned the details of her attack and that she was a student at Copperfield University. Originally from Brookstone, New York, she was the daughter of Carmen Davenport, the head fashion designer and CEO of Flame, Inc. The news alone almost made him choke as he realized how dangerous the situation was.

Anyone who wasn't living under a rock knew the history between Carmen Davenport and Jay Santiago. Victor knew his life was on the line if his paths were to ever cross with the notorious drug dealer. It was one thing for Blu to get on his bad side, but it was another for him. He most definitely couldn't hold his own against Jay. He didn't own a weapon and never had the urge to get one. Now that he knew Kristian's connection, he was ready to get her out his place. "Look, um, I need to look for you a ticket. The quicker I find it, the quicker we can have you on a plane."

"You're going to let me repay you, aren't you?"

Victor shook his head as he rose from the table. "Don't worry about it. Why don't you get some rest?" He picked up his plate and put it in the sink before going inside his room. He could hear Kristian moving around the kitchen, but he didn't let it distract him from securing her flight. He quickly went to Expedia and ordered a one-way ticket to Brookstone. After an eight o'clock flight was secured, he printed out the confirmation page, which he set on his bedside dresser. By that time, his apartment was completely silent and he assumed Kristian had gone to sleep. Done for the day himself, he quickly stripped down to his boxers and got inside his bed.

***

Only a few hours had passed, but Kristian believed she had missed a much larger gap in time. Everything happened so quickly she couldn't even grasp what was going on. All she remembered was turning over in bed and feeling a cold hand clasp tightly over her mouth. She made several attempts to bite it until a thick wad of duct tape was placed firmly over her lips. With the room being completely black, Kristian felt as if she was fighting against the darkness as the person's hands slid underneath her legs and picked her up.

Automatically, she believed she had been set up. She had trusted Victor and yet he had failed her as well. His motive was hard to decipher until she reminded herself he was Blu's business partner. The whole entire thing, from him saving her in the basement to feeding her and helping her get cleaned up, was probably all a set up. Blu had probably told him to check up on her and to make sure she wasn't wasting away. Now that Victor's assignment was done, it was time for her to be transported to the basement.

Kristian became certain of it as she squirmed in the person's arms. From the way she was positioned, it was hard for her to get a good look, but she could see it was a male who was dressed in all black whose hair had been braided in cornrows. A pair of shades covered his face and he carried her into Victor's living room where he set her on her feet.

At that moment, she knew she hadn't been set up. She stared in shock horror at Victor who was in the living room as well wearing only a pair of black boxers. He was in a headlock while a silver pistol was at his temple. Blood trickled from his lips and she could tell from the scratches on his face he had been in a scuffle.

"She ain't got shit to do with Santiago," he yelled.

Kristian gazed across the room until she saw Blu walking from Victor's bedroom.

"This was the ticket you bought for her?" Blu asked, holding a sheet of paper. "You're the last person I expected this from. I guess you wanted to play hero, huh? Shit, why couldn't you save those motherfuckers at The Kingdom? Those New York motherfuckers dropped four bodies at my spot. You could've been a hero over there."

"She's a kid, Blu. Leave her alone."

Kristian watched the two men as they stared each other down. She could tell words were silently being exchanged though neither of them was speaking verbally. When Blu looked her way, she saw Victor struggle up against the man who was holding him. He didn't even care that a gun was pointed at his head.

"I'm not going down for this shit," he yelled, struggling against Blu's goon.

Kristian shook her head repeatedly as Blu came towards her. The duct tape must not have been quite enough because she watched as he pulled a black bandana out his coat pocket. She tried to maneuver away from him, but his goon had a good grip on her. He held her in place as Blu covered her eyes and bounded her arms. She could hear the sound of someone finishing Victor off, which was followed by his body dropping to the ground. Then, she felt someone's hands all over her as they dressed her. Although she wasn't sure where she was headed, she knew someone had to find her soon. Blu had mentioned he was under attack, which meant Jay knew she had been kidnapped. In due time, he would find her and Blu's demise would begin.

12

Meet the Parents

Blacksburg, South Carolina

Carmen tapped her knee repeatedly as another image of Kane flashed in her mind. The idea of him made her nervous yet she didn't vocalize it. Jay was already dealing with a lot, from the warrant for his arrest to the massacre at Blu's clubs. Not to mention, he had killed one of his right-hands at the Ritz. His stress was probably mounting, which was why she remained silent.

Jay faced the window while Linx was still in the driver's seat not saying a word. Carmen expected for their demeanors to change when a black car drove behind Waffle House, but still no one spoke. When the black car pulled directly beside them, Carmen held her breath until the window rolled down and she saw King's face. Nicholas was beside him, both of them dressed in all black and wearing gloves.

"Switch places," Jay whispered, finally speaking.

Carmen peered at him because she was confused about the request. She understood him wanting to have a conversation with King, but asking her to leave was out of the question. If their son had gone and killed a bunch of people, they both needed to have a conversation with him. If King was to get caught, she would be the one signing a check to her lawyer, Clement, while Jay sat in his own prison cell. "I'm not going anywhere," she replied.

"The clock is ticking. Switch places," Jay ordered. He met eyes with Carmen just so she could see how serious he was. His expression was straightforward and stern, which seemed to do the trick because Carmen got out the car. Seconds later, his firstborn was sitting across from him. King held his jaw tight, giving off the impression he was still ready for war. Everything about his son made Jay believe the Santiago curse was upon him. King had received his thirst to kill, which meant his son's actions might become repetitive.

"His restaurant is our last chance at finding Kristian."

Jay scratched his chin as he realized King's mind was still set on going after Blu. Even after killing a slew of men and learning less than nothing of Kristian's whereabouts, King still wanted to continue the hunt. "Under normal circumstances," Jay began, "I would kick you in your neck.

Considering the fact that every cop and federal agent is on my ass right now, I'll add your ass whooping to the other ones I owe you. Right now, we need to talk business." Jay rested his elbows on his knees. "I need you to take your ass home. Everything we have is about to be stripped of us and I need you to handle business, our legal business. I already got someone lined up to find Kristian and handle this whole situation."

King didn't respond to his father's plans. The main reason why was because he knew the words were already going to be spoken. Jay had every intention to send him to Brookstone the moment he laid eyes on him. That was the reason he went ahead and retaliated against Blu.

"You know I'm looking at life."

King looked at his father, hearing his words. It was just yesterday, he threatened to part ways with his father. If Jay went to prison, he would never feel the effects of his abandonment. In actuality, it would be the other way around. He would be the one left alone.

"That's why I need you in Brookstone and away from this shit with Blu. If I can't get out from behind these bars, I need you to make sure we don't lose our shit. In my will, everything is yours, not your mother's, not your sister's, not your brother's. It's yours. When I went in the first time, I didn't expect to get out. I wrote my will and gave everything to you. I haven't changed it since my release and I don't intend to. You're a natural when it comes to business and that's where I need you to be." Jay looked at his watch and then at King. "We gotta go and you have a plane to catch. You need to get out this city just like I do."

King wiped his face and even took off his black skull cap. The right words still hadn't come to mind so he let his actions speak for him. He held out his hand to his father, not as a truce, but as an agreement he would go to Brookstone. Jay accepted it, allowing him to part ways. He crossed paths with his mother, giving her a hug before joining Nicholas. They peeled off in a matter of seconds leaving his parents alone behind the restaurant.

"What did Nicholas say?" Jay asked once Carmen was in the car.

Carmen mumbled a few choice words under her breath due to the short amount of time she had with King. "He didn't pull the trigger."

"Exactly what I expected him to say," Jay admitted as the limo's engine came to life. "Well, now that I have King squared away, I just have to take care of you."

"I got this," Carmen told him.

Jay chuckled at the 'tough girl' act Carmen was trying to wear. He knew she wasn't going to let up or abandon any secret plan she had so he went ahead and made arrangements to have her link up with Gully. His cousin would take his place while he paid his debt to society. Once Kristian was found, he would use the kidnapping as part of his defense and hopefully get out of prison. In addition, he would pin the missing coke on Blu.

Only seconds away from the interstate, Jay met eyes once again with his fiancée. The words, *I love you*, were on the tip of his tongue until he saw Carmen's eyes bulge. Simultaneously, her arms became wrapped tightly around his neck as she pulled him violently towards her. The move caught him off guard until the sound of crushing steel sounded from behind. It was soon followed by a hard thrust in Carmen's direction, which landed him directly on top of her. The impact forced the limousine to swerve to the right, running off the road and involuntarily, coming to a halt.

With the limousine at a standstill, Jay was able to hear everything around him, from the sound of shattering glass to the helicopter overhead. Time moved faster than his thoughts and before he could think of a plan, he was dragged out the vehicle by his legs. Blue and white lights flickered around the entire highway almost blinding him as he stared at his surroundings. He studied the area as he was pulled away, piecing together the events of the last minute. A metallic gray Acura had crashed directly into the left side of the limo, explaining the impact he heard. Carmen had seen the car coming and pulled him towards her to keep him from being crushed.

Quickly closing his eyes at the thought, he was forced on his stomach as his arms were pulled behind his back. Prison was closer than he intended and he opened his eyes, hoping he could meet eyes with Carmen. When he spotted her, Linx was beside her, and federal agents had them surrounded. With no time to spare, he blocked out the voice yelling his rights in his left ear. He continued to stare at them even when he was placed on his feet. Then, their image became blocked by Kane.

The mere sight of him made anger form in the pit of his stomach. It rose from his chest to his throat before forcing its way out between his lips. Before he could give Kane the upmost disrespect, he was pulled away and pushed into a black van. Armed federal agents awaited him, binding his legs upon arrival. There weren't any windows on either side of the vehicle so he couldn't see Carmen or Linx. Once the news of his capture was leaked, he knew Gully would find his way to his fiancée. His cousin was sometimes selfish and stubborn, but he always kept his word. Jay knew he was going to come through for him. He only prayed they found Kristian before it was too late.

13

Capo

Both of Carmen's wrists were handcuffed behind her. She had stopped shaking only minutes ago and was now sitting calmly on the hood of a police car. Linx was beside her, his wrists handcuffed as well, not a single word being spoken between them. Both of their eyes were focused on the black van where Jay was sitting. Federal agents including Kane were still around it, talking amongst themselves as well as searching Jay's limo.

Ten minutes passed before they realized their only catch was Jay. Carmen could tell they were expecting to find much more when Kane wandered over to her. He pulled out a small key, undid her handcuffs as well as Linx's. "Where are they taking him?" she asked him.

Kane's face was tight, an obvious sign something didn't go right. He didn't answer her until the black van started to move, continuing on 85 North. "The airport," he replied.

Carmen placed her hand on Kane's chest, pushing him away from her so she had room to stand on her feet. About to speak, he interrupted her before she could begin.

"I'm going home on a separate flight," Kane announced. "I'll be in Brookstone for a day or so and then I'll be back."

Carmen folded her arms across her chest just as a dark blue Honda Civic pulled up beside them. Linx stood on his feet once he saw the car, prompting Carmen to look at him. When he remained in place, she assumed he didn't know the person. Therefore, she turned to Kane. "I'm staying here so I can find Kristian. I'm not coming back until Jay's bond hearing."

"You can save yourself the trip. It's going to be denied. It's already in the cards."

"That's because you want it to be. You want to take him down so bad, and for what? You think that if you put him behind bars we'll magically fall in sync? Taking him away is not going to make us get back together."

"Not a problem," Kane responded. "I'm content just knowing the son of bitch is behind bars. Are you still going to marry him if Kristian pops up dead?"

Carmen gritted her teeth at the question. Her eyes locked in on Kane's even as he held up the handcuffs for her to see. Her lack of response was obviously miniscule to him because he turned away from her. He faced the Honda Civic beside them, his face scrunching up. Unsure of why, Carmen watched impatiently as the driver stepped out the vehicle. She didn't recognize the man, but he instantly reminded her somewhat of Jay. Kane stepped towards him, as if to attack, but distance was put between them by another agent. A nonverbal exchange took place between the two before Kane backed off. Unsure of what was going on, she turned to Linx only to have the driver of the Honda address her.

"Get in the car," the guy barked.

Carmen raised her brow before looking at Linx who was walking towards the vehicle. She followed his lead only because she thought the guy was part of some unknown plan of Jay's. "And you are?" she asked the guy, eyeing him from head to toe.

"Get in the car," he muttered.

Carmen watched as the man got inside the Honda. She turned towards Linx who responded with a single shrug of his shoulders. Not quite sure what was going on, Carmen decided to trust her gut. She got inside the car, Linx following suit.

"Hell fuckin' no," the guy spat. "I said I was taking her, I didn't say shit about you."

Carmen looked behind her at Linx who was in the backseat. Once again, a nonverbal exchange took place until Linx left the vehicle. She left him there on the interstate while she headed south down 85.

"Name," Carmen pleaded after minutes of silence.

The guy peered at her before putting his eyes on the road. "And this is who my cousin can't let go of. I tell you, pussy will make a man do *some* things."

Carmen rolled her eyes before peering in the guy's lap. While she thought her fiancé didn't have any family, it was obvious there was something he didn't tell her. *More like someone,* she thought. Desperate to get answers, she quickly reached down in the guy's pocket. He pushed her off him with his right hand while the other controlled the wheel. To distract him, Carmen grabbed the steering wheel as well, turning it to the left. The Honda almost collided with another car, which forced him to put both hands on the wheel to regain control of the car. When he did, Carmen reached into his pocket again to grab his wallet. Once it was in her hands, she opened it to reveal his ID. "Guillermo Perez," she read out loud, staring at his picture.

"Nice to meet you." She flung the wallet in his lap, the billfold landing right between his legs.

"Gully," he corrected. "I don't go by Guillermo."

"Jay never told me he had a cousin."

"I never claimed him. I use Perez because Santiago is a hindrance. It's my mother's maiden name. My father was Hector's brother."

Carmen looked at Gully out the corner of her eye. "So, what am I supposed to do with you?" Carmen's question was met with another chuckle. "Oh, I see, you're babysitting me. I don't need a babysitter. I have my own plans."

"Let me guess, you were going to meet up with an old comrade, buy a bunch of weapons, and go on the hunt for Blu?" Gully chuckled only because he knew Carmen thought her plan was a secret. "Let me tell you something, princess. No one can buy a bunch of heat in Georgia and let their order slip past me. Your secrets aren't secrets, baby girl."

"Where's my shit?" Carmen yelled, taking off her seatbelt. She charged at him, but he quickly slammed her in her seat with his forearm.

"Do you think I want you in this fuckin' car with me?" Gully's volume increased as his anger heightened. "Jay begged me to help him. I'm not doing this shit for you or your fuckin' daughter. I'm doing it for him. Now that we've made that clear, you'll think more wisely before you pop off. I already want to drop your ass with the quickness."

Gully pressed harder on the gas, speeding past several cars. He was going nearly twenty-five miles over the speed limit, but he didn't care. Carmen had him on ten especially since he didn't want any part of her or her situation. If it wasn't for Jay, he would've watched everything go down from a distance. Now, he was forced to help.

"So we're both in places we don't want to be," Carmen observed. "I don't want to be with you, you don't want to be with me. So, let's end this. I go my way, you go yours."

Gully shook his head. It wasn't as simple as Carmen was trying to make it be. She thought she could handle Blu on her own, but she couldn't. A few weapons were only going to go so far. She could kill every man on Blu's team, but it wouldn't benefit her if she couldn't give Blu what he truly wanted. Since she couldn't, they were glued at the hip until Blu was dead and Kristian was found.

"No one's going anywhere," he told her. "Sit back and enjoy the ride."

Whatever, Carmen thought, her lips pursed together. She stared at the road ahead of them, wondering what was to come. Her guns were gone, courtesy of Gully, Linx was somewhere in Blacksburg while Jay and Kane were headed for New York. In her opinion, she was officially on her own. It was the way she initially wanted it. She told herself the minute she could get away from Gully, she would. He may have wanted her to play by his rules, but he would soon learn he was second in command.

***

A white two-bedroom house, tucked away in a quaint suburban neighborhood, was where Gully called home. No fancy décor decorated the house, only the basics, and it was also free of photographs. From what Carmen could see, Gully lived a life of a loner and it was obvious he didn't associate with any of his family. He only had enough for himself which was evident when he tried to scrape together a meal for them. She offered several times to order takeout from Waffle House, but Gully declined the offer. Therefore, a bowl of SpaghettiOs and Texas Toast was dinner. She barely touched her food until Gully pointed towards her bowl.

"I guess you're too sophisticated to eat canned food."

Carmen's face was frozen on her bowl yet she knew Gully saw her when she rolled her eyes. The food wasn't the problem although she would've preferred something else. The problem was the time she was wasting. If she wasn't being held up by him, she would've been meeting with Troy, an old friend, to confront him about her heat.

"Not at all," she replied, finally addressing what he said. To please him, she ate a spoonful of SpaghettiOs and finished the rest of her toast. "Yum," she muttered.

Gully overlooked her response by saying, "Tomorrow, we're staking out Blu's restaurant. It's the only spot that wasn't touched. Blu is going to show his face there if he hasn't already. If you ask me, he probably got extra security watching the place because he thinks Jay is going to hit. Pretty soon, he'll learn it isn't Jay who's coming for him. Well, not at the moment."

Carmen looked at Gully only because he confused her. While she could see the similarities between him and Jay, she thought he wanted to stay away from all things Santiago. By going on a manhunt, he was following in his footsteps. "I don't get you," Carmen said, dropping her spoon in her bowl. "You come out of nowhere, you steal my shit, and I'm supposed to trust you because you're my fiancé's cousin?"

"I'm the only person in your corner right now. You don't have a choice."

"I do have a choice," Carmen argued. She stood up from the table, but Gully quickly motioned for her to sit down. She ignored him, continuing her rant. "Ever since I came to this city, I've been doing everything except finding my daughter. I'm sitting here, eating stale SpaghettiOs, staring you in the face, when I need to be knocking on some doors. You took my heat? So what? I can get more. My money is longer than you'll ever see."

Gully chuckled once again, something he did whenever she tried to play tough on him. "You want to be Superwoman so bad," he joked. "You want to take charge, do everything by yourself. It doesn't work that way, Carm. You're one woman going against a whole bunch of men. See, going after people is my shit. That's what I do. Uncle Sam needs someone gone? They call me. I move in, move out, like smoke. That's why Jay put you with me. He knows I can get Kristian back. Stick with me; you'll get your daughter. I certify that shit. If you do this by yourself," Gully paused for a second, "well, I would start planning two funerals—yours and Kristian's."

"Don't doubt me."

Gully let out another small chuckle as he pushed his chair away from the table. He grabbed his empty bowl and quickly dropped it in the sink. "You're hardheaded, Carmen. Do what you do, but please believe I'm a light sleeper if I sleep at all. You'll only get so far before I find you. The choice is yours. You can let yourself in your room."

Carmen got the impression the conversation was over when she saw Gully head for the hallway. She wasn't done with him, which she made known when she spoke. "You don't know shit about me," she yelled at him.

Her frustration was coming to light, her voice shaking, and her volume increasing. "That's my fuckin' child out there. It's not Jay's, it's not yours; she's mine. Y'all want me to sit here and be pretty, and let y'all handle shit, but nothing's happening. I'm tired of wasting fuckin' time. We should be at Blu's restaurant right now. What are you waiting on?"

"Everything happens in due time, Carmen. I know when to move."

"Due time?" Carmen questioned. "Is that your answer for everything? What about your relationship with Jay? Y'all were going to link up in due time?"

Gully walked in the kitchen at the sound of Carmen's words. In his opinion, she didn't have the right to speak on his relationship with Jay. She never knew he existed while he always knew about her. If she continued to test him, he would be forced to put her in her place. "You don't know shit about what happened between me and Jay."

"And you don't know shit about me. You sit up here and judge me based off what you see on TV and in a fuckin' magazine like I can't do anything."

"Because you can't," Gully spat. "You don't know shit about this game." Gully hurriedly walked in his living room and grabbed a small mirror off the wall. In seconds, he was in the kitchen, the mirror directly in front of Carmen's face. "This is your fuckin' enemy," he yelled, allowing her to study her reflection. "That motherfucker doesn't care about your daughter. Y'all are dollar signs. If Blu gets you, he'll have Jay in the palm of his hand."

"I don't care about money," Carmen huffed. "Is that what you're here for?"

"I'm doing this because Jay asked me to. He's never called me for anything. For him to pick up the phone now, I know he needs me."

"So you feel like you owe him? I bet you treated him like shit."

"He deserved what I gave him." Gully dropped the mirror at his side. "Keep fuckin' with me, you'll get what you deserve, too." He attempted to walk away yet Carmen wouldn't let up. Before she could finish her statement, he threw the mirror at her feet, allowing the glass to shatter. The fear he wanted to see appeared on her face. "He killed my bitch," he whispered, harshly. "That's what you wanted to know, isn't it? There it is."

Carmen's mouth was already open, but grew wider with Gully's revelation. Not quite sure what to say, she waited for him to elaborate. He didn't, leaving the kitchen and going into the hallway. Shortly thereafter, he slammed his bedroom door.

Unsure of what to think, she sat at the kitchen table. She didn't touch her food, allowing it to grow cold. More and more questions arose in her head, which she knew she wouldn't get answers to. Gully was in his room reliving the memory and she knew the topic wasn't one he wanted to discuss. He had reason not to talk to Jay and he was right in telling her she shouldn't get involved.

Carmen made the decision to let the whole thing go. To ensure it, she picked up the bowl of SpaghettiOs and dumped the remaining food in the trash can. She then set the bowl in the sink before departing to the guest room. She remembered Gully's warning about him being a light sleeper as she plotted her next move. She could either ditch him all together or she could stick with him. With pros and cons to both, Carmen weighed out each option. Although she expected for the decision to be final before she closed her eyes, it wasn't. If she was lucky, she would know where she was headed once the sun came up.

14

Disclosure

Brookstone, New York

Kane was barely inside the county jail before he stopped and wiped his brow. He had been on the move since landing in New York with little time to catch his breath or even sleep. His Jeep had been parked at the airport since he and Carmen had departed for Copperton City, which worked to his advantage. While Jay was being transported to the county jail, he headed home for a quick shower. There wasn't any time for a nap so after getting dressed, he headed downtown. Now, he was walking inside the jailhouse, about to be face to face again with the man responsible for his daughter's kidnapping.

"I knew I would find you here," a voice said. Not surprised to see Sanders, he wondered what he wanted. "We have a meeting to attend. Can your interrogation wait?"

Kane rolled his eyes before checking his watch. It was almost eight-thirty in the morning. "I'm on a strict schedule. Is this about the coke? I haven't forgotten about it. I know we have a deadline. The quicker I get to Jay, the quicker we'll get the coke back."

"No, it's about BNYC Media, the registered owner of the black car that was outside Flame yesterday morning. They are also the owner of the black cars that were outside Blue Magic. We have a meeting with the manager. His name is Joseph Waters. I set it up."

Kane twisted his mouth in confusion. He could've sworn they were leaving everything with BNYC Media in the past since the company was only a bunch of paps. It was obvious Sanders had done more digging since he had linked them with Blu.

"Do you still think they're paps now?" Sanders asked the question as he pulled a manila envelope from behind his back. He opened it and showed Kane several photos of the vehicles that were found outside Blue Magic. The images were proof there was more to the company than either of them expected.

"So either Blumington has something to do with this company or he stole their cars."

"I drew the same conclusion. However, we need to know which one it is."

Kane exhaled before looking past Sanders. While his intention was to head straight for Jay, he was now being turned in another direction. Not to mention, he still needed to link up with Jean. *Duty calls first,* he thought. "What time is the meeting?" he asked, handing over the photos.

"Now," Sanders replied. "You know how we do, just pop up and start asking questions."

A slight snigger escaped Kane's lips. "Let's do it," he responded. He made the conscious decision to put his conversation with Jay on the back burner. He would meet with Joseph Waters then head back to the jail for a one on one. Then, if time permitted, he would try and see Jean.

They made it to the company's headquarters in less than ten minutes. Kane walked in first, approaching the receptionist who was seated directly in front of the entrance. Kane got straight to the point, flashing his badge and requesting to see the manager. The receptionist didn't hesitate in paging him and in no time, they were in front of Mr. Waters' desk.

"These cars are registered to your company," Sanders began, setting the photos in front of the manager. "These pictures are from the shooting at Blue Magic, the soul food restaurant downtown, which is owned by Jay Santiago. Do you want to explain how those cars got there?"

Mr. Waters picked up the top photo. He stared at it for a second or two before going to the next one. "I don't know anything about this. We're not missing any cars."

"You're not missing any cars?" Kane picked up one of the photos and moved it closer to his face. "Take a closer look. This is a Mercedes Benz. If you lose one, you're going to know."

Mr. Waters jerked the photo out of Kane's hand. He threw it to the side, which proved the pictures hit a sore spot. "My brother has a car dealership," Mr. Waters started to explain. "We work together with our businesses. Sometimes I send my reporters out in his cars so people can see what he has to offer. It's a marketing scheme. So, yes, sometimes, our reporters drive around in expensive cars."

"Do they also eat at Blue Magic?" Sanders asked.

Kane looked at his partner as they waited for Mr. Waters to answer. He didn't respond, which Kane took notice of. "Your actions speak for you. What do you know about those black cars that were at Santiago's restaurant?"

"I don't know anything. These photos show the cars outside a restaurant. Yeah, we have Benzes, but there aren't only four in America. I can't see a license plate in any of these shots. These cars have bullet holes in them. None of my reporters are dead."

Kane took a deep breath at his words. He had a point, but Kane knew he was only stalling. "The cars were impounded. We can easily leave here, get the license plates, and bring them to you as proof. We're only showing you what we already know."

Mr. Waters stood up from his desk and proceeded to pace the floor, a ploy to buy himself some time. Kane made the conscience decision to give him a few minutes to think.

"We did purchase those cars. The lawsuit with Mastermind Records was a win for us and to help out my brother, the company purchased the cars. Long story short, we got involved in another lawsuit and the cars had to go. The company needed quick money so I made a deal with a business owner who was visiting the city from Georgia."

"His name is Shawn Blumington," Kane replied.

"I guess that's his name. I called him Blu. Two men came in with the money. He paid for the cars in cash. The cars were picked up about ten minutes after the transaction was completed. I never worried about the vehicles after that. I was too focused on the lawsuit. Now, this shit happens." Mr. Waters sat in his seat. He stared at the two men in front of him as he wondered which one was going to tell him the fate of his company.

"If you can confirm the gentleman's identity, we can make sure everything with BNYC Media disappears. We're actually looking for this man. You can say he's wanted."

Mr. Waters shrugged his shoulders. "I wouldn't know where to start."

"Start where you ended. Try and remember what those men looked like who handled the deal. Write down details. We can get you a sketch artist if need be, that's not a problem," Kane offered. "Find us the evidence we need and we'll get you the clearance you need. Otherwise, we're holding this company partly responsible for those deaths at Blue Magic."

Kane knew he had Mr. Waters where he wanted him. He watched the man drum his fingers on his desk as if he was thinking things over. He thought rather quickly because seconds later, he was telling them he would work on it. Satisfied with the answer, Kane signaled to Sanders it was time to go and they excused themselves.

"If we can identify Blumington as the man behind what happened," Sanders began once they were outside, "we'll know for sure he sent that car to Flame."

"I just want to find out what's in that FedEx truck. What I know for sure is that it has something to do with Jay and whatever it is, he's housing it in Carmen's building." Kane paused in his step once they were in front of Sanders' car. "I know Blumington's men were shooting at Jay. I also know Blu kidnapped my daughter. However, I refuse to believe he did it because Jay kicked him out his camp."

"Yeah, there's more to it."

"And I'm about to find out." Kane opened the passenger side door and got inside while Sanders took the driver's seat. They headed to the county jail where they went their separate ways. Kane proceeded to Jay's cell while Sanders drove to the precinct.

Kane wasn't quite sure what to expect when he saw Jay. The last image he could remember was the deadly expression on his face when he arrested him. He also remembered how easy it was to handcuff him. Jay didn't put up a fight, not even when dragged out the limousine. It was unlike him, but Kane told himself not to look too deep in it. Nonetheless, when he looked inside Jay's cell, the thought came back. There was only one window on the door, the space big enough to catch a glimpse of his wife's fiancé. Jay was seated on his bed, slightly bent over with his hands clasped together as if he had been praying. Kane watched him for a minute or two before signaling the guard to open the door. Jay's pose didn't change although the doors were now unlocked.

Deep down, Kane knew he needed Jay. He had a wealth of knowledge when it came to Blu, making him valuable. However, he would never ask for his help.

"I never expected for her to get in the middle of this," Jay replied, not looking in Kane's direction. "I'm responsible for this shit and I can't do anything about it." Jay unhooked his hands, wiping his sweat on his pants. "He owns Soulshock in Copperton City," Jay continued. "He also has two clubs, The Kingdom and The Sphinx Club."

Kane shifted his feet, somewhat surprised at Jay's words. He wasn't expecting for him to disclose anything, yet there he was telling him exactly what he needed to know.

"I've never been to any of those places," Jay quickly added. "I just know that in order to find Kristian, we have to start at his businesses."

Kane stuffed his hands in his pants as his mind went to work. While he was appreciative of Jay's willingness to help him, he also saw the bigger piece of the puzzle. Jay was in a delicate situation, which caused for desperate measures. He was about to spend the rest of his life behind bars and was probably looking for anything to aid his case. *If he thinks giving me information on*

Blu is going to make me go easy on him, he's mistaken, Kane thought. *I deserve that information.*

"Do you think that's a plus for you?" Kane asked, finally speaking. "You think telling me something about Blumington is going to make your charges disappear? You don't want to get out of these walls so you can find my daughter. You want to get out so you can marry my wife. That shit bothers me. Well, maybe I should say it *bothered* me. You should tell me what I need to know because I *need* to know, not for some fuckin' freedom."

Jay's tone and volume remained constant. "This isn't about Carmen anymore. It's about Kristian. I only did what I would've wanted you to do for me."

"I don't believe you," Kane admitted.

Jay turned his head to the right so he could look Kane in the face. A comeback was on the edge of his tongue until he heard a new voice in the doorway. It belonged to another officer who for some reason was whispering. Unsure of what was being said, Jay listened as Kane left his doorway. Since their conversation was cut short, Jay assumed there would be a second visit. If so, it was destined to happen sooner than later.

15
The Blindside

An abrupt meeting with the oldest judge in Brookstone wasn't on Kane's task list. The Honorable Judge L. Ernest McCallum had specifically requested his presence and the answer to why was still unknown. With only a small window of time open, Kane was forced to put his conversation with Jay on hold. From what he did know, Judge McCallum was almost ninety, if not already so, and headed towards retirement. He had seen his name a couple of times in documents related to Hector Santiago yet he was never a person of interest to him. Somewhat nervous, Kane wished he brushed up on the judge's involvement in Hector's case. That way, he wouldn't have been walking in his office blind.

Upon entering, the first thing he noticed was the age in the man's face. There were uncountable wrinkles, only strands of white hair on his head, and he was even slightly bent over. Judge McCallum's eyes were focused on a piece of paper in his hand, which he was viewing with a monocle. He didn't lay the paper down until his receptionist introduced Kane's presence.

"Mr. Michael Kane," the judge said with surety. "Close the door behind you, sir."

Kane did as the judge asked and closed the door after the receptionist left. When he turned towards the judge, he noticed a videotape in his hand. A smirk was on the judge's face as he raised a regular, black, unlabeled VHS in the air. Kane was unsure of the tape's contents. He searched the judge's desk for a clue, but he couldn't see anything in detail.

"This is gold, you know. Hector Santiago was my first case in Brookstone," the judge admitted, setting the tape on his desk. "My very first," he continued. "To be honest, it was the reason I stayed in this city. I worked with the DEA for years trying to get him. Then, the Triad took over and I had to try and work my way in their good graces. We never got him, though. The closest we ever got was when you took down his son. We had Jay for seventeen years and one stupid son of a bitch overturned his sentence." The judge let out another slight chuckle. "You got him back for us, though. That's why I called you here. I wanted us to watch this together."

Kane folded his arms across his chest. The tape in the judge's hands was the footage from Blue Magic. It was the key source of evidence which he planned on using when Jay had his day in court. "The shooting," Kane whispered. The judge handed the tape over to him and then pointed at a television which was in a corner of the room.

"You can do the honors."

Kane took the tape from the judge's hands with little to no hesitation. He headed towards the television and slid the tape in the VCR before turning the television on. *His ass could've watched this by his got damn self. This isn't the time for celebration. We celebrate when he hits the fuckin' gavel and Jay's ass is locked away for good.* Kane had watched footage from the shooting a hundred times so he barely paid attention to the current viewing. Not that it mattered because the judge had to stand in front of the entire television in order to see. His monocle was over his right eye yet Kane believed he may have needed a pair of bifocals when he started to rewind the tape.

"Everything is there," Kane told him. "I've got some leads on who he was shooting at—" Kane's words were interrupted when the judge let out an even louder chuckle than before. Not to mention, he was replaying the tape at exactly the point where Jay was firing the most bullets. His laughter confused Kane and when the judge turned around to meet eyes with him, he couldn't help but question his behavior.

"They always win," the judge muttered in response. He walked slowly to his desk as the tape continued to play behind him. "Always," he repeated.

"There's no winning this time," Kane disagreed. "You saw the tape for yourself. He killed those men."

"How many times have you watched this tape, Mr. Kane?"

Kane shrugged his shoulders. "I've watched footage of the shooting like a hundred times," he responded. "It's Jay, right there in the flesh, standing in the parking lot of his restaurant, shooting a whole bunch of men."

Judge McCallum's face became filled with agitation as he walked to the television. He rewound the tape again then set it on pause. "That is Jay," the judge blurted, pointing at the image frozen on the screen. "This," he said, pointing at another figure, "is a baby."

Kane's forehead became wrinkled as he tried to focus on the blurry image. He had to take a few steps closer to the television to see what Judge McCallum was pointing at. The driver's side door was open, allowing him to make out part of a car seat which had been set at the front of the limousine. Then he noticed Nyla whose mouth was wide open as if she was in a fit of tears.

"He had a baby in the car," the judge yelled. He hit the television with an open palm right over Nyla's face. "Y'all are trying to paint this picture of him attacking someone. From what I see, he was the one being attacked while a baby sat inside, screaming for its dear life." The judge paused for a second or two so his words could sink deep into Kane's mind. "He's going to get off on a self-defense plea, because that's what the tape shows. It shows a father who did everything in his power to ensure his daughter wasn't harmed. Do you have a daughter, Mr. Kane?"

Kane's eyes narrowed at the question because his very daughter was being held against her will because of Jay. He wanted to tell the judge he did, but he remained quiet.

"I know you do," Judge McCallum replied, answering the question. "If it was you, you would've been shooting, too." The judge stopped the tape and ejected it from the VCR. "Here," he told Kane, handing it to him. "It's the original from the precinct. It's no good to either of us."

"He killed those men," Kane argued, not taking the tape.

The judge proceeded to walk towards his desk, which is where he set the tape. "Mr. Kane, I postponed my retirement because of this case. I could never get Hector Santiago because someone killed him before I could. However, this one, this one was mine." Judge McCallum slowly turned around, still slightly bent over due to old age and bad posture. "Look at me." The judge raised both his arms horizontally. "I lived my life trying to take down one man. One man," he screamed, his voice echoing off the walls. "The war is over," he muttered. "I'm calling Gomez so he can file the papers for an emergency bond hearing. I'm also going to put in a personal request to the President for a pardon."

"Whoa, whoa, whoa," Kane roared, marching up to Judge McCallum. The judge's hand was already on the telephone as if he was preparing to make the call that very moment. Kane slammed his hand down on the judge's to prevent him from doing so. Kane's words were stern as he tried to change the judge's mind. "It's not just the bodies at Blue Magic; we also have a missing kid, Jarrod Luis, who I know Jay murdered. Then, a million dollars' worth of coke was stolen from the Brookstone PD's vault."

"The coke is still missing," Judge McCallum shot back. "The clock is ticking on the Brookstone Police Department. How much time do y'all have left? Is it even forty-eight hours before the Triad shuts you down?"

"Don't do this," Kane begged. "He won't get off for self-defense. I'll make sure of it."

The judge grabbed Kane's arm, pushing him away. "I'm too old for dirty work, Mr. Kane. If that's your idea of keeping an innocent man in jail, you're on your own. I'm making this call. I suggest you get with the lieutenant. Someone will need to make a statement to the media once a bond hearing is confirmed. If I can get to my contact at the White House in the next ten minutes, I can have this tape on the President's desk by noon."

Despite the cool temperature in the room, sweat started to pour profusely from Kane's forehead. Words spat out his mouth left and right in an attempt to coerce the judge into reconsidering the pardon. When the judge continued to dial an unknown number, Kane knew all hope was about to be lost. Now desperate, he pushed Judge McCallum away from the phone. As a result, the receiver hit the desk with a loud thud. It didn't take much for the man to nearly topple over; however, the chair beside him broke his fall.

"Mr. Kane." Judge McCallum started to make a threat as Kane hovered over him. "You will not get away with this. That tape will be played in court."

"Try me," Kane taunted. He stared Judge McCallum in the face, their eyes frozen on each other until the judge's eventually closed. It took longer than usual, but when Kane removed his hands from the man's neck, the job was done. He changed the judge's position in the chair, placing Judge McCallum's hand slightly over his heart. He then stared at his own hands before wiping them on his pants. Well aware he couldn't walk out the room in a calm manner, he sprinted to the door. He opened it, allowing the door to hit the wall as he screamed for help.

Judge McCallum's receptionist was the first to run to the judge's chambers. The woman screamed at the top of her lungs when she saw the judge's lifeless body. Kane ran to her desk, making the 911 call as more people appeared. When the operator answered, he told him the judge had a heart attack and requested an ambulance. At this point, the entire hallway had become the center of mass hysteria. People were rushing in and out the judge's office as if they didn't believe what everyone was saying. The attention immediately caught the eyes and ears of a police officer who had been patrolling the courthouse.

Kane knew the cop was going to be pointed in his direction so he was prepared when he approached him. He quickly explained the situation, the cop hanging onto every word he told him. "He just started grabbing his chest. I didn't really know what was going on. It all happened so fast. I went into shock for a little bit," Kane was telling him. "Then, he fell in the chair." Kane pretended to get choked up and even turned away, pretending to wipe a tear from his eye. In doing so, he noticed a middle-aged gentleman slipping inside the judge's office. Not quite sure what he was doing, Kane started to follow him until the cop cut off his step with more questions.

Kane rattled off a few quick answers yet time wasn't on his side. The man emerged from the judge's office, this time, his hands weren't free. The VHS tape, which contained the footage of the shooting, was in his left hand. Kane failed to grab the tape before he ran out the judge's office. Now, he was watching as it disappeared from him. *No coke, no tape, no job,* Kane thought. His jaw tightened as the man walked down the hallway, farther away from the judge's office. Then, as if the man sensed him, he turned around, allowing them to meet eyes.

Since he only retrieved the tape from the office, Kane knew he was aware of Judge McCallum's plans. The tape would somehow make its way on the President's desk and the bond hearing that was supposed to send Jay to the state prison would release him into the free world. Jay would be unchained while he would be the one behind steel bars.

"Mr. Kane," a voice said, interrupting his thoughts.

Kane looked at the officer in agitation. "I told you everything that happened," he mumbled. "I don't know anything else. The paramedics should be here soon." The officer was still talking yet he tuned him out as his eyes searched every inch of the hallway. The man was indeed gone. Without a doubt, Kane knew if he didn't find him, his career would be, too.

***

Copperton City, Georgia

Not a light sleeper, Gully was surprised to learn he had slept as long as he had. He figured the argument with Carmen weighed on him more than he thought. Ready to put the quarrel behind him, he climbed out of bed. A quick shower soon followed before he was walking down the hall to her room. The door was closed, making him suspect it was locked. He knocked once only to make sure she was decent yet a sound didn't register. He knocked once more before trying the knob. The door opened easily allowing him to see the room was empty.

The bed wasn't made while her pajamas were strewn across the floor. With the house being dead silent, Gully knew she made a run for it. He remembered seeing his keys on his bedside dresser so he knew Carmen had left on foot. While he knew she had a head start, he wasn't worried. He knew where to find her. It would be only a matter of time before she would prance around to one of Blu's spots. When she did, he would be right there.

Certain of it, Gully walked further in the room, examining everything. He got more than he bargained for when he pulled the covers back on the queen-sized bed. Right there, in plain view, was a small amount of blood stained on his sheets. Either Carmen had started her menstrual cycle or she had injured herself. *Shit,* Gully thought, gazing around the room. *The bitch walked to the corner store. She could've asked me for a ride.* A smile crossed his face at the thought. *Nah, she didn't want that. She wanted to get away. Her period was just the reason for her to do so. It's cool, Mrs. Davenport, we'll catch up soon.*

The smeared blood left on the sheets in Gully's guestroom went unnoticeable to Carmen. It wasn't quite daylight when she made her exit so she wasn't able to see much. She used her cell phone as a flashlight to locate her purse and luggage. Everything else was forgotten.

Carmen had walked four blocks up the road from Gully's house to call herself a cab. If she had the taxi pick her up at Gully's, the car's engine would've woke him if not the headlights. By putting distance between them, she was able to leave without interruption. She requested the cab driver to take her to the nearest homeless shelter. The driver, stunned by her request, did as she asked and pulled in front of a brick building named The Goddard Home. Carmen knew what she needed so she told the driver to wait for her while she went inside.

When she emerged, she had an older gentleman with her. He talked in rambles yet he seemed to understand her when she told him she wanted to put him in a room. He didn't ask any questions, simply following her into the cab and getting inside. He even thanked her repeatedly as the driver took them to the city's local Super 8. Once there, Carmen kept her promise, booking two rooms in his name, one for him, and one for her. With this arrangement, she wouldn't leave a paper trail if Gully started looking for her. A plan she believed would work. She walked the man to his room, left two hundred dollars on the nightstand before retreating to her own.

It had only been a few hours since she had left Gully's, but she was long overdue for a shower. While the motel wasn't the Ritz, it was a small sacrifice for her current situation. To prove to herself she was comfortable, she went in the bathroom and stripped down. It was then she noticed the small circle of blood in her underwear. Embarrassed by the sight, she quickly checked her pants, noticing the same stain of blood in the crease of her jeans. With nearly back to back pregnancies, she had slacked in keeping up with her cycle. Still well prepared for it, she headed in the room and grabbed a pad from her purse.

Now with a stop at a convenience store on her task list, Carmen hurried to the bathroom. She quickly showered, changed into a tee and jeans, before calling herself another cab. Her next stop was a corner car dealership where she could purchase a four-door vehicle with little questions asked. A suitable vehicle was easy to find in Copperton City. In less than two hours, she drove away in a light blue Honda Accord. After a quick stop at Walgreens, she finally made it to the second major stop on her task list, the Hilton Gregory salon.

Gully put a mirror in her face, using her reflection to support his argument on why she wasn't fit to go after Blu. A valid point, Carmen took the gesture to heart. Plastic surgery wasn't an option or a thought, but she knew it was time to make a change in another area. She had spent most of her life growing her hair so cutting it wasn't an option either. However, she didn't have any reservations about changing the color. Naturally jet black, she knew it was a stretch for her to go all the way blonde. Therefore she settled for a two-tone hair color—honey brown at the top which slowly transitioned into a medium golden blonde at the bottom.

To add to her disguise, she swept her hair into a tight bun once she returned to her room. An all-black outfit was already on the bed with a pair of black shades. Almost everything was set except for her arsenal of heat. Contacting another connect was out the question so she quickly called Troy, who she had initially purchased her weapons from. They agreed to meet that night, which was music to Carmen's ears. She was beyond ready, and nightfall couldn't come quicker.

16

Face Off

Brookstone, New York

A television was mounted in the right corner of the lobby of the county jail, displaying a report of Judge McCallum's death. Kane ignored the story as he made his way to Jay's cell. A guard was still in front of it as if Jay needed extra supervision. From what Kane could see, he hadn't changed positions since he left only hours ago. "Open it," he barked at the guard.

"Sanders came by here looking for you," the guard announced, opening the door to the cell. "Things are getting real tense at the station. The coke is still missing."

Kane overlooked the guard's comment. In due time, he would have that situation fixed. Time was ticking yet there was only so much he could do with the obstacles in his path. He planned on asking Jay about the coke amongst other things now that he was in his presence.

"The cars," Kane began, stepping in the doorway. "The cars that were at Blue Magic, the Benzes," he continued. "They were bought by Shawn Blumington from a company called BNYC Media. Word on the street is that he tricked himself into thinking he worked for you. You fired him, and now he wants to retaliate. I believe it, but there's more to it."

"Your reasoning," Jay stated, calmly. "Why do you think there's more to it?" He kept his eyes planted on the wall, not giving Kane a single glance. He knew from his first visit he wasn't finished with him therefore he waited patiently for his return.

"A black Benz was outside Flame today. It was following a FedEx truck. I can put two and two together. You're storing something in Carmen's building."

"You were married to her for seventeen years before I came around. You should know her building in and out. If I'm storing something there, where am I putting it?" Jay turned his head towards the doorway. "You know how I roll, Kane. You studied me, remember? If I'm using her building as a storage house, what am I storing, and where am I putting it?"

"What does Blu want from you?" Kane yelled.

Jay shrugged his shoulders. "I don't know what he wants. That's for you to find out. I gave you the means to do it. Use what I…" the blow to Jay's right temple was enough to make him retaliate. Without any handcuffs on his wrists, he didn't spare Kane any mercy. His knuckles connected at least four times with Kane's nose before the guards were able to separate them. Blood was trickling from his face yet he couldn't feel the pain over his adrenaline.

He didn't put up a fight against the guards, knowing any sudden movement would land him in confinement. Instead, he simply stood there as Kane was ushered out the room.

"No matter what happens," the guard on Jay's left said, "he's not allowed in here. The lieutenant has already spoken. We're not to give Kane any more passes. It's because of him the whole Narcotics department is about to be unemployed."

The guards dropped Jay's arms, allowing him to sit on his bed. A part of him expected for them to address him, but they didn't. They simply left his cell, taking their post outside his door. Officially alone again, he turned once again towards the wall.

Jay knew Kane was on to something when he mentioned a FedEx truck. What Kane didn't know was that Flame's basement was completely clear of everything. He made the call when he was in the bathroom at the Ritz right after the warrant for his arrest became public. His diamonds were currently in the tunnel underneath the building while the machinery had been transported to a warehouse owned by a friend of Linx's. He didn't have time to give word to his friend in Africa that he was closing down shop. So, another package could potentially be sent. With no one there to sign for it, the driver would send it back. When his comrade received the package, he would know something was wrong. Although he couldn't help him, the least he could do was keep the packages at bay until everything was straightened out.

Unfortunately, things weren't coming together as quickly as he wanted. Based off his conversation with his lawyer, Gomez, a bond hearing hadn't been set and even if it was, the outcome wasn't in his favor. To Jay, it seemed everything was up in the air. The only thing he was certain of was that Gully would have Kristian home within forty-eight hours. That's if Carmen didn't beat him to it first.

***

Copperton City, Georgia

Troy was the only man in Georgia who Carmen knew to get weapons from. She was first introduced to him in her early twenties when she used to run the streets with Jay's former best friend, Carlos. Originally from the Bronx, he made his way down South and so did his business. Carmen never kept up with him until she started looking for weapons of her own. While Jay and Malik were busy tending to King's shenanigans when they were in Brookstone, she was in the house with Tiara getting Troy's phone number. Since Tiara was Carlos' ex-girlfriend, she was certain her friend still kept in contact with some of his friends. She thought right and in minutes Tiara slid the number her way. Without hesitation, Carmen called him, gave him a quick reminder of who she was, and put in her order. Then, the inevitable happened. He double-crossed her, giving Gully access to everything she asked for.

Salty wasn't a strong enough word to describe how Carmen was feeling. If she knew of someone else she could go to, she would have. Instead, she decided to deal with Troy, and give him his punishment later. She agreed to meet with him at a small mechanic shop which was about five miles away from the Super 8. It was nighttime, nearing nine o'clock and the place looked somewhat deserted except for a white Mustang, which was parked in front of the building. The lights were on inside, which soothed Carmen's nervousness as she entered.

"Troy," she shouted, her saltiness exhibited in her tone. She paused at the door and listened for any sudden movements. When she heard something towards the back of the shop, she proceeded to head towards the sound. "Troy," she repeated.

Carmen raised her brow when she saw him slide from underneath an apple red Mitsubishi Lancer. Her expression became stern because she was ready to remind him of what he'd done.

"Long time no see," he shouted, gazing towards her from the floor. "You look different. That's a nice color on you," he continued, staring at her hair. "Sad thing what happened to Carlos." Troy stood on his feet before grabbing a rag off one of the many toolboxes in the shop. He wiped his hands as he continued to greet her. "You did real well with yourself. Even Jay ended up on top. Well, after that long stint in prison."

"My shit," Carmen asked, ignoring his comments. "I wired you the money."

"I was going to call you about that," Troy stated, his voice becoming softer than before. "I had everything you requested. It was all set and ready to go. Then, there were some complications." Troy paused for a second or two. "Look, some dude took your shit. It was like he knew about our deal."

Carmen bit her lip. Troy's words confirmed that Gully had everything she purchased. If she wanted any kind of heat, she would have to go to Gully's house or ask Troy to refer her to someone else. Then again, she wouldn't trust his reference since he still hadn't coughed up the money she wired him. *Speaking of that,* Carmen thought. "Where's my money?"

"I got it in the back," Troy replied. "Let me get it."

Carmen rolled her eyes as he headed towards the back of the shop. She could tell he was unaware she knew about Gully, but he would be in for a rude awakening when she brought him up. Until the moment came, she stood there impatiently, exhaling every now and then as she waited for him to return. He was taking longer than expected so Carmen started peeking around the shop. About three different cars were inside with parts of each vehicle missing. From the looks of things, Troy was preparing for more than a normal ride down the road.

She pondered on his plans as she picked up a nail gun which had been set on the hood of a Nissan Skyline. She held it tightly in her hand until she heard Troy returning from the back. At the sound of his footsteps, she dropped it on the hood as if she had never touched it. When she looked in the direction of his steps, she saw him with a duffle bag in his arms.

"I actually was able to dig up some stuff for you," he told her, setting the bag on one of the cars. Carmen watched as Troy unzipped the duffle bag. She took a peek inside and saw about three weapons. Her forehead furrowed because she knew the money she gave him didn't equate to what was in the bag. "I know it's not much, but—"

"This isn't my money, Troy." Her anger was on full display, evident by the bulging vein in the middle of her forehead. "This doesn't even equal the money I gave you. Either give me my shit or give me my money."

"I got fucked up, Carm. Your shit is gone. I got this, though."

Carmen knew she was wasting her time. Troy's plan was to give her heat to Gully, leave her with three pistols, and take off with the money. Just like Jay's cousin, he thought she was weak and not fit for the war she was trying to fight. "You know what, Troy?" she asked him, grabbing the nail gun. She quickly compressed the safety on the tool, firing a nail in his trachea. Troy's hands immediately flew up from the impact. He lost his footing when the second nail hit, and shortly thereafter, lost his balance at the impact of the third. "Now, you're fucked up," Carmen whispered as he shook violently on the floor.

Blood trickled from Troy's lower neck, slowly creating an outline around his convulsing body. When his facial expression became frozen, she didn't bother to check for a pulse. Instead, she set the nail gun inside the duffle bag for safekeeping. Time was even more of the essence so she didn't hesitate to head towards the back of the shop where Troy had been. In a small corner, she found an office, which was cluttered with several papers and a large stack of bills. Carmen didn't need to count the money to know it was the payment she had sent him. She simply grabbed the money and stuffed it inside the duffle bag as well.

Just like Jay, her actions could lead her down a road of imprisonment. The thought of being locked up prompted her to look at each corner of the ceiling. She didn't spot a security camera, but she knew not to press her luck. She walked quickly into the main shop area and looked for any sign of a camera. In the process, she spotted a red gas can that had been set directly behind the Nissan. Just like her initial plan was to never kill Troy, she also didn't plan on setting the shop on fire. Somehow, she ended up doing both. It was like she was on a roll. Before the madness was over, Carmen knew she would do more damage. With weapons, thousands of dollars and a nail gun in her passenger seat, the party was only starting. Troy was the first attendee, but he definitely wouldn't be the last.

Intermission

Blood and Chocolate

A cool breeze swept through the room, the slight wind tickling Kristian's nose. The sudden touch made her eyelids flicker until her eyes were wide open underneath the blindfold. Once again, she found herself completely wrapped in darkness. The floor was cold and hard underneath her, which didn't aid the sudden chill pouring through the room. Unsure of where she was, Kristian stretched out her legs. She couldn't remember much from earlier except for a lot of whispering. She did remember being placed in a car, hearing the sound of the engine and then a long ride. Shortly thereafter, she felt a hard prick in her side and then everything went black.

Now that she was awake, she was curious to know where she had been placed. The space was big enough for her to stretch out, which meant she could possibly stand. She raised her arms over her head, her arms still bound yet able to be fully extended. When she didn't feel anything, she stood on her feet. Her hands went overhead a second time, which told her the space was probably equal in height to the basement of Soulshock. To make sure the width was similar; she took a few steps, forward, backward, and then side to side. The space wasn't that confined so she proceeded to move to the left until she ran into a wall. Like she had done before, she traced the wall until the feel of it became different.

Her hands found an opening, then steps, which told her she was in the basement of Soulshock. While it did soothe her mind for a few seconds, it also made her remember Victor's fate. He was the only person who knew where she was with the exception of the kitchen staff. She couldn't count on them to rescue her so she was as good as dead. *I'm not even hearing their voices,* Kristian thought. *They could be long gone by now.* Kristian balled her right hand into a fist with the idea of striking the door. The second the two were about to connect, she paused when she heard the sound of footsteps, which was followed by an all too familiar voice.

"That smell is still here," Blu said. He was rather close, right outside the door yet he was no longer walking. Kristian assumed he was trying to figure out where the smell was coming from. The stench was strong, dancing around her nose even more than before.

"These boxes weren't here a couple of days ago," Blu said, pointing in front of him. "It might be something in these boxes." He reached inside his suit jacket and grabbed a handkerchief. "It has to be," he mumbled, picking up the box at the very top of the stack. He looked at his right-hand who was standing there quietly. "Are you still mad at me?" he asked Victor. He chuckled for a bit when his partner didn't answer. "Ahh, you didn't get roughed up too bad, just enough for it to be believable. Shit, if anyone should be mad, it should be me. You were the one who fucked up."

"I'm not doing this shit, Blu."

"Yes, you are," Blu replied, opening the box. "You most definitely are. By the way, keep your voice down. She's probably awake. That shot doesn't last forever, you know." Blu wrinkled his face when he saw the box was empty and tossed it aside. "Nothing," he whispered. "It's something here I'm telling you. This hallway has been fucked up since this morning."

"What is your plan after you get this man's shit? Are you going to let her go?"

"Too many questions," Blu responded, grabbing the second box. This particular one was a little bit shorter than eye level so he didn't bother to pick it up. He simply pulled it closer to him, proceeding to tear off the white wrapping paper and the red ribbon which decorated it. The stench was much stronger so he knew something was rotting inside. "Too many questions," he repeated. "Kristian is too much of your concern." Blu planted his hands on the flaps of the box as he looked at Victor. "She made your dick hard, too, huh?"

Victor raised his brow only because Blu had figured him out. He did find Kristian attractive, but she was younger than him, which meant she was off limits. Not to mention, she wouldn't be pleased to know he helped Blu secure her in the basement a second time. If she found out, he could lose her trust and potentially catch a charge. "I don't know what you're talking about," he quickly said. "She's a kid."

"That body isn't," Blu muttered. He placed his eyes on the box and proceeded to open the flaps as the stench grew. "I promise you, if they left food out here to rot…" he didn't finish his sentence as he opened the box. At the sudden glance of its contents, he backed away at the gruesome sight in front of him. Victor did the same, both of them backing up against the wall.

Blu heard the message loud and clear that Jay was sending. He knew the work was of no one but him. For one, the severed head belonged to House, one of his runners from the outskirts of Chicago. He was one of several men he had sent to Blue Magic in an attempt to kidnap Jay. It pained Blu to see his death up close although he had gotten word that Jay had murdered him. To make matters worse, House's penis had also been cut off and was shoved inside his mouth. Both body parts were decomposing in his restaurant without anyone's knowledge, until now. In addition, there were three more boxes decorated exactly the same underneath the one he opened.

"Santiago moves like this?" Victor whispered, harshly.

Blu didn't respond to Victor's comment. Instead, he motioned for him to go towards the front of the restaurant where two of his men were. "Tell them to get this shit out of here. I'm going to check on Kristian. We don't have much time before the raid begins." Blu didn't hear any apprehension from Victor so he continued to the basement while Victor headed towards the front. The image of House's rotten head was still in his mind yet it quickly faded at the sound of several gunshots. Blu was quick, pulling out his glock and the key to the basement at the same time. He heard Jay's message even louder as the gunshots came closer.

With little time to spare, he unlocked the basement door only for Kristian to fall in his arms. He grabbed her, pressing his gun up against her forehead and giving her a stern warning to follow his instruction. The blasts were coming from the front and were soon matched with the sound of Victor's footsteps. Guns in hand, they proceeded to the nearest exit, the exact same location they previously entered. His black Benz was still parked outside, untouched. "Take her," he told Victor, throwing Kristian in his arms. Since he was certain two of his men were dead in his restaurant, Blu decided not to add himself to the body count. Therefore, he took the driver's seat while Victor and Kristian headed to the back.

He sped out the parking lot, going the opposite way in which he came. He ran two red lights in the process, almost colliding with a black Toyota. Once he passed the car unscathed, he looked in the rearview mirror to check on Kristian. Her entire body was centered on Victor, his arms wrapped tightly around her frame. Blu's jaw tightened at the sight, but he knew he couldn't do anything about it. All he could do was focus on his next move. Not yet in process, Blu had given the order for things to start on time whether his men received word from him or not. In addition, he needed a place to house Kristian. Soulshock was completely out so the next place had to be chosen strategically. Jay was moving in on him and time was gracious to no one.

17

Remember Me?

Two bodies were dead at the hostess stand, but Carmen knew the restaurant wasn't completely empty. She heard footsteps in between the gunshots, which meant someone was there. Still standing at the front of Soulshock, Carmen knew the person was probably long gone or in hiding. She walked slowly behind the hostess stand, her finger tight on the trigger in case she needed to fire.

From what she could see, the kitchen was directly ahead. She moved slowly to it, pausing between steps to listen for any sudden movements. The restaurant was completely silent so she pushed open the double doors to the kitchen. Upon entering, she was met with a foul stench. More surprised than disturbed, Carmen covered her nose as she walked through the kitchen. She didn't find anything out the ordinary until she entered a long corridor. The hallway was littered with boxes and there was even torn wrapping paper in the middle of the floor. Nonetheless, it was when she spotted a long red ribbon she stopped in her tracks.

"Shit, I didn't even tell you about the phone call I got from Cesar, she remembered Jay saying. *"All of the bodies that were left at Blue Magic ended up at Jimenez Funeral Home. You know what that means? I get another chance to show Blu who he's fuckin' with. I shipped two of those corpses to his restaurant in a fuckin' box. I gift-wrapped it; put a bow on it and all."*

Carmen took a deep breath as she took another step forward. More fearful about what she was going to see, she moved like a snail. The stench was stronger with each step and the closer she got, the more she could see inside the box. At the first sight of ghastly eyes, Carmen turned away, almost vomiting. She tried to keep everything down, but it was hard. *I have to move. I have to move.* She listened to her own voice, moving away from the area. A door was opened to her right so she went to the doorway, which led to the basement of the restaurant. The light in the hallway was rather dim yet it was strong enough for her to see down into the space.

A different kind of smell entered her nostrils as she walked down the steps. The stench wasn't as potent as the smell of decaying bodies, somewhat more manageable. The basement was completely empty, which wasn't exactly what Carmen expected to find. However, the open door told her one thing. There was someone down there before she came. More than likely, they went to the basement, got whatever they needed, heard the gunshots, and jetted. Certain of it, Carmen went up the steps and into the hallway. She didn't look in the direction of the severed head, walking past it and towards an exit sign. The door was slightly cracked, giving her more confirmation that someone else had been at the restaurant.

When she opened it, no one was in sight. Cars were passing behind the restaurant, but no one was going at an alarming speed. Everything was completely normal so Carmen knew it was time to go. While the empty basement was somewhat of a dead end, the severed head wasn't. Someone had been there to open the box. It could've been opened by one of the men who were now dead in front of the restaurant. Carmen knew once the bodies were found, police reports would be made, and eventually, funerals would be planned. Not only would family show up to pay their respects, but friends as well, including Blu. If he didn't show, she would know he was dodging all chances of a showdown.

Certain of it, Carmen walked towards the front. The bodies were in the same place she left them as well as her car. Unlike what she had done at the shop, she didn't torch the restaurant. She wanted the bodies found in solid condition despite the bullet holes. Carmen walked steadfastly to her car, well aware sirens would be wailing soon. About to slide in, her plans were halted when she felt someone grab her right ankle. With a pistol still in her left hand, Carmen pointed the weapon downward yet she didn't fire for fear of shooting herself. Instead, she tried to jerk her leg out the person's grasp until she fell on the ground.

Sirens were distant in the background, the clock ticking more than before. Desperate to get away, Carmen pointed the pistol underneath her car until she met eyes with Gully. It was only then she allowed the gun to fall from her grasp. Simultaneously, he let go of her. The sirens were getting closer so Carmen moved fast, getting inside the car where Gully joined her uninvited. Instead of arguing, she started up the car, leaving the scene. She didn't ask him why he was there, where his car was, or even where they were headed. She simply drove until the sirens could no longer be heard.

"Remember me?" Gully asked once she had drove about two blocks. Carmen didn't reply to him only because she didn't want to remember. She thought she had rid herself of him. "Take the right at the light," he ordered. "You don't know where the hell you're going. You're driving all over this damn city and going to have us in College Park before you know it." A slight chuckle sounded out his mouth. "What happened in my bedroom?"

Carmen raised her brow only because she didn't know what he was talking about. "Nothing happened. Are you mad because I didn't make up the bed?" Carmen made the right turn as Gully had instructed.

"I'm talking about the blood, Carmen."

"My period came on," Carmen replied, quickly. "I'm sorry. I'll wash the sheets. If you want, I'll buy you a new set. I'll even make sure it's 1500-thread count."

"Cool, now what about the bodies in the restaurant?"

Carmen looked at Gully whose eyes were frozen on her. She didn't admit to the murders although she knew Gully was aware she had killed Blu's men.

"You killed two men without getting any information. You could've killed one, wounded the other, and at least got something before you killed him. You made a mistake."

"You can fix mistakes," Carmen shouted. "Don't make me feel like I failed."

"Take the left at the stop sign," Gully instructed. "What did you find out?"

Carmen swallowed as she started noticing an area she had walked through earlier that day. Gully was leading her to his house as if she was going to stay with him. If anything, she should've taken him to his car so they could go their separate ways. "Look, Gully, we both have plans," Carmen told him, slowly pressing on the brake as she approached a stop sign. "I just don't believe they include each other."

"Jay didn't want this, Carm. He didn't want you out here doing this shit by yourself. Maybe, deep down, he knew you would, but those weren't the words expressed to me. He wanted us together. You're just making it a little bit harder for me."

"Don't talk about him like he's fuckin' dead," Carmen yelled. She pressed her foot on the gas, making a left turn, which took her into Gully's neighborhood. "Jay wants a lot of things and so do I. Nobody gets everything they want."

"You're right, we don't." Gully sunk down further in the seat as he tried to piece together his next move. It was obvious Carmen wanted to do her own thing by her actions. She had made major moves in a short amount of time without even the slightest bit of help. "Look, if I let you do this, at least stay with me. The room is all yours."

Carmen looked at Gully out the corner of her eye. Her money was already spent on a room at the Super 8 and while it wasn't the Ritz, it would make do until her daughter was in Brookstone. "When I left this morning, we both knew this Bonnie and Clyde thing Jay wanted was over. I think I've proven myself to you. I can handle a whole lot more than what you give me credit for. Thanks for the offer, but no thanks."

Gully gave her a single head nod. "Fine then, if that's what you want. Just sit tight for a minute. Let me get your shit." Completely wiping his hands of everything, Gully opened the passenger side door and stepped outside. He retrieved his keys from his pocket as he walked towards his house. He also debated about whether or not to tell Carmen about his own discovery. He knew he needed to, but a part of him wanted to hold back because of the wall she had put up. Then again, giving her the information would be the only way he could help her.

By the time he was inside, his mind was made up. He moved quickly, heading in his bedroom and grabbing the duffle bag from underneath his bed which held Carmen's guns. He didn't know her plans, but he could make sure she was well equipped. He would watch from a distance like he had done that night, staying put until his presence needed to be made known.

"This is it," he told her once he was inside the car. The duffle bag was in his lap, which he opened so she could see the contents. "Everything from Troy is right here." He moved some of the guns aside so she could take a look at everything before he zipped the bag up. "Where would you like it?"

"The backseat," Carmen told him, promptly.

Gully did as she requested sliding the bag into the backseat of her car. Although he gave her what was rightfully hers, he wasn't going to leave so soon. "I understand you want to run the streets alone, but I have some info for you. I didn't take a car to Soulshock on purpose. You can see more on foot than if you're hiding behind a steering wheel." Gully waited for Carmen to react, but she remained mum. "Blu was at his restaurant tonight. He came with another man. They went in through the back, which is the same way they exited. I know because I was there and I saw them. About ten minutes later, you started laying bodies out. He went in empty-handed, but that doesn't mean he left empty-handed."

"The door to the basement was open," Carmen admitted. "Nothing was down there and it looked as if it had never been used."

"Your daughter was in that basement," Gully assumed. "He came to see her, heard the gunshots, grabbed her, and ran. I bet my life on it."

Carmen swallowed as she began to piece together the details. Gully's assumption could very well be true. She knew for sure she heard someone running in between the gunshots. She would've known for sure if she had taken the time to scope out the area before going on a killing spree. "If it wasn't for me, you would've been able to see if Kristian was there."

Gully didn't want to voice his agreement for sake of her feelings so he remained quiet. Tears were streaming down her face as she realized how close she was to finding her daughter. A witness to her pain, he didn't speak even as her phone rung from the glove compartment. "Do you want me to get that for you?" he asked. He waited until she nodded her head before he retrieved her phone. He handed it to her after seeing it was her husband. "I'll excuse you," he told her, about to head out.

Carmen grabbed his arm to hold him in place as she answered Kane's call. "Hey," she said, softly, trying to control her tears.

"Are you in Georgia?"

Carmen swallowed at the sound of his tone. He sounded somewhat out of breath so she wondered where he was. "I am," she replied. "Have you heard anything from Detective Morris?"

"Great," Kane said, promptly, not answering her question. "Stay there."

Carmen parted her lips, but before she could reply, Kane hung up. His reaction was enough for her to know he was up to something. Not quite sure what it was, she debated about going to Brookstone or staying in Copperton City. She looked to Gully for advice as if he heard Kane's words. "He told me to stay in Georgia."

Gully narrowed his eyes only because he didn't know what Kane had up his sleeve. Due to the attack the other day, he knew Kane wanted retaliation for what he had done. Since he wasn't coming to Georgia any time soon, Gully figured there was something in Brookstone more important than him. "He's up to something for sure. Whatever it is, he doesn't want you around for it." Gully got comfortable in the seat although he needed to be getting in the house. He was breaking ties with Carmen yet he was still sitting in her car. "Look, it's late; we both had a long night. Can we at least remain cordial?"

Carmen grabbed the steering wheel despite the car not being on. She was having second thoughts, which was why she was hesitant. "Two sometimes is better than one," she told him.

"The room is yours," Gully muttered, sensing she had changed her mind. "Come on in."

Carmen didn't rush to park, doing it at her own pace. Gully still hadn't fully earned her trust, but he was closer than he thought. She knew she had to do her part, too, which is why she decided to stay. She had somewhat of a slip up tonight, but with Gully's help, things could potentially turn around. Before she knew it, Kristian would be home and the nightmare would be something of the past.

***

Back in Brookstone, Kane was stuffing his phone in his pocket when Sanders called him. He had been dodging him since his scuffle with Jay as he worked out a game plan regarding the FedEx truck and Flame. Now that he had things figured out, he was ready to put everything in motion. He was currently at Tiara's house; the one person he knew had full access to Flame when he received Sanders' call. His wife's best friend didn't know about his presence so he told Sanders, "Lay it on me," when he answered.

"Joseph Waters called the station a few hours ago. Detective Brockman met with him at his office with a sketch artist. I'm looking at the drawings now and the images match two of the men who were killed at Blue Magic. He most definitely sold the cars to Shawn Blumington."

"Perfect," Kane replied. "On to other things, though. Carmen is still in Georgia. I don't know what she's found out, but I have a new plan to get some answers. As long as she's in Georgia, this'll work."

Sanders exhaled loudly on the phone. "What about the coke, Kane? I know you're dealing with your daughter, but our jobs are on the line. If we don't get this coke then everything we're working on is for nothing."

Kane knew the future of the department was on his shoulders. Everyone was expecting for him to come through before the Triad shut them down. If he told Sanders his plan, he would soothe his mind all while getting him to join him in his mission. "I think Jay is housing his coke in Carmen's building. I'm at Tiara's house now. She's Carmen's best friend and the Vice President of Flame. If I can get her to cooperate, we can get a team inside tonight. I want to tear the place apart."

"So," Sanders pondered, "you think the FedEx truck is delivering drugs?"

Kane knew the idea was somewhat farfetched only because Jay swore up and down he was no longer a drug dealer. Still, there was something he was doing to bring in income aside from his two businesses. Blue Magic and Sapphire only brought in so much, and with Iceland still being prepped, Kane knew money was coming from somewhere. "What else could it be, Sanders?"

"Your wife lets Jay get away with a lot, but housing drugs in her building isn't one of 'em."

"Look, it's the only lead I have at the moment. Do you have something better? Let's not forget, it was your idea to give Jay his shit back." Kane didn't want to place the blame, but at this point, he had to. His partner was the one who had confiscated a million dollars' worth of Jay's coke. After the shooting at Blue Magic, Sanders raided Jay's penthouse apartment to arrest him for the murders at his restaurant as well for selling and distributing illegal drugs. He also arrested Carmen for conspiracy. To get out of jail, Carmen threatened to disclose every secret she knew regarding the Triad. In an attempt to keep her quiet, Sanders agreed to give the drugs back to Jay. That way, the Brookstone PD no longer had evidence against him. At the time, there also wasn't any footage from Blue Magic, which showed Jay shooting anyone. His wife's fiancé made bail and was freed.

"Look, sit tight for a few minutes," Kane ordered. "I'm going to try and work this whole thing out. We don't have time to get a warrant so you better hope and pray Tiara will cooperate. It's worth a shot."

Sanders had no choice but to agree. It was worth a shot. If they did find drugs in Flame, the whole department would be saved. Whether it was a million dollars' worth or a couple hundred thousand, they had another charge to place on Jay's ever growing list. "Do what you have to, Kane. Keep me informed."

"I will." Kane ended the call, starting the short trek towards Tiara's front door. He could see a light on in the living room, which made him assume someone was awake. If it was Malik, he would have to deal with him before getting to Tiara.

Ready for the battle, he pressed the doorbell. He didn't receive an immediate answer, having to press the doorbell a second time before Malik showed. His face was one of annoyance, which quickly turned to anger. There was already tension between them so Kane prepared himself for an argument.

"Do you know what time it is?" Malik spat, stepping outside. He closed the door behind him so if things escalated he wouldn't wake Tiara or the kids.

"I need to talk to your wife."

"Tiara isn't talking to you. I know y'all have Jay in police custody. I've already spoken to Gomez and I know he's getting the runaround on a bond hearing. Besides, you have enough on your plate. Didn't the city's oldest judge just die on you? You should be running around somewhere else."

Kane tried to control his temper with Malik's comment. The mention of Judge McCallum was only a reminder of the crime he committed and the stolen surveillance tape. The longer the tape was out of his possession, the greater the chance of it turning up in the hands of Jay's defense team. "We can do it this way, Malik, or we can do it the politically correct way. I need to see Tiara because I need to get into Flame. Now, you can deny me access to her or I'll call a judge in the morning, get a warrant, and get in the building my damn self. Maybe I need to remind you that your goddaughter is still missing. Or do you believe that protecting Jay is more important than finding Kristian?"

Malik dropped his hands at his side, his demeanor changing. Due to his differences with Kane, he forgot to ask how the search was coming. With the reminder right there in his face, he had second thoughts about letting Kane speak to his wife. "What have you found?"

"I know a man named Shawn Blumington who used to work for Jay orchestrated the hit at Blue Magic. He also had a black Benz trailing a FedEx truck that was at Flame yesterday. Something was in that truck that Blumington wants and it's also in that building."

Malik chuckled only because he knew Flame was completely empty. Jay wasn't hiding anything there. The last thing his friend would do is compromise Carmen's business. "You're wasting your time," he told him. "I promise you that. The only thing you'll find in Flame that belongs to Jay is a few unfinished suits. Carmen designs suits for him. If he wanted, he could have his own collection. No one else wears those designs."

"Cool," Kane said, happily, "then Tiara and I won't be gone long. Can you get her for me? We'll be back before you know it."

Malik took a step forward because Kane's adamant nature was starting to bother him. It was already late and Malik wasn't thrilled to hear Kane's demands. "I know this is about the coke. The coke is gone. The Narcotics department *will* be shut down because we can't give you shit we don't have. Jay didn't lie when he said he was cutting all ties to the drug game. He's out. We all are. You're not going to find any drugs in Flame."

Kane scratched his chin only because he wasn't quite sure what he was looking for. Although there weren't any drugs, there was still the possibility Blumington thought there was. As long as he did, he would keep coming until he discovered he was fighting a losing battle. On the other hand, Kane wasn't certain he could trust Malik. "I want to see for myself."

Malik took a deep breath only because Kane wasn't letting up. Instead of continuing to argue with him, he decided to let Tiara make the decision. "I'm going to wake her. Stay here." Malik didn't wait for a response, turning around to enter his house. He closed the door behind him, even locking it to ensure Kane stayed outside. Their friendship was beyond rocky and practically hanging by a thread. The only reason Malik felt he needed to somewhat comply is because Kane knew his secret. If Jay knew he was behind his seventeen-year incarceration, he would kill him dead. Certain of it, Malik went to his bedroom, waking his wife.

"Kane is here," he whispered once she stirred. "He needs you to help him get inside Flame."

"What?" Tiara wiped the sleep from her eyes as she tried to digest Malik's words. "He needs me to help him get inside Flame? What's in Flame?"

"He thinks something is in there that Blu wants."

Tiara shook her head in disbelief. "Are you serious, Malik? We don't have time for this. We have three babies in this house, Malik, three," Tiara fussed. "We're trying to keep up with Malachi, Akaila, and Carmen's mother. Not to mention, I still have to phone into the office to make sure Flame is straight. I don't need him trying to make allegations against my company."

"Baby, I know, but if you don't go with him, he said he's going to get a warrant. Maybe if we do it this way, if he does find anything, he'll go easy on y'all."

Tiara continuously shook her head. If there was something in Flame, she knew Carmen didn't tell her. A loud sigh escaped her mouth as she studied her husband's face. "What could be in Flame?"

"Nothing is supposed to be there. We're out the game, I told you that. I made a promise I wasn't going back. All that shit is long gone."

Tiara sighed again, but only out of frustration. She was worn out and going on a hunt wasn't something she was up for. Still, she would prefer to go in the building with Kane than with a bunch of nosy ass detectives. "Alright, I'll do it," she said, pulling the covers back. "Tell him, I'm getting myself together. I'll be down in ten."

Malik told her he would and retreated downstairs. A part of him was slightly nervous about them going in Flame, but he told himself to calm down. Nothing was in the building that could hurt either of them. Kane would come up empty-handed and Tiara would return home making a big fuss about how she had wasted her time. In two hours or so, they would be in bed sound asleep or at least that was the way Malik wanted to see it.

"She'll do it," he announced to Kane.

A smile flew across Kane's face at the news. *I knew she would,* he thought. *Tiara is no one's dummy. She knows when to move. Let's just pray Jay does, too. If I find anything in that building, his ass is going to the wolves.*

18
ASAP

Kane could feel Tiara's eyes burning on his the entire time he was driving. He knew she wanted to jump down his throat, but for some reason, she was sitting there quietly. The silence was almost too much for him so he decided to address the issue. "I do appreciate this, Tee. I know you have your hands full. It's not like I wanted things to come to this."

Tiara didn't respond to his words although her eyes were planted on him. Kane could say whatever he wanted, but her feelings weren't going to change. His motive was to always keep Jay in jail and he didn't care who he had to take down to do it.

"Look, we're almost there, Tee. You haven't said one word during this whole ride. I'm not trying to do anything to compromise Flame. I know this is your bread and butter. I'm just trying to do everything I can to find out what Blu wants so I can get Kristian back."

Kane's eyes flickered to Tiara in hope she would say something. When she didn't speak, he turned his eyes to the road. The turn for Flame was only a few seconds away so he decided to remain mum. Tiara didn't want to talk so it was best if he stopped trying to make her. She wasn't there to converse with him, anyway. She simply was his key.

She proved it to him when she let him inside the building and on the elevator. She didn't ask him where he wanted to go, allowing him to press the buttons. When he went to the executive floor, Tiara knew he was headed straight for Carmen's office.

He didn't know if she had a key, but since she wasn't stopping him, he figured she did. He got his answer when he stopped at his wife's door and Tiara let him inside.

All the lights were off, which he turned on upon entering. The first place he went was to her desk, opening a few of her drawers. He started at the first drawer, noticing how neat and organized Carmen was. The drawer was actually a file cabinet filled with several labeled folders. From designs to sale reports, business contracts and even fashion magazines, Carmen had everything in its proper place.

Tiara didn't bother to join him in the search. Instead, she chose to remain in the doorway in a stance which said she didn't want to be involved. Kane purposely ignored her behavior so it wouldn't distract him from what he was doing.

When he moved to the second drawer, he expected to find similar documents only to find a rough sketch of a wedding dress, a mix between a trumpet and mermaid-styled gown. He stared at the dress in disbelief. It was designed to be all white, strapless and even had a sweep train. *We're not even divorced yet and she's planning a fuckin' wedding. This is some bullshit. Is this what she's been working on?* Kane grabbed the paper from the drawer and immediately went to Carmen's shredder. He turned it on and passed the sketch through the machine, shredding the document. At the sound, Tiara came in the room, obviously intrigued.

"What was that?" she asked, finally speaking.

"Nothing of importance," Kane whispered. *Carmen isn't wearing that shit. I bet my life on it. Jean or no Jean, Carmen isn't getting married again.* His voice remained low as he went to the drawer. There weren't any other wedding details inside. The rest of the drawer was filled with large notebooks of past sales reports. Still not satisfied, he moved on to another drawer. This time, Tiara was breathing down his neck as she watched his every move.

"There's nothing here, Kane."

Kane didn't reply to her comment. He hadn't finished checking the drawers, which meant there was still a chance something would turn up. Therefore, he kept looking, moving on to the third drawer located in the upper right-hand corner of Carmen's desk. He grabbed the handle on the drawer yet it didn't budge. It was then he noticed the keyhole. "I need a key," he told Tiara, looking behind him. "This drawer is locked for a reason. There's a keyhole."

"I don't have the key. I only have a key to her main door in case I need to access files."

Kane sucked his teeth, but only because he was going to have to pick the lock. He knew he didn't have a lock pick on him so he started to look for the next best thing, a paper clip. Not hard to find, he picked up the first one he saw, bending the clip inward so it was flat. It took him awhile to get the clip the way he wanted since he didn't have a set of pliers, but he still managed to squeeze it together enough to get into the lock.

"You don't even know what you're looking for," Tiara muttered as he twisted the clip in the keyhole. "You're just going off some stupid hunch."

"Remind me to tell you the same thing when Robin gets kidnapped."

"This isn't about your daughter, Kane. This is about Jay. If it was about your daughter, you would be with Carmen. Instead, your ass is here, trying to make sure Jay stays in jail."

"I want that, too," Kane admitted. "I'm multi-tasking." He shot Tiara a smile just as he heard the drawer unlock. She rolled her eyes and even walked away from him when he opened the drawer. At first glance, the drawer appeared empty until he noticed a black velvet bag in the upper left-hand corner. The only thing inside, he pulled it out, feeling the weight of the bag. "Come here," he told Tiara, who had gone to the doorway. Impatient, he didn't wait on her as he loosened the bag's strings and dumped the contents on Carmen's desk.

"Jackpot," he muttered. Kane looked at Tiara to see her mouth wide open. He then pointed at Carmen's desk where a wide array of diamonds laid. "Blumington didn't cause this much damage for one bag of diamonds. There has to be more. I bet my life on it."

Tiara walked further in the room, approaching Carmen's desk. Pink, white, blue, and even a few green diamonds were right there in front of her. She knew Jay was opening a jewelry store, but she never expected for Carmen to be in on it, too.

"Jay and Carmen both love diamonds," Kane said in a low tone. "Carmen most definitely wouldn't let him house drugs in her building, but diamonds?" Kane chuckled at the thought. "She most definitely would let him put a shitload of stones in her spot."

"So what are you thinking?" Tiara asked. "I know she's not hiding stones in any of the executive offices. There is nothing in our mailroom."

Kane knew Tiara had a point. He drummed his fingers on Carmen's desk as he thought about another place to check. Simultaneously, he studied the diamonds on her desk. The colors drew him in, leading him to notice a rare stone in the pile. One single black diamond was in the bunch, the only one of its kind. A diamond he had only seen in photographs, the stone intrigued him more than the others. He picked it up, turning it over in between his fingers. *A black diamond,* he thought. *Carbonado.* Kane looked up at Tiara who was still in the same spot. "What is the darkest part of this building?"

Tiara's lips parted yet no reply came out. The question was rhetorical so Kane spoke for her, telling her he wanted to go to the basement. "It's the place no one goes, a place no one has probably ever seen." Kane picked up the diamonds and put the stones inside the bag. He then slid the bag in the drawer and closed it. "I've been married to Carmen for more than twenty years and I promise you, I've never seen the basement of this place."

"Neither have I," Tiara admitted. "So you think there are diamonds in the basement?"

Kane gave her a small smirk. "I *know* there are diamonds in the basement. Jay was hiding his drugs in the basement of Continental, so of course he would put his diamonds in the basement of Flame. He knows no one is going down there." Kane moved quickly, heading out of Carmen's office. Tiara was right behind him, turning off the lights and locking up.

"So you think Blu is after the diamonds?"

Kane nodded his head as he pressed the button to call the elevator car. "For some reason, I think he's just after the black diamonds. Carmen only had one, but Jay probably has plenty more. Blu knows about the diamonds, he just wants the black ones. That's why he took Kristian, my..." Kane paused at the statement he was going to make. "Black diamond." He looked at Tiara as the doors opened to the elevator. Once on board, he pressed the button labeled B for the basement. The doors closed in front of him yet the elevator didn't move.

"It lit up," Tiara noticed, moving closer to the control panel. "We should be moving." She pressed the button again, but nothing happened. "This thing has never gotten stuck," she claimed, pressing the button labeled one. The elevator came to life, starting to take them to the first floor. Not quite sure what was going on, once they stopped on the first floor and the doors opened, she hit the button labeled B again. The elevator doors closed, but the car didn't move.

"Jay isn't dumb," Kane expressed. "If he is hiding diamonds in Carmen's building, he's not going to give everyone access to the basement. It won't be that simple. If you ask me, there's a combination of buttons you probably have to use. Unfortunately, we don't have time to play around. Let me ask you this. Can I get to the basement using the steps?"

Tiara wasn't quite sure. She had never been to the basement and only used the steps during fire drills. She never made it to the basement because she always stopped on the first floor and exited through the lobby. "I don't think you can. If we can't, what are we going to do?"

"*We're* not doing anything," Kane stressed. He held his hands up and pretended to beat on a drum. "*I'm* going to knock down some doors."

Tiara's eyes grew big at Kane's plan. While the company could afford some reconstruction, the timing was off. Carmen was gone and wouldn't be pleased to know her building was being torn apart. However, if locating the black diamonds was going to get Kristian back then she was all in. Not bothering to express her thought to Kane, she followed him to his Jeep. He was now on the phone with Sanders, giving him the 411 on their find.

According to the conversation, Kane was planning on breaking into the basement tonight.

From the looks of things, he needed to find drugs to save his job and diamonds to save Kristian. How he expected to use the latter for his job, Tiara didn't know. She also didn't have the time to find out. She learned her time was up when Kane brought her home. "So this is it?"

"This is it," Kane responded, not turning off the car. "The only thing I need is your badge and keys. I'll return them in the morning. By that time, we should've been in and out." He held out his hands with the expectation Tiara was going to give up the goods. She did so, planting the items in his hand as easily as he had asked. "Thank you, Tee. I know this isn't easy for you."

"It's a very small price to pay. Besides, you're right, if it had been Robin, I would've done everything you're doing and probably more. I never asked, but how are you holding up?"

"I work through my shit," Kane told her. "I'm worried, but when you have so much shit on your brain, you simply stay focused until the job is done."

"But Kristian is your only child."

Kane stared at Tiara, the image of his daughter becoming clear in his mind. "She is," he admitted. "I know how this shit looks, Tee. I know what y'all are thinking. Yes, I'm doing a lot of this to keep Jay out the picture. At the same time, I have a child to bring home. Kristian is the glue between me and Carmen. Our relationship may be fucked, but we're still parents to her, and two other kids. I'm depending on Carmen just as much as she's depending on me, and," Kane continued, "Kristian is depending on all of us."

Tiara agreed with him. "You're right. We do have our opinions, but deep down, we know you want your daughter back. That's why I don't need to be holding you up. You have a long night ahead of you. Call us whenever you're done or if you find something."

"I will." Kane planned on sticking to his word regardless of the outcome. It was the least he could do for pulling Tiara out her bed. With his wife's best friend headed in her house, he pulled out his phone and dialed Sanders. His partner answered on the first ring as if he was waiting for the call.

"You may have found the golden ticket for saving your daughter," Sanders told him, after hearing the plan. "But, we're not looking for stones. We're looking for coke. That's what we need to save our asses."

"We don't have anything to save our asses," Kane shot back. "If we make good with this diamond thing, maybe we can get something at the Triad or DEA. According to Malik, the coke is gone. He couldn't give it back to us even if he wanted to."

"That's bullshit, Kane. You know why? I can't go to the Triad or DEA. I don't have the same resume as you. You can't say that to a rookie detective in the Narcotics department."

"Well, what do you want me to say? You want me to sugarcoat the shit? Right now, my main concern is getting in Carmen's basement, finding these diamonds, and getting my daughter back. Everything else can take a backseat."

"Of course," Sanders responded in anger. "Get your daughter back and worry about everyone else later. I knew that was the plan. Now, what do you want me to do?"

Kane decided to ignore the sarcasm in Sanders' voice. He knew what his partner was up against, but like he said, he couldn't worry about the Narcotics department. "I don't need you to do much. Tiara gave me her badge and keys to get inside Flame. The basement is only accessible from the elevator. The steps don't lead to the ground floor."

Sanders was in complete shock at the task. Not only was the feat costly, Kane was implying he wanted it to be completed that night. "Are you going to run this by Harris? You can't just go in Carmen's building and start tearing shit up because you're her husband. There has to be certain documentation."

"I'm doing this with or without Harris. If I have to call the captain at the Triad and get a favor from him, I will. All I need is a man or two. I'm a wiz with ropes and a harness."

Sanders exhaled. He wasn't quite sure what Harris was going to say when the news hit. He had already spent most of the day with Harris up his ass because the coke hadn't showed. In addition, he was growing tired of having to be the main one covering for Kane. Although giving Jay his coke back was his idea, he didn't think it was going to cost him his job. "We need anything at this point," he replied. He gave in, knowing that finding a black diamond or two was the only lifeline they had. If it didn't work, he would be unemployed as soon as the sun came up. "This whole thing is on you. I'm not taking the fall."

"Not a problem." Kane didn't mind carrying the project on his shoulders. He knew he was trying to do a lot in a short amount of time, but things had to get moving. Detective Morris never called him with an update so he had every right to move forward with the case. For all he knew,

Kristian's kidnapping was the last thing on the detective's mind. Since it was the first thing on his, Kane was ready to dive in head first.

19

Lil' Drummer Boy

Numerous officers were inside the precinct, which Kane ignored as he entered. He headed straight for the locker room, taking a quick shower, before changing into a pair of black trouser pants, a T-shirt, and flak jacket. His next stop was his office where he had a small personal closet. Upon entering, he was caught off guard when he saw Harris sitting at his desk.

The lieutenant didn't speak right off, but when he did, his voice was stern and low. He also spoke slowly as if he wanted Kane to catch every single word. "There is too much going on in this city with your name on it. To add on to the list, I get a call that you want to break into your wife's company. You do know that when the clock hits 12, the Triad is shutting our operations down."

Kane knew he couldn't deny all, but he could deny some. "It is a lot," he admitted, "some of this wasn't caused by me, though, like the coke. My daughter, her kidnapping is the result of a drug war between Jay Santiago and a drug dealer named Shawn Blumington. As far as my wife's company goes, I believe she is allowing Jay to hide diamonds in her basement. I think he's getting the diamonds delivered in a FedEx truck."

"And you say that because?"

"I found a bag of diamonds in a drawer in her office. She even had a black diamond. If you ask me, I think Blumington kidnapped my daughter because he's after the stones. I think his business relationship with Jay soured, he found out about the diamonds, and he wants in."

Lieutenant Harris sat up straight at Kane's accusation. "It makes sense, I'll give you that. I just want you to say something that will make me give you permission to do this. I mean, let's be honest, you've caused more damage than good."

Kane didn't exhibit any sign of nervousness from the lieutenant's statement. He wasn't concerned about coming up with a good reason. His concern was in getting the diamonds. "Harris, you've been working with me for years. You know me personally. What is more important to me than my child? Kristian is my only child, my *only* biological child. You witnessed my breakdown when I learned I was the problem my wife couldn't get pregnant.

What father wouldn't do everything in his power to make sure his child was safe?"

Harris stood up. He was a witness to Kane's struggles and his glory. He was there for it all, which is why he knew he was going to help him. "Take Sanders with you. Use your time wisely. You need to be out before the Triad shuts us down."

Kane gave Harris a single head nod right before the lieutenant walked out the room. Only a few hours away from being midnight, Kane rushed to his closet, throwing several items around until he was able to pull out a medium-sized duffle bag. He opened it, seeing a full-body harness, a few pistols, and a rarely used machine gun. Not quite sure if he would need it all, he decided to take everything with him and zipped the bag. He carried it out his office, running into Sanders in the process. He was about to leave without him, which he knew Sanders noticed. Instead of openly admitting it, he simply told his partner to come on as he kept moving.

For Kane, the drive to Flame was the longest minutes of his life. Due to the lack of a plan, he made the trip in silence. Once at the building, he swiped Tiara's badge to unlock the door before running to the elevator. He already knew the car wouldn't take him to the basement so when they boarded, he immediately hit the button for the second floor. The car moved without a problem and after a few seconds, he pressed the emergency stop button. Despite the hard jolt, the car remained in place.

"Can you at least tell me what we're doing?" Sanders asked.

Kane didn't bother to look at Sanders as he spoke. "When I need you, I'll tell you. Right now, stay put." Kane gazed upward, noticing there wasn't much distance between him and the ceiling. Most elevator cars had a service hatch on the roof, but since he was unable to see it, he assumed it was on the side facing the elevator shaft. That meant only one thing, he would have to blast his way through.

"You're not prepared for this, Kane. You don't have anything to help you get up there. Not even a—" Sanders was silenced by the loud rounds of gunfire. He moved quickly to the left of the car as the middle of the ceiling started to cave in. He coughed from the dust, covering his mouth as he peered up. A large gaping hole was now there, the entire elevator shaft now completely visible. When he looked at Kane, he was stuffing a machine gun in his duffle bag. "So I guess you're going to have that fixed before the work day starts?"

Kane ignored the comment, looking up in the hole. He had destroyed a good part of the ceiling, but he could still see part of the roof's steel frame which he planned on using to connect his rope. He moved expeditiously, putting on the harness and adjusting the straps. "I'm going to need you to lift me up. I'm going to try and grab the edge so I can get on top of the car."

"Are you serious right now?"

Kane was growing impatient. "Are you going to do this or not?" He shot Sanders a scary look, one that made him come to Kane's aid. His partner bent down, allowing Kane to place his right foot on his bended knee. He knew his weight was heavy so he moved quickly, grabbing the roof of the elevator car. The material wasn't stable so when he grabbed it, it became loose in his hands, causing him to lose his grip. He fell down to the floor missing Sanders by a few inches.

"Another way," Sanders suggested. He stood up, wiping off his pants where Kane's shoe had been. He waited until his partner was on his feet before he rushed him. He grabbed Kane by his legs lifting him so he could try and grab the edge again. This time, Kane managed to grab a more stable part and pull himself on top of the car. While Kane balanced himself, Sanders grabbed the rope from the bag. He tossed it up to Kane who quickly connected it to the roof's steel frame and then to his harness. "Make sure you're secure before you turn into Spiderman."

"I got it," Kane yelled, checking all areas of his harness. He pulled on the rope hard to ensure the steel frame didn't move. If it was weak, he would know the moment he started to climb down to the basement floor. "Toss up the machine gun."

"Are you going to commit a murder, too?"

Kane looked down into the hole. The commentary was about to make him use the machine gun on him. "Just toss up the gun," he told him. "The basement doors aren't going to open on their own because the car isn't there. Both sets of the doors work simultaneously. I'm going to have to blast my way in."

Sanders knew he had a point. He grabbed the machine gun and tossed it up to Kane who slid it behind the chest straps of the harness. He kept his eyes on him until he saw Kane grab two steel cables. In a flash, he was gone and Sanders was forced to listen to him as he made his way to the basement floor. He could see the rope moving as Kane climbed down and he positioned himself in the elevator so he could have a direct view of the steel frame. It wasn't moving, which was a good sign that it was holding Kane's weight.

"I'm almost there," he heard Kane yell. "I just passed the first floor."

Sanders covered his face because he knew his entire career was resting on something being inside the basement. There was only a limited amount of time before the clock struck twelve. The Triad was clear in their promise to halt everything with the Narcotics department if the coke didn't show. There was a rumor some of them would be transferred to a different department, but that was only if they weren't placed under investigation. If so, the Triad would be charging a bunch of innocent men and women with a crime they didn't commit.

The matter weighed heavily on his mind until a large blast sounded from below. It was followed by two more large blasts and then silence. Sanders knew it was the sound of Kane creating a hole within the doors of the basement. One more large blast sounded before he heard the sound of the elevator doors being crushed.

Kane was standing in the doorway of the basement kicking in the lower portion of the doors. From what he could see, the entire basement was dark, the only light coming from the elevator car above him. Upon entering, he climbed out the harness, leaving it where he stood. Without a flashlight in hand, he was forced to use an app on his phone to look around the space. The area was completely empty although he could see an image of something in the middle of the floor. Not quite sure what it was, he searched the walls for a light switch. When he found one, he flipped it on. The image, now much clearer, jogged his memory.

"What do you see?"

Sanders' voice was faint yet Kane could still make out his words. He didn't answer him, moving closer to the mural in the center of the floor. He heard Sanders yell something else, which he also ignored. Unsure of what was going on, he scanned the walls until he noticed a door. He ran to it, quickly opening it only to find another empty room. There wasn't anything there to aid the Narcotics department or Kristian. Nonetheless, there was something there, which impacted his relationship with Carmen. In the middle of the floor was a large painting of a female's full lips. In the center of her mouth was a red rose, making the artwork a replica of the mural on the ceiling of his clothing store. It was an ode to his favorite song, "Kiss of a Rose," by Seal. He knew the painting was there on purpose because directly underneath it in large black letters was the word *Production.* The store was a business front he used during his undercover operation twenty years ago when he was working to take down Jay.

The image forced him into a state of reminiscence. He remembered seeing Carmen outside his store, his proposal at the precinct, and then connecting with her for the very first time on the night of their wedding. The images were strong, but he knew he had to dismiss them. She was up to something, but it didn't have anything to do with their relationship. It also didn't have anything to do with Jay's diamonds or drugs. Carmen had simply stolen an idea from him.

The idea of bringing *Production* to life was something he had to confront her about. He had to come with evidence so he quickly took a photo of the painting. About to stuff his phone in his pocket, he almost lost his balance at the sound of several unexpected gunshots. The blasts continued longer than expected, his hands quickly wrapping around the machine gun. There was a period of silence, which was followed by another large blast which shook the building. The elevator car shook as well before two more gunshots sounded. Then, just as quickly as the noise had come, it disappeared.

The silence made his adrenaline increase. The longer it lasted, the faster his heart raced. No other sounds were coming from the shaft so he started to move. His footsteps were soft, but quick to the doorway. He quickly grabbed the harness, pulling it back on. Once everything was secure, Kane tugged at the rope, making sure the steel frame was secure as well. Certain it was, he climbed into the shaft and grabbed the steel cables, making his way up towards the car. He caught a peek of Sanders on his way up. Half of his partner's body was covering a gaping hole at the very bottom of the car, an obvious result of the blast. A small breath escaped Kane's lips, but as quickly as it came, it left. He continued climbing the elevator shaft, using the steel cables until he was on top of the car.

Footsteps sounded below him, belonging to more than one person, leading him to grab the machine gun in his hand. Then, he heard the voices. He could only catch bits and pieces, but it was enough to know they were looking for the same thing he was. Unfortunately, everyone was going home empty-handed if they were going home at all.

Kane rested his body upon a section of the roof that was still intact. Both hands wrapped around the machine gun as he pointed it in the direction of the hole. Although he wasn't sure how quickly he would be waiting, he stayed in position. Neither the voices nor the footsteps had returned, which told him the men were listening. They were waiting for him to make a move so they could make theirs. He stayed in place, concentrating hard, until he saw a shadow. Automatically, his hands pulled the trigger, firing. The space became bigger, Sanders' body sliding down into the hole. His body hit the bottom of the elevator shaft just as the fire was returned. He automatically reacted to the sound of gunshots and fired back.

When the gunshots stopped, Kane knew to move quickly. He jumped in the elevator car, the rope allowing him to plunge directly inside. Three armed men were standing in the doorway of the first floor and he fired repeatedly as he passed them falling in the hole they created at the bottom of the elevator car. Two of them he knew he placed on their backs. If he had gotten all three, he would know in a few short seconds. He waited for any sign of movement after he landed on his feet at the bottom of the elevator shaft. Now standing directly above Sanders' body, he took a quick peek at his partner. Sanders' legs had nearly been blown off right at the knee caps. Gunshot wounds were on his chest, which he suspected killed him.

The silence lingered longer than expected so Kane pulled his phone from his pocket. He made the call to the lieutenant, the conversation lasting less than two minutes. Not ready to disclose Sanders' death, he only requested back up. Harris asked a million and one questions, but Kane only told him, "In due time." Harris didn't want to accept the answer yet Kane wasn't going to be pressed. His partner was dead, the basement was empty, his wife's company had been deconstructed, and there were three dead goons in the building. On top of all that, severe trauma was starting to set in.

With each minute that passed, Kane knew his career in law enforcement was going down the drain. Without anything solid, the Triad would shut them down. Once the Triad pulled the plug, the chances of him ever getting in Harris' good graces was questionable. His eyes closed at the thought, but reopened when he heard the loud sound of pattering feet above him. A ton of yelling followed, his name being rattled out the mouths of many. The voices forced him to stare at Sanders yet he couldn't bear to announce his partner's demise. Instead, he yelled for a paramedic.

"We're coming down," a voice said. "Paramedics are here."

Kane rubbed his lips together as he felt the temperature in the elevator shaft increase. Due to his nerves, he hadn't felt the heat until that very moment. To make matters worse, he could hear chatter about the three dead men on the first floor. Then, it wasn't long before Kane recognized Harris' voice amongst the others.

Detective Davis was the first to show and see Sanders' state. The space, being small and square-shaped, wasn't even big enough for Sanders' body. Half of his partner was flat on the floor while the other half was bunched up against the wall.

"Put this on," Davis told him, giving him a new harness. "They're going to pull you up."

Kane took the harness, somewhat pleased Davis didn't speak on Sanders' condition. Not quite sure how he could explain, he busied himself with the harness. When he had it on, Davis ordered for him to be pulled up and he was immediately carried out the elevator shaft and to the first floor. Once on solid ground, he watched as Forensics photographed and investigated the scene. Harris, although in the middle of the hoopla, was the first to approach him. Before he could speak, he went ahead and gave him the worst. "Sanders didn't make it." Then, he gave him the rest. "The basement is empty. I didn't find any diamonds."

Kane met eyes with Harris, but he wished he hadn't. He had just broken the news to him about Sanders and now the proof was there for him to see. Three paramedics were passing them with Sanders on a stretcher. "I fucked up," he admitted. He stared Harris in the face just as the lieutenant folded his arms across his chest. "This wasn't supposed to happen."

"We both fucked up," Harris replied. "I should've made sure you had back up."

Kane parted his lips again yet his words came out in fumbles. A crew of paramedics was directly in front of him, examining Sanders. The guilt continued to pile on. He attempted to take a step, but when he stumbled, Harris caught him.

"Take it easy," the lieutenant whispered. "This isn't something you're just going to get over." Harris waited until he felt like Kane was somewhat stable before he loosened his grip. He knew Kane needed a moment to take it all in, but he couldn't give it to him. While everything was still fresh, he needed Kane to give them a play by play of what happened. After nearly an hour of Kane going back and forth with the details, Harris allowed him to leave.

Still, Kane didn't move an inch. He knew he was responsible for the scene at Flame. Sanders' blood was on his hands and any time away from the force wasn't going to change that. While his intentions were to try and persuade Harris to let him stay, his words didn't come out as such. Everything ran together, from apologies, to what happened, to how they could move forward. Harris didn't want to hear any of it, which was obvious when the lieutenant personally escorted him to his Jeep. At that point, all hope was lost.

Intermission

House

Copperton City, Georgia

It was after midnight and the last place Blu expected to be was in the parking deck of one of the city's local banks. He was stuck in his car along with Victor and Kristian, unsure of where to go. All his businesses were now targets, completely taken over by police, reporters, and paramedics. He knew a few owners of some chop shops, but no one was answering. It was as if the scarlet letter was now written on his forehead. He had the idea of letting Victor call some people he knew, but the move was pointless. Victor didn't know the type of people he was in need of. In fact, Soulshock was the only commonality between them.

Then he had to remind himself that Victor was against everything he was doing. His partner's unwillingness was a major concern. It led Blu to scroll through the contacts on his phone for the fifth time trying to think of anyone he could call. He was halfway through the list when he saw the name Jerome. The name struck a chord because he hadn't heard from him since the kidnapping. Jerome had simply done the job and disappeared. Unsure of where he was, he dialed his number. He learned within seconds it had been disconnected, a sign Jerome didn't want to be found.

"I think I found a place," Blu announced as he started the car. He looked in the rearview mirror at Kristian who was resting beside Victor. The bandana was around her eyes and her wrists were still bound. Despite her position, Blu knew she was hanging on to every word. Therefore, he was careful with what he said.

He pulled out the parking space, his mind focused on finding Jerome. His plan was to stop at his house and if it was empty, break in. Jerome may have worked for Jay, one of the hardest men in the game, but he didn't have balls. Jerome was easily intimidated so Blu knew if he found him, he wouldn't run. Not to mention, Jerome rented a house in one of the city's quietest neighborhoods, which he was reminded of when he pulled in front of his house. "Stay here," he ordered. There wasn't a car in the driveway, but that didn't mean Jerome wasn't home. In the event he was, Blu wanted to prep him before he brought Kristian inside.

He walked to the front door and knocked loudly. He didn't hear any movement or sounds from inside so he continued to knock until he was certain the house was empty. With Jerome not being home, Blu took it upon himself to use the property. He made his way to the car, starting it up once he was inside. He drove into the driveway until he was at the back of the house. Once there, he got out. He didn't have a key, but just his luck; he saw an old bottle of Budweiser on the back porch. He used the bottle to break one of the door's windows, sticking his hand inside to unlock the door. Then, he went to the car to get Kristian.

He helped her out the car and inside, Victor following from behind. From what Blu could see, Jerome hadn't been home in a couple of days. The sink was clear of dishes, the trash had been taken out, and everything was in its proper place. Still standing in the kitchen, he tried to think of where he could hide Kristian. He hadn't fully explored the house to know if there was a basement or attic and he needed that chance. He pulled out a chair and pushed her in the seat. "Watch her," he ordered, sneaking a peek at Victor. "Don't do anything else."

Victor looked at Blu questionably unsure of what he was getting at. He didn't respond to him, remaining silent as Blu started to check out the house. He was only gone for a few seconds before he sat at the table next to Kristian. She still didn't know he was there or if she did, she wasn't showing any signs of it. Nonetheless, he was ready to make his presence known yet he was silenced when Blu came in the kitchen.

"Basement," Blu mouthed. He pointed downward, letting Victor know they had a place to put her. The basement wasn't as clean as Soulshock's, but it would make due until he could figure out a plan. He moved quickly, pulling her out the chair by her right arm and practically dragging her down the hall. Victor followed him until they came to the door of the basement. "Watch your step," he told her, starting to lead her down. The area was wet so he told her to remain standing as he went upstairs to grab a mattress. He passed Victor on his way up, giving him a look that told him once again not to try anything.

Victor complied, resting himself against the wall until he heard Kristian's voice.

"How much is he paying you?"

Victor turned to his left where Kristian was standing. She was looking straightforward as if she didn't know exactly where he was in the room. He was scared to answer because he didn't want her to recognize his voice and get the wrong idea. While it was true he had a hand in her ordeal, he wanted no parts of it. Thankfully, Blu came with a mattress before he could say anything. He placed it in the middle of the floor before directing Kristian to it. Unsure of his plans, Victor watched him carefully. When Blu turned to face him, he mouthed the words let's go.

"We're going to leave her here?" he whispered.

Blu looked at him in disbelief. "Do you have another plan?"

Victor shrugged his shoulders. "You don't know when Jerome is coming back."

"I don't care either. What I do care about is the situation I have going on in New York. You should be caring about it, too."

Victor peered at Kristian who was sitting quietly on the mattress. "I don't," he muttered under his breath. "I'm not down with any of this." Victor spoke the words as he started to head up the steps, brushing past Blu until they were both standing in the kitchen.

"You know what we have riding on this, Vic. Don't let the panties make you soft."

"What panties?" Victor yelled. "I'm thinking more about a kidnapping charge and jail time. I know there's another way for you to get those diamonds."

"Do you know how much black diamonds are worth?"

"How does that compare to life in prison? The minute they find your ass, you're going to be locked up with the quickness. How long are you going to keep moving her from place to place? At some point in time, you have to tell them where she is for the payout."

Blu shook his head. His plan was to never ask for ransom. It was too easy. Besides, ransom would be giving his freedom away. He wanted to find Jay's stash and then somehow dump Kristian in Brookstone. Then, he would be on his merry way to an exotic country never to be seen or heard of again. "That's not my plan."

"Well, this shit isn't my plan either."

Victor turned on his heel, but he was forced to stay put when he felt a cold object up against his throat. For the past twenty-four hours, Blu had used violence to get him to comply and he didn't seem to be letting up. As long as Blu thought he feared him, he would continue to use it. "Is this what you want to do?" Victor calmed his nerves as Blu pressed the knife further on his skin. "You're already in this shit by yourself. Why carry me along for the ride? Do me the honor." Victor turned his head so their eyes could meet.

Blu could sense his anger, but before he could speak, they both heard the sound of a car door closing.

Blu pulled the knife from Victor's neck before pulling his gun from his jacket pocket. Meanwhile, Victor stood still as Blu walked to the front door as someone, presumably Jerome, started to unlock the door.

Victor was certain Jerome knew someone was inside since there was a car in his driveway. He just didn't know who it was or what the intruder wanted with his house. He was about to find out soon, though. Before he saw Jerome, he saw his silver glock. Jerome didn't shoot, keeping the gun pointed as he stepped in the house.

"Fontaine?" Jerome called Victor by his last name.

Victor pointed to his left so Jerome would know they weren't alone. Jerome stepped all the way in the house and saw Blu standing behind the door.

"What is this shit, Blu? You're gunning me?" Jerome asked.

"You weren't answering your phone," Blu explained, putting his gun in his jacket pocket. He watched as Jerome put his heat away as well before closing the door behind him. "Where have you been in the last two days?"

"Keeping a low profile," Jerome answered. "You did this to my door?" He pointed towards the broken glass. "Did you think I was dead or something?"

"You're running your mouth like you don't know shit about what's going on. I got cops all over my damn spots. Santiago shot up everything."

From what Victor saw, Jerome didn't look surprised. He simply stared at Blu as if he should've expected it. When he turned to him, Victor sat at the table as a way to say he was staying out of it. Jerome took the hint and sat down as well.

"Everything is gone," Blu continued after several seconds of silence. "I got men in Brookstone right now, trying to get in Flame and they're not answering their phones. I don't even know what the fuck is going on."

Blu walked towards the table as if he was going to sit down, but quickly changed his mind. "I don't even have time for this." He took a step, scratched his head, and then started to pace the floor as if he had thought of something else. "Look, Jerome, Santiago got my men dropping like flies, the blue lights got all my spots on lock. I need to keep Kristian here for a while until I can figure something out."

"She's here?" Jerome jumped from the table, but before he could take off, Blu grabbed him. "I told you I was out, Blu. I told you I would get her for you and then I was out."

Blu let go of Jerome once he realized he wasn't going to run. "We don't always get what we want, do we? She's in the basement. I got some stuff to take care of so I need y'all to keep watch. Hopefully, if someone answers their phone, it'll save me a trip to New York."

Jerome turned towards Victor, a person he had met only a handful of times. "So you're after Santiago, too?"

Victor shook his head in response.

Jerome looked at Blu who was on his way out the door. "So you just want us to sit here and babysit? What do I do if 5-0 comes knocking on my door? Take the fall? You're bugging, man. Santiago is locked up. They're not even giving him bail. I say you go ahead and tie this shit up. Just plant her ass on campus."

Blu's hand froze on the doorknob. "Y'all can pin this shit on me all you want, but I didn't work alone. Jerome, if I remember correctly, you were the one who busted out her window. You brought her to me. As for you, Victor, you didn't have a problem helping me get her in Soulshock once you learned it was going to keep a bullet out your ass."

Jerome looked at Victor, learning blood was on his hands, too.

"I'm done here," Blu retorted. "Watch her."

Jerome rolled his eyes as he watched Blu leave his house. Not quite sure what to do, he looked at Victor for an answer.

"You and me both know this shit is about to hit the fan," Victor began. "Whether we like it or not, both of our hands are dirty. If we have Kristian in our corner, it'll be our word against Blu's."

Jerome looked through the window of his back door, not responding. While he wasn't keen on Kristian discovering his involvement, he didn't have many options. He could always make a run for it, but Blu would put a bounty on his head. He would be on the run until Blu finally caught up with him. Too young for that kind of life, Jerome decided to take his chances. "What's your plan?"

Victor stood from his seat so he was at eye level with Jerome. "I wanna talk to her."

Jerome shook his head. The last thing he wanted was for Kristian to think he was involved. While he did have an issue with Jay, he didn't harbor any ill feelings towards her or King. However, if Kristian learned he was partly to blame for her kidnapping, his relationship with her and her brother would sour.

Lost in his thoughts, Jerome didn't notice when Victor walked past him. It wasn't until he heard the sound of footsteps heading towards the basement, he realized he was alone. He thought about following him, but it would work in his favor if he stayed put. As long as Kristian was clueless about him, he was safe.

In the meantime, Victor stood at the bottom of the steps, his eyes planted on Kristian's frame. She was seated on the mattress, both of her knees at her chin. He neared her, moving slowly, unsure if Blu would reappear. Upon reaching her, he crouched down in front of her immediately grabbing the ends of the bandana which was tied around her face. The knot was tight so it took longer than expected for him to undo. Once he was finished, he watched as a look of confusion appeared on her face. Her eyes were somewhat bulging, which made him believe she was recalling the last memory she had of him.

Unsure of how to explain the situation, he grabbed her arms, starting to undo the bounds around her wrists. "Your brow," were the first words out her mouth. It took him a second or two to figure out what she was referring to until he remembered the gash at his temple. He had forgotten about the wound, a direct result of being pistol-whipped. He took a quick look at Kristian before putting his eyes once again on the rope.

"Does it still hurt?" she asked.

Victor shook his head as the rope started to loosen. He kept working at it as he tried to think of what to say. After a minute or so, he softly mumbled the words, "A small price to pay." He peered at her again before the rope fell from her wrists. The moment it hit the floor, he rose. "Still a hero," he muttered.

The slight grin which was on Kristian's face turned into a frown. Somewhat confused, she remained silent as she started to take everything in. Victor claimed he wanted to be a hero, but the last time she saw him, he couldn't even save himself. Now, once again, he was trying to save her. In order to do that, he had to get in Blu's good graces. "It was you, wasn't it?"

Victor narrowed his eyes at her question. He didn't know what Kristian was accusing him of, but he knew it wasn't good. He waited for her to elaborate before he replied.

"It was you," Kristian repeated. "When I asked, 'How much is he paying you?' it was you. You were the one who was standing beside me."

Victor moved to put some space between them. Kristian's stance hadn't changed, but the more suspicious she became, the more her wrath could grow. "It's been a long day and an even longer night. I know you're hungry so I'm going to find you something to eat."

Kristian stood up from the mattress and took a few steps in Victor's direction. At this point, he was heading towards the stairwell, running from the conversation. When his foot hit the first step, she spoke, hoping her words would convince him to admit the truth. "How much is he paying you?" she asked him as he climbed the stairs.

Victor paused on the top step before turning to look in Kristian's direction. For a brief second, he was going to respond until a voice in his head told him not to. He left the basement without another word. When he returned to the kitchen, Jerome was seated at the table.

"I'm going to get something to eat," he said, holding out his hand for Jerome's keys.

Jerome chuckled in disbelief. Blu had already taken his house and now Victor was asking for his car. He wanted him to stay with Kristian. The last thing he was about to do was risk his freedom by having Kristian see him. "You want something to eat, fine, but I'm going to get it. You stay and babysit." Jerome stood up from the table and hurried towards the door before Victor could persuade him to do otherwise. It seemed to work because he was out the door with Victor standing dumbfounded in the kitchen.

In actuality, Victor felt more stuck than dumbfounded. He was trying to find a way from Kristian's suspicions and questions, and his one way out, Jerome took. Unsure of what to do, he steadily drummed his fingers on his leg, a clear sign of his nervousness. The condition worsened when he heard a sound coming from the basement. Kristian easily could've been on her way up the steps. If so, he was forced to deal with her.

When he heard the noise again, something told him to get moving. He didn't know what she was doing, but if she disappeared from the house, he would have to disappear, too. Blu wouldn't let him live if he lost the one thing that was going to get him millions of dollars in diamonds. Thus, Victor made his way to the basement. Hundreds of thoughts came in his mind about what he would find, but only one made sense. Kristian was simply trying to do anything she could to get away.

20

Tables Will Turn

Brookstone, New York

Far away from Copperton City or the scene at Flame, images of the night continued to dance in Kane's head. Currently experiencing the worst headache of his life, each flashback was matched with an intense throb of pain. It kept him awake, tossing and turning in bed until he finally sat up. Moreover, gun blasts sounded in his ear as if he was still standing in the elevator shaft. Kane grabbed the remote, attempting to turn the TV on to create background noise. The remote shook in his hands until he threw it on the other side of the room.

Time continuously passed yet the headache and visions weren't letting up, only getting worse by the second. Kane made the decision not to get up. An image of his daughter flashed in his mind, followed by Carmen, and then eventually Sanders. He had failed all three of them and the guilt stabbed his heart, a feeling even more painful than the throbbing in his head.

Then, unexpectedly, his phone rang. He looked at his bedside dresser where his phone was. The ringing didn't come from his cell, but the house phone, which made him wonder who was calling him. All the people he suspected it to be wouldn't have been calling him at his condo. They would've dialed his cell. Since the person hadn't, he allowed the call to go to his voicemail. After it did, the phone rang again. This time, he knew to answer. He picked up the phone and mumbled a low hello. When Harris' thunderous voice sounded, he took a deep breath.

"I need you to come by Brookstone General," Harris told him. "I know it's been a long night, but we need to talk. This couldn't wait until sunrise."

Kane wasn't sure if he said yes or no, but whatever he said was sufficient enough for the lieutenant. The phone hung up and before he knew it, he was in his Jeep on his way to the hospital. Most of the city was still awake, not a single beat missed. Twenty-somethings roamed the street while loud music blared from outdoor speakers of the city's local bars. Kane gave it only seconds of his attention, choosing to keep his focus on his meeting with

Harris. Unsure if he could take much more, Kane braced himself when he finally walked through the hospital's doors.

The lobby was fairly empty with only the security guard at the front desk so Kane was quick to pull out his cell. He dialed Harris' number and when the lieutenant answered, he quickly told him to come to the eighth floor. Kane followed his instruction and when he walked off the elevator, he ran right into Harris who was at the nurses' station. Harris looked as if he hadn't slept so Kane knew something was going on.

"I really thought when I sent you home it was going to be for good," Harris told him once he was in earshot. "Or at least I wanted it to be." A few seconds of silence passed before Harris continued. "I'm not going to beat around the bush with you. You're bound to find out anyway so I'm going to be straightforward. The surveillance tape from Blue Magic got into the hands of a man named Howard Grendel. He works closely with Amnesty International. He turned the tape in, which led to a meeting with the most prominent judges in the state. They reviewed the tape and requested a bail variation."

At first, Kane's demeanor didn't change. He knew the tape was stolen from Judge McCallum's office and now he knew the identity of the man who took it. He just didn't know what Amnesty International had to do with Jay. Also, he didn't expect for the other public counsels to notice the same thing as Judge McCallum.

"Every judge in New York is petitioning for his release. I've already received word he will have a bail variation," Harris continued. "He'll probably get off on a self-defense plea when this whole thing goes to court. So tonight, we may have lost our department, but Jay, well," Harris swallowed, "he won his freedom."

"There's got to be something," Kane began, wiping his face as sweat beads formed.

"There's nothing, Kane. This whole thing, this battle, this war, between you and him, the Triad, and the Brookstone PD is over. We all need to stop. No one can keep going after the same man their whole entire lives. This thing has eaten you to the core and to tell you the truth, there's nothing left to be eaten. Let it go."

Kane rested his arms on the counter for extra support so he could maintain his composure. He shook his head at the lieutenant's words not wanting to accept that once again Jay had a way out.

"That was the bad news," Harris continued, interrupting Kane's thoughts. He grabbed his shoulder and gave it a slight tug to get Kane to look at him. "Maybe, it's time for the good." A smile had formed on Harris' face, which quickly faded when he notice the scowl on Kane's. It caused him to remove his hand once he saw Kane needed a moment to absorb the information. While a part of him wanted to let him be, Harris knew he couldn't. He had worked alongside him for a number of years and knew when Kane needed sound advice. Although he wouldn't always be receptive, it didn't stop Harris from speaking his mind.

"It's not giving up, Kane. It's taking a step back and attacking from a different perspective. Or maybe you just need to examine what you're really fighting for. Is it worth it?"

Kane punched the countertop, but Harris didn't let him do it a second time. He grabbed Kane's arm the second he tried to strike again. "What is it?" Harris stressed, saying the words directly in Kane's ear. "What is keeping you from giving up? You have no backing. You have no job. You have no wife. If Jay stayed in jail, two more years, guess what? You still won't have a job or a wife. The shit hurts, but it's not going to kill you. *You're* going to kill you."

Harris pushed Kane away so he could stare him in the face. "Carmen isn't coming back. If she's the reason you want to keep up this war, you're better without her. She's not coming back because she wasn't there in the first place. You were married to her for almost two decades and how many days did it take for Jay to come and take her? She didn't give up on him even with a life sentence on his head. She waited before, she's waiting now, and she'll wait again. In the end, he'll still win. You view it as a loss, a failure, but God is trying to tell you it's a blessing. You let Jay be, you'll get the rest you need. You'll leave this hospital with only one thing on your mind, getting your daughter back. Kristian will come home and you'll start anew."

Harris released his grasp allowing Kane to slide away from him. Only a few inches separated them yet Harris made the space larger to give Kane more breathing room. "The Triad shut us down. We both have to find something new. Before we do, I need you to follow me."

Kane heard the lieutenant's voice yet he didn't move. There was already too much on his plate to digest. The flashbacks returned tenfold making him almost comatose. Then, as if enough time had passed, Harris emerged in front of him, repeating his words. This time, Kane did as he asked, following behind him until they were standing in a patient's room. A curtain blocked them from seeing the person, which Harris pulled back once it was in arm's reach.

A man, somewhat unrecognizable due to the bandages across his face, appeared to be laying in-state until Harris pointed at the heart monitor.

Despite what his body language showed, the man was alive and breathing on his own.

"Sanders didn't give up. He remained a fighter," Harris disclosed. "God gave him a second chance and He's giving you one, too."

Kane was directly in front of the man, his eyes focused on the man's closed eyelids. Not once did he see Sanders in the man's face yet the lieutenant claimed he was his partner.

"He still had a pulse, Kane."

Harris' words were as clear as the image in front of him yet Kane found it hard to believe. For one, he had seen Sanders' condition. His partner had multiple gunshot wounds, broken legs, and fell to the absolute bottom of an elevator shaft. Although only a small portion of the man's face was visible, Kane didn't see any similarities.

"The pulse was weak, but it was there. He's paralyzed from the waist down, but he's breathing on his own. I wish you were there when we got the news."

Kane placed his hand on the man's shoulder. The more he stared at the patient, the more recognizable his partner became. Relief poured over him, but even more than that, he felt a sense of hope. It was almost like he had a reason not to give up. Jay was no longer the target, his dart was now set on Shawn Blumington, the man responsible for Sanders' condition and his daughter's kidnapping. Like Harris tried to tell him minutes ago, his focus needed to change.

"I'm going to stay updated on his progress. If there are any changes, I'll let you know. For now, I would advise you to go home, get some sleep, and plot your next move. If you ask me, you should be on a flight to Georgia in the morning."

Kane nodded his head in agreement. He then met eyes with Harris just as he moved his hand away from Sanders' shoulder. "I hear you." He didn't bother saying goodbye, heading quickly to the elevator. The ride down was short yet Kane used the allotted time to do exactly as Harris had suggested, plot his next move. More optimistic than before, there was a sense of calmness about him when he walked in his condo. As a result, he kept the lights off. The street lights, peeking in through the blinds, lighted the living room. There was just enough light for him to see the pictures of his kids on the bookshelf including a shot of him and Kristian. He stared at the photo for several seconds, envisioning his daughter as a baby in his arms until he could no longer bear the image.

Halfway up the stairway, a soft knock at the door stopped him in his tracks. Not quite sure if his ears were playing tricks on him, he preceded up the steps until eventually the doorbell sounded. Kane assumed it was Harris trying to check up on him or possibly deliver more news. Whatever he was there for, Kane figured the visit would be quick. He sped down the steps just as the doorbell sounded a third time. Before Harris could ring it again, he opened the door.

Jean was standing in front of him, clothed in a white jacket, an Ann Demeulemeester design, nude pumps, and barelegged. Vintage earrings hung from her ears as she walked forward forcing herself in the condo. Caught off guard, Kane remained in the doorway as she entered, staring out into his front yard. Jean was the last person he expected to see, thus creating a debate in his mind about whether or not to send her home. He had promised to call her once he was in town, but the events of the night didn't allow it to happen. If it wasn't for her abrupt appearance, Kane was certain he wouldn't have any contact with her. Although he cared about her, other things took precedence at the moment.

A small exhale escaped his lips as he closed the door. When he turned to face her, he took a second to study her demeanor. Her jacket was buttoned all the way up to her neck, but she was now shoeless, her nude pumps to the left of her. Her face, not at all expressionless, held a smile that was quite devilish and innocent at the same time. Almost making him lose his words, the thought of Sanders and Blumington reminded him of why she shouldn't be there. He parted his lips to explain, but before he could, he saw her tongue glide across her lips. The move silenced him and as if it wasn't enough, she walked towards him, shortening the distance between them. Less than a foot apart, she dropped to her knees, not bothering to remove her jacket.

Kane learned quickly what her plans were when she stripped him of his boxers. The tip of his manhood escaped into her mouth and she immediately went to work. Sex was nowhere on his mind, but he didn't stop the embrace. He simply stood there, his hands placed at the crown of Jean's head as his fingertips tussled through her hair. She worked on him for a solid three minutes until he felt as if he was about to explode. At that moment, Jean's tongue was massaging his urethra, sending an electric thrill through his body. It eventually led to an intense explosion. He couldn't warn her but Jean didn't seem to mind the guest.

In fact, when he looked at her, she seemed somewhat pleased. He smiled at her before parting his lips to finally say hello. Unfortunately, the ringing of his phone stopped him before he could. A hint of surprise appeared in Jean's eyes, which grew slightly when Kane pulled away. Considering the events of the night, he knew he had to take the call. Not quite sure how Jean would react, Kane made sure to stare at her as he answered. She remained rather content and she headed in the kitchen to clean her face as he took the call.

The moment she was out his sight, he greeted the person on the other line. The person didn't say anything so he said hello again. When the person didn't answer, he remained quiet and listened. The sound of a television was in the background so he checked his caller ID only to see that the number was blocked. Not in the mood for games, he hung up the phone and set it on the coffee table. Jean appeared a few short seconds later, having heard the silence. She had cleaned her face up, and was now waiting for an explanation.

He didn't know where to start so he sat on the couch before patting the space next to him. She joined him but when he got ready to dispel the details of the night, she swayed his attention again. This time she was nibbling on his left earlobe.

"I thought you were going to call me when you got in," she whispered before planting a kiss on his cheek. "I haven't heard anything."

Kane separated himself so he could concentrate on his words rather than her affection. "Things were complicated," he replied. "I wasn't ignoring you."

Jean gave him a small smile. "Any change with your daughter?"

Kane responded with a simple shake of his head. For all he knew, Kristian was still missing and Carmen was still in Copperton City. It wouldn't be until tomorrow when he would be able to get more answers. "I'm going to Georgia in the morning," he announced, placing his hand on Jean's thigh. He gave it a slight rub just as their lips connected for the first time that night. When she broke apart, he was somewhat surprised.

"I know you have a lot going on, which is why I really didn't want to bother you. It's just that, I couldn't stop thinking about that night. I..." Jean's voice trailed off as she tried to form her words. "I don't want to pressure you into anything. You're dealing with a divorce, a missing child, and I know they shut down your division. I just... I wondered if there was, you know, any time you had that you could devote. That's if you want to devote, of course."

Kane blinked. Jean wanted time, something he was giving at the moment, but also something that was about to be stripped. He didn't know what kind of time he had. He had already entered Brookstone with a bang, devoting his time to discovering Blumington's hidden agenda, which eventually left her on the backburner. While time wasn't something he could give at the moment, declining her offer was out the question. Jean was his relief and he needed her if he ever wanted to successfully get over Carmen. The only logical thing he could do was ask her to wait.

"I want a lot of things," he began. "Right now, though, I can't give you the time you want. Not now, no, but if you wait, once this stuff blows over, I can." Kane looked in her direction to see how she was taking his words. If anything, he expected her to be understanding. She couldn't expect for him to go full throttle into a new relationship when he was still burning away the old. He also had a daughter who needed his attention and support.

In the end, what he got was the same look, which was just as content as before. Jean hadn't verbally responded yet her eyes told him she accepted. Her lips were straight, showing neither a smile or frown, and her face was relaxed. If there was any question in her mind, Kane believed he answered it when he said, "I want this." It seemed to do the trick because Jean's lips turned upward. Then, as if she was waiting for the right moment to do so, she brought her face towards his, their lips reconnecting and sealing the deal.

Intermission

On The Run

Copperton City, Georgia

The door to the basement was cracked just enough for Victor to peek inside. While he could hear Kristian more clearly than when he was in the kitchen, he couldn't see her as good as he thought. What he did see and hear was the mattress being pulled across the floor. The image alone made him open the door and step in the stairwell. Water was quickly spreading into the room and he followed the trail until he saw a busted pipe in the left-hand corner.

A curse word sounded out his mouth as he raced down the steps. He pulled Kristian behind him so he could better examine the area. A puddle had already formed where he was standing and he was at least two yards from the mattress. Certain the area wasn't that bad when they came in earlier, he traced the pipelines with his eyes until he noticed a rusty wrench lying only inches away. His eyes narrowed until he heard loud steps on the stairwell.

When he turned to face Kristian, she was already headed out the basement. He took off after her, but she was quick. By the time he was in the hallway, the backdoor was slamming closed. The sound alone made him stop in his tracks. Both Jerome and Blu were gone, which meant her disappearance was on him. Blu already had a bullet with his name on it and now he had reason to have two. Eighty percent of him was glad Kristian was free while the other twenty knew he needed to find her before Blu did. With the latter overruling, he ran out the house and into the backyard.

The street lights were barely lit while the neighborhood had fallen completely silent. He studied his surroundings, knowing if Kristian was nearby she was doing her best to not make any noise. He knew she wasn't far yet he didn't even hear her breathing. It was almost like she had vanished into thin air. Certain she couldn't have gotten far, he walked hastily around the house until he was standing in the driveway where Blu and Jerome's cars had been. Neither vehicle was there so Victor expected to at least see or hear her running down the street. When he approached the sidewalk, he realized he was coming up empty again.

He took a small breath as he scanned the area, trying to pay attention to the smallest detail. He even walked two blocks up the street in both directions before going to the house. Everything Blu wanted rested in him having Kristian in his possession. With her gone, he was now fighting a losing battle. *I just won't be here to see it,* he thought. More anxious than ever to get away, he started another trek up the street, walking as far away from Jerome's house as he could get.

21
Bloodline

Carmen wasn't quite sure what to expect when she walked in Gully's kitchen aside from breakfast. She could smell the scrambled eggs and cheese from her room as well as the bacon which he had fried on the stove. It had been a while since she had last eaten so she was ready to dive in. Now that she and Gully were on the same page, she was more confident about working with him than when they first met.

"Morning," she greeted, stopping in the doorway. She gave Gully a slight smile, which was instantly returned. Unsure of what to do, she walked in the kitchen and sat down as Gully opened the oven door. He pulled out a pan of biscuits, which he set on the table. "I tried to check on my kids this morning," she told him, "but Akaila was the only one up."

"When was the last time you spoke to your husband?"

Carmen rolled her eyes at the way he referenced Kane. He was still legally her husband, but the word bothered her. "I talked to him last night, remember? He told me to stay in Georgia."

"I saw your husband," Gully announced as he pulled two plates from the cabinet. *I also called your husband,* he thought, referring to the phone call he made last night. *Do you even know he's still in Brookstone?*

"Can you stop calling him that?"

Gully turned around with the plates still in his hand. He ignored her question, moving in on what he really wanted to talk about. "I may not have kept in contact with Jay, but I followed everything about him. Since you're the main person in his life, I also followed you. I know who your husband is." Gully handed Carmen a plate, which she kindly took. "I saw y'all when y'all got here. I even saw him that night. He had a girl in his car. They were staking out a house."

Carmen became more than suspicious. "He was with a girl, staking out a house? That doesn't make sense. He doesn't know anyone in Georgia. Maybe you saw another black man with a baldhead who you thought was him."

"I've studied your husband's face and work for seventeen years. It was him." Gully pointed towards the food so Carmen would fix her plate.

Their conversation wasn't going to end any time soon so he figured they might as well eat. "He was with her for a reason and he was looking for something. I remember the house he was parked in front of."

Carmen held her plate in her hands, not having moved an inch towards the stove. She wasn't quite sure what Gully was getting at yet he sounded very certain of himself. "What do you think is in the house?" Carmen shook her head as she realized her error. "What I meant to ask is, who do you think lives in the house?"

Gully shrugged his shoulders. "I don't know. I know the area, but I never got the house number. If I had that, I could see who owns the place." Gully looked directly in Carmen's eyes so he could see her expression when he made his first request. "You and Jay have an older son, right?" He watched as Carmen nodded her head. "I want to meet him."

"You'll meet him eventually."

Gully made his request again because he knew Carmen didn't know what he was getting at. "No, I want to meet him now. I want you to bring him here."

"Hell fuckin' no," Carmen spat, setting her plate down. "I'm not about to bring King here so he can get caught up in this." Carmen set the plate on the table suddenly losing her appetite. "I'll get Linx."

"I don't want Linx. I want King."

"You're not getting—" Carmen wasn't able to finish her sentence because Gully cut her off as if he was never finished with his.

"Someone did a number on Blu's clubs. I want whoever did it and I think it was King. When Jay initially called me, all he wanted was guns. This other stuff came about when he realized he was headed to prison. I got a shitload of stuff thrown at me in less than twenty-four hours. I didn't ask for anything in return, but I'm asking for this."

Carmen folded her arms across her chest. She even narrowed her eyes to let Gully know she wasn't budging. "I understand, but that's not what we want. King is responsible for the deaths at Blu's clubs, which is why we want him to stay in Brookstone. You want to meet him, fine, but not on these terms. Once this is over, you can come to New York and you can meet him. In fact, you can meet the whole family. It just won't be tonight."

Gully started to fix his plate not replying to what Carmen had said. Once he was done, he started to fix hers. After placing one of the biscuits on her plate, he slid it towards her. She didn't take it so he simply shrugged his shoulders before grabbing his own. He wasn't going to let up, but he figured he would end the conversation until they were done with breakfast. To make her think the conversation was over, he headed in the living room, leaving her at the kitchen table. To his surprise, she followed him, entering the living room as he turned on the television.

The channel was already set to CNN from where he had been watching the news story announcing the warrant for Jay's arrest. Currently, the reporter was discussing a new healthcare bill so he tuned her out as he ate. The news wasn't something he watched on a regular basis unless he needed to see how good he cleaned up one of his messes.

"Did you see that?"

Gully blinked his eyes at the sound of Carmen's voice because he hadn't been paying attention to the TV. Once he took notice, he dropped his plate on the couch, standing on his feet to get a better look. Naturally, he cracked a smile.

As for Carmen, her face became rather blank as she watched Jay disappear behind the tinted windows of a black limousine. No one, not Gomez, Linx, or even Malik had called to tell her about his release. If it wasn't for Gully turning on CNN, they both would've been in the dark. "So what does this mean?" she yelled. She stared at the screen as the camera focused on the limousine. Due to the angle, she couldn't see who the driver was, but she assumed it was Linx.

"Let's see what the boss says," Gully replied. He dialed Jay's number, automatically getting the voicemail. "His phone isn't on yet."

"I know I should, but I don't want to wait on him," Carmen revealed. "If you think that house has something to do with Kristian, I think we should check it out. We don't have to go inside, but what is it going to hurt to drive by?"

Gully shrugged his shoulders. "It won't hurt at all until we see who lives there. Then, we might have a problem on our hands. That's why I want King. "

"You can do this without him."

Gully looked at Carmen, their eyes meeting for probably the twentieth time that day. She sounded so sure of herself yet she forgot Blu had men at his beck and call. At the moment, she only had him. With Jay being released, it was a possible aid to them, but neither of them knew where he was headed. They assumed he would be joining them in Copperton City, but Jay could always throw them for a loop. Since he could, their best bet was to work as if he was still behind bars. "Still hardheaded," Gully responded, breaking the glare. He turned towards the television again as the reporter transitioned to the next story. Out of all the words she said, the one that stuck out the most was Flame.

Gully watched as Carmen moved closer to the television, both of her hands in her hair as if she was about to pull it out. According to the report, only a few short hours ago, there was a shootout at Flame, which nearly destroyed the first floor. Blu had struck again yet Gully knew there was more to the story. "What are you hiding?"

"What am I hiding?" Carmen squealed. She turned to face him, her hair falling on her shoulders. "I'm not hiding shit. Are you hiding something?"

"Blu's men tried to tear apart your building. Oh, you're hiding something."

Carmen turned towards the television screen as video footage of a stretcher being pushed out her building appeared. The person was identified as Sanders, Kane's partner, who was reportedly at the scene during the shootout. While nothing was said of Kane's condition, the reporter made it known that Sanders sustained severe injuries.

"You have to be hiding something. Kane was there for a reason. He got a lead and he made his way to Flame because he was looking for something. So, do you want to tell me now or do you want me to find out when Blu hits again?"

Carmen walked past Gully wanting to clear her head. Unfortunately, Gully didn't let her leave his presence, following her into the guestroom.

"Blu is going to hit again. You know that, right?"

Carmen grabbed her duffle bag off the floor and opened it. She started unpacking her guns, setting the weapons on the bed, in order of smallest to largest. Once the bag was empty, she stared at each gun as she tried to choose which one she would use on Blu.

"It's something to do with Jay, isn't it? It's not even about you. You're protecting him."

Carmen picked up a gold-plated Uzi, which was immediately pulled from her hands. Automatically, her eyes shifted to Gully who was wearing a look of annoyance. Her face read the same as she jerked the gun from his hands. "If he didn't tell you then you don't need to know. That's our biggest problem right now. People have their noses in too many fuckin' places. Your job is to find Kristian. Do that and leave everything else the fuck alone."

Gully sneered at her words yet he didn't utter a response. He knew to let her have her moment. Jay might not have told him everything, but there were enough pieces floating around for him to complete the puzzle.

***

Brookstone, New York

The temperature was nearing eighty-five degrees yet Jay didn't bother to roll up his sleeves or unbutton his shirt. He even ignored the sweat trickling down the sides of his face. Linx had offered him a handkerchief, which he didn't decline or accept. In fact, he had said nothing to him aside from telling him to head to Malik's house. Even when they arrived, he exited the car without a single word. Linx didn't press him, knowing he would speak when he wanted to.

His presence was speedily known because Malik appeared at the door before he even made it up the driveway. His best friend ran to meet him, asking question after question about his release, his plans, and Kristian. Jay ignored the interrogation as he continuously walked towards the house. His focus was on Rakim and Nyla, and getting to them as quickly as he could. It was the one reason he pushed past Malik who tried to block the door.

"They're still sleeping," Malik yelled, following him up the steps. "Carmen called this morning, but they weren't even up for her to talk to them."

Jay didn't speak, first heading in Robin's room, thinking all of them were together. The room was empty so he went further down the hall to the master bedroom. When he opened the door, he found Tiara inside, still in her pajamas. She jumped when she saw him, his presence shocking her. He closed the door, continuing down the hall as Malik continued to speak.

"There was a shooting at Flame last night. Kane's partner almost died. You won't tell me what's going on, but you need to say something. How are you going to explain that?"

Jay opened the door to the guest room to find toys on the floor and three small bodies in the middle of the bed. His eyes gazed over the room until he recognized Rakim and Nyla's luggage set. He started to pack their things as Malik continued to whisper beside him.

"You've got to tell me something, Jay. You got Linx and Cesar at your beck and call, knowing more shit than I do. What caused that shooting at Flame? Why was Kane and Sanders even there? Then, Blu's men showed up. What do you have in Carmen's building?"

Jay set the luggage by the door still remaining mum. Malik could ask question after question yet Jay wasn't responding to anything. For the moment, everything with Kane, Flame, and even Kristian was taking a backseat. Proving it, he went to Rakim who was on the left side of the bed. He picked him up causing him to stir yet not waking him. His son sensed his presence and Jay felt Rakim latch onto him. Jay then attempted to lift Nyla in his arms, who, unlike her brother, started to fuss the moment he touched her. Her cries made Malik continue to persuade him to let them be.

Jay ignored him, removing his right hand from underneath Nyla's abdomen. He then ran his fingers through her hair, calming her until he could lift her in his arms without her making a noise. With his hands full, he peered at Malik, telling him with his eyes to get the luggage. Malik hesitated, but after a few seconds, he complied. He then followed him to the limo.

Linx was standing outside the car, the trunk already open, ready for the next move. When Malik approached the vehicle, Linx took the luggage from him and put it in the trunk. He assumed Jay was getting inside until he noticed a silent conversation going on between him and Malik.

Jay knew he was moving quickly, but he didn't expect to forget the car seats. When he looked at Malik, he was asking him for another favor. Although Malik didn't verbally refuse, he wasn't budging. Jay waited for a minute or so and when Malik didn't move, he looked at Linx and then at his kids. Linx took the hint and started making his way up the driveway.

"I got it," Malik retorted, blocking Linx's path. "You don't order anyone in my house."

Jay spat on the ground at Malik's response before resting himself against the limo. It took his right-hand five minutes too long to come back, but eventually he emerged from the house. Malik put the car seats in the limo and even took Nyla out his arms to buckle her inside. Once he was done, Jay got Rakim settled before joining them. By this time, Linx was in the driver's seat and Tiara was standing outside. When Jay went to close the back door, Malik stopped him.

"Robin got attached to these two. You're going to let her wake up and see her friends are gone? Who's going to watch them when you go after Blu? Carmen isn't here. Tiara has to take care of Flame. Everyone else has their own shit going on. What are you going to do with them?"

Jay stared at his kids who were sleeping beside him. Deep down, he knew Malik was right. While Silvas would be more than welcome to take care of them, his age didn't allow him to give them the attention they needed. Jay trusted Tiara and Malik when it came to his kids so he knew they would have to take them when he went to Georgia. His mind made up, he finally parted his lips. "I'll be back in the morning."

22

New Blood

San Juan, Puerto Rico

Nearly three hours had passed since Jay set foot in San Juan. During that time, Rakim and Nyla had awoken, taken their baths, ate, and now were sleep yet again in the next room. Only he and Silvas were awake, his butler busy putting the finishing touches on lunch while he checked in with King on his businesses. From what he learned thus far, Blue Magic was still in the red, Sapphire was right on track, and Iceland was progressing as normal.

Unfortunately, when it came to Flame, Carmen's entire first floor and elevator were under construction. He blamed himself for the damage so he made Linx return to Brookstone to check on things. He also sent him with a suitcase of money so the building could be fixed before Carmen returned to New York.

"Pork chops with a bourbon-peach sauce," Silvas announced, interrupting Jay's thoughts. His butler set a plate of food in front of him, thwarting his attention away from his laptop and cell phone. "It was one of your favorites growing up." Jay took a peek at the plate seeing the glazed pork chops, mashed red potatoes, and asparagus. His butler was right; it was one of his favorite meals so he dove right in.

"So, how are things looking?" Silvas asked, taking a look at the papers on Jay's desk. "Do you think you'll be opening your restaurant any time soon?"

Jay finished chewing before he responded. "It'll probably be open in December. It's tied up in my trial so you know how the Girl Scouts are. They want to keep their hands on it."

Silvas sat on the couch, watching Jay as he continued to eat. "Well, I know your workers are really feeling the effect. Aren't they on unemployment?"

"It's only temporary. King came up with the idea to move Blue Magic into Sapphire until we can get in the building. In a week or so, Sapphire will be a restaurant by day and a club at night. Once that is complete, everyone will be back at work. Their hours will be shortened, but at least we can give them a paycheck."

"Do you think you have room for one more?"

Jay dropped his fork at Silvas' question. His butler had never asked anything of him and at the most delicate time was asking him to give someone a job. "Do you owe someone a favor?"

"Cesar isn't with you," Silvas replied, not directly answering Jay's question. "I see you're down a man, so I figured, maybe, you had room for one more."

Jay pushed his plate away only because he didn't know the person in question. He trusted Silvas with his life and he was certain he knew everyone in his butler's circle, but it was obvious he didn't. "Who is he?" Jay watched as Silvas started to reply yet the doorbell kept him from doing so. When his butler stood up to answer, Jay did as well. "How long have you known him?" he asked, following Silvas to the door. "He's obviously someone you trust."

Silvas wanted to tell him more, but he had a feeling their guest was the person in question. When Silvas first saw Roman, he knew the man was just like his godson. Rough around the edges and stern, but carried a warmness about him that made him approachable.

"Who's on the other side of my door, Silvas?"

Jay pressed the palm of his hand on the door to prevent Silvas from opening it. He was only stalling because he didn't need another surprise. All he wanted was the man's name.

"Roman Soliz," Silvas told him. "He's in his late thirties, single, and needs a job."

"So, we're doing a job interview? Silvas, you know what I have on my plate. I got thirty employees right now on unemployment because of me. I just lost one of my good men."

"Which is why I'm giving you this one," Silvas gave Jay a small smile before tapping his hand. "Excuse me, Mr. Santiago. We don't need to be rude to our guest."

Jay moved his hand so Silvas could open the door. While the last thing he wanted was to meet someone new, Silvas was pressing the issue. He didn't know the reason and it really didn't matter. His butler was asking for a favor so he had to come through. When he saw Roman, he took a long look at him as he stood in the doorway. He was inches shorter than him, had the same complexion as Jesse Williams with a buzz cut. He looked tough partly due to his muscular physique, which explained why Silvas thought he was fit to take Cesar's place.

"Roman, this is Mr. Santiago," Silvas introduced, closing the door. "Jay, this is Roman Soliz. If you would like, I can take your plate in the dining room and have Roman join you. You two can talk while I check up on the little ones."

Jay nodded his head yet he didn't follow Silvas. Instead, he stayed in the foyer with Roman who hadn't moved an inch from the doorway. In fact, he acted as if he was waiting for permission to step further inside. Jay gave him permission by leading the way to the dining room. Once inside, he found his plate already in its usual spot. Jay sat at the head and pointed to the right of him, directing Roman to his seat.

"Roman was coming by the estate for about a month before I took a meeting with him," his butler began. "I wasn't quite sure what he wanted so I met him at the security gate."

Roman picked up where Silvas left off. "I needed a job. I couldn't find one in the states so I came home. Unfortunately, my line of work doesn't look good on a resume."

"So what is on your resume?" Jay asked. "And who told you to come here?'

"I was a bounty hunter. Gully referred me. I guess you can say we're colleagues. I got out the business after my wife got pregnant. It wasn't something I wanted to put a family through."

"Then you don't want to work for me. If you got out so you could protect your family, being with me is like going back in." Jay looked at Silvas and rudely pointed at Roman's plate, asking for his butler to make it to-go.

"My wife and daughter died during childbirth," Roman explained. He grabbed his plate although Silvas never took a step towards him. "That's why Gully referred me."

Jay looked at Silvas. A 'do you get it now' expression was on his butler's face, which made him more compassionate. He quickly mumbled his condolences as he started to see the similarities between them. Roman had given up his career for his family just like he had done with his cartel. They both were protectors, which Silvas realized. Jay wasn't sure where to take the conversation so he proceeded to finish his meal. When Silvas brought in dessert, ten minutes later, he resumed the conversation. "You don't want to be a murderer anymore, do you?"

"Only when necessary," Roman replied. Silvas placed a slice of cheesecake and a clean fork in front of him, but Roman didn't touch the dessert. He planned on celebrating after he secured employment.

"We're on the same page," Jay agreed. "Did Gully give you any idea of what you were getting yourself into?"

"Are you referring to the news reports?" Roman waited until Jay nodded his head before he continued. "Gully didn't tell me anything. After he told me where to find you, I did my research. Your fiancée's daughter has been kidnapped, you've got a murder and drug charge on your plate and your restaurant has been shut down. You obviously need help and so do I."

A weak smile appeared on Jay's face until he saw Silvas step in the room. His butler was holding his cell phone, which he layed in front of him. When Jay saw the number was marked as Private, he knew who was on the other end. He hadn't spoken to his comrade in Africa in a matter of days and he knew his release had reached his ears. Not quite sure how the conversation was going to go, Jay took the call in the foyer while Silvas entertained Roman.

"Everything is under control," Jay greeted.

"I sent you a courtesy gift and I received notice the package was undeliverable. You know I don't do returns. I'm sending it back because everything *is* under control. The package should be reaching the coast of Florida at this very moment."

"I need you to put a hold on it." Jay tried not to show any concern in his voice although everything wasn't under control. Carmen's building was in shambles and he was in San Juan. Not to mention, Blu had picked up on where his deliveries were being made. He could try and seize the package before he could get to it.

"I don't do holds, Santiago. You said everything was under control."

"Everything is—" Jay wasn't allowed to finish.

"Don't let me catch him before you do."

The phone immediately hung up. A loud sigh escaped his lips as he realized the timeframe he was working against. His best bet was to head to Brookstone before the package arrived. The only downfall was that he would have to fly commercial. With his plane in police custody, Jay figured out Roman's first assignment. He slid his phone in his pocket and walked to the dining room where Roman was sitting. His butler wasn't in the room and Jay figured he went to the nursery to check on Rakim and Nyla.

"I need you to start now," Jay ordered.

Roman clapped his hands to show he accepted.

"Your first assignment is to locate a fifty-five thousand pound girl. We need to get to Florida." Jay reached in his pocket, pulling out his wallet in which he retrieved a small piece of paper. Several routing and account numbers were written on it, giving Roman access to a large amount of money. He set it on top of his cheesecake so he would know dessert was over.

***

Brookstone, New York

Jay wasn't the only one looking forward to an evening flight. It was almost five o'clock and exactly two hours and ten minutes before Kane's flight was scheduled to leave for Georgia. Jean had spent the day with him, most of it spent in bed as they sexed in between news reports of Jay's release and the shootout at Flame. Throughout the duration, Harris had called twice, updating him on Sanders' condition. His partner was showing some improvement, which soothed Kane's nerves.

"I guess we're both hoping this will be your last trip," Jean stated.

"We are," Kane responded. "I'm hoping to nail Blu in the next twenty-four hours. After this, I hope I don't have to go to Georgia for anything." Kane zipped up his duffle bag and picked it up by the shoulder strap. When he turned to Jean, in a way, he was asking her to gather her things as well. Too early to give her a key to his place, he waited patiently as she placed her feet in her nude pumps and slid on her white overcoat.

"You'll call me when you land, right?"

"As promised," Kane replied.

Jean gave a nod of approval before grabbing her purse. She took her time leaving the bedroom and even opening the front door. A cab was already on its way for her and Kane agreed to wait until it arrived. By the time his duffle bag was in the car, the cab was out front. While she didn't want to leave his side, she knew it was for the best. His daughter needed him and she would only be in the way like she had been for the last several hours. Once everything with Kristian was settled, they could start building a relationship and eventually a life.

"I'll be in touch," he told her, giving her one last embrace. "I promise."

"Me, too," Jean whispered. She then gave him one final smile before walking towards the cab. She got inside while Kane went to his Jeep. Once she heard his car start, she told the driver to pull off. If she watched him leave, it would only be a reminder she was on the backburner.

"Home?" her driver asked, reminding her she hadn't specified her destination. The question alone brought her to reality. At that very moment, she was no longer living in the world of Jean Monet. She was now Monifah Harris, the Psychology major who escaped to Florida after her fiancé's murder. Now, a clinical psychologist with numerous honors and awards, she returned to Brookstone to confront her past.

If only my demons were here for me to face, she thought, picturing Carmen.

She shook the image from her head, remembering to answer the driver's question. "The Lofts," she finally replied, "Downtown, at the corner of 84th Street." Monifah watched as her driver gave a single head nod in her direction. Once he turned around, she took a look behind her. Just like she hoped, Kane's Jeep was nowhere to be seen. *It'll all be over once he gets back. This double life will end so the real fun can begin.*

23

Addresses

Copperton City, Georgia

The word hardheaded was repeated continuously in Gully's mind. Carmen was in the passenger seat of his car, still refusing to have King join them in Copperton City. He had spent most of the day trying to persuade her, but to no avail. Even after seeing firsthand what they were up against, she felt they could do everything on their own. Gully tried to thwart her plans by repeatedly calling Jay, but his cousin always sent him straight to voicemail.

"Are you going to start the car?" Carmen asked with an attitude. "I've been rushing you all freakin' day. You should be ready to go."

Gully shot her an agitated glance, turning the engine over at the same time. When he backed out the driveway, she already had her phone at her ear as if she was trying to contact Jay. When she didn't get an answer, he knew Jay was dodging everyone. Something either had his cousin tied up or he was too in his feelings to talk to anyone.

"Are we going about this thing on foot? I mean, you were the one who said you saw more when you were walking." Carmen looked Gully's way until her phone started to vibrate in her hand. A burst of excitement shot through her until she saw Kane's name on the lock screen. While it wasn't the person she wanted to speak with, she still answered.

"What were you doing in my building?" she asked, not bothering to greet him. "Sanders nearly lost his life and you couldn't even pick up the phone and let me know my business was under investigation? Oh, let me guess, that was the reason you wanted me to stay in Copperton City. You knew you were about to tear my shit apart. I hope you have a damn good lawyer. Please believe. I'm suing you and the Brookstone PD for every damn cent y'all got. I know you didn't have a warrant."

Kane allowed Carmen to get out her anger before he said anything. He took her threats and insults until she had used every derogatory statement known to mankind. When he realized she was done, he decided to speak, using a calm tone. "I'm about to board a plane to Georgia. We need to meet up. Have you spoken to Detective Morris?"

"Fuck Detective Morris," Carmen shouted. "I haven't heard from him since we left the precinct. He's not working this case, I am. Our daughter has been gone for longer than forty-eight hours so you know what those fuckers are doing, nothing. She's dead to them."

"Keep your phone on," Kane responded, ignoring her f-bombs. "I'm coming straight to you the moment I land. No games, Carmen. I know Jay was released. I don't give a fuck if he's with you. We'll be three deep if need be."

Another f-bomb was about to sound out Carmen's mouth yet Kane hung up in her face. As a result, Carmen dropped her phone in her lap. Unable to get her thoughts out, her anger raged inside, seeking a way to unleash. When the moment didn't come, the anger ceased until it was almost nonexistent. Time obviously helped and now she was noticing they were in a different neighborhood. "This is it?" she asked, looking at Gully.

"Yep, the crash happened right there. We're on Central Avenue."

Gully pointed in front of him so Carmen's eyes could focus on the yellow tape that was still in the area. In addition, there was visible debris from the accident.

"Crash," Carmen questioned, somewhat confused. "What crash? Wait, are you talking about Kristian's car? Her car wasn't found here."

"I'm talking about the crash that occurred when I ran my car into your husband's. I told you about it this morning." Gully paused only because he realized he hadn't. "I actually didn't tell you. See, Jay told me to stop whatever Kane was trying to do so I trailed him here, crashed my car into his, and jetted."

Carmen covered her face because she knew Kane never mentioned an accident. He also didn't tell her the rental car now had an auto claim on it. "The car wasn't his," she explained to Gully. "I rented the car. Kane never said anything about a crash." Carmen watched as Gully started typing on his phone. "Who are you contacting?"

"No one," Gully replied. He showed her his phone so she could see the news story. "The girl died in the crash. Kane fired at me and one of the bullets caught her in the head. She was eighteen with a history of run-ins. The death was ruled an accident and he wasn't charged. I guess he forgot to tell you he killed someone."

Carmen rolled her eyes, not at Gully, but at Kane. Even if the death was an accident, he still murdered a girl who was the exact age of their daughter. "So, it happened in front of this house? The one we're scoping out?"

"That's it." Gully stared at the house, examining the outside to see if there was anything that could serve as a lead. He knew he needed a closer look, but before he could suggest it to Carmen, he heard her phone ring. He heard her muster out the word hello before the other party took control of the call. He tried to listen in but the person's voice was inaudible. Then, after five minutes, the call was over and Carmen's phone was in her lap. "Who was it?"

Carmen swallowed as her nerves became settled. "Your cousin," she replied. "He's in Puerto Rico and he has Nyla and Rakim with him. He said he had some things to handle before he could get up with us." Carmen looked at Gully, scrunching up her face so he would know the details were scarce. "He got his hands on a plane so he's planning on going back to Brookstone. He thinks Blu is going to hit again so he wants to stop him before he does. Long story short, it's just me and you."

"Not quite," Gully argued, tapping her leg. "Who's that?" He pointed at a car that was currently pulling up in the driveway. A young black male got out the car, walked to the back of the house, and assumingly disappeared inside. "I think we found the owner." Gully glanced at Carmen, her face somewhat suspicious. "You know him, don't you?"

Carmen's face tightened because she did. Jerome had been King's best friend since elementary school. They had gone to juvie together, even for the same crimes, and now their relationship was about to be tarnished. From what Carmen was seeing, it was obvious Jerome had a hand in Kristian's kidnapping. It would also explain why none of her stuff was taken. Jerome didn't need or want any of it. He just wanted her.

"King can't come," she finally answered. "He can't come because that's his best friend. His name is Jerome McFadden and Jay murdered his cousin, Rico, earlier this year. Jerome disappeared right after it happened, but now we know where he went." Carmen prayed her response would help Gully understand why King needed to stay in New York. "This will kill him, to learn his best friend did this to him, King was in jail when Jay killed Rico. He had nothing to do with it, but Jerome is retaliating by kidnapping his sister."

Gully understood where Carmen was coming from, but he knew they needed a third person. He thought of his friend, Roman, but he was already in San Juan trying to find a job. "There's got to be someone else."

Carmen drummed her fingers on her thigh as several people came to mind. She knew Linx was busy with Jay, Jerome was playing for the other team, and then there was Phase, another one of King's friends, who she didn't know that well. *But Nicholas,* Carmen stopped when the name sounded in her head. "I got it," she shouted. "Nicholas went with King to shoot up Blu's clubs." She turned towards Gully, grabbing his shoulder. "I can call King and get Nicholas on a plane to Georgia."

Gully picked up Carmen's phone from her lap and handed it to her. Once she took it, he set further in his seat, his eyes focused on the house. He didn't plan on taking his eyes off the property until he necessarily had to. Based off Carmen's conversation with Nicholas, that wasn't going to happen until he landed in Copperton City. "So we wait," he told her once she hung up. "We wait until Nicholas gets in town or something pops off."

"We wait," Carmen agreed. "And once he gets here, well, then it begins."

Gully looked at the house again almost expecting to see Jerome. When he didn't, he had a feeling there was a third person involved on their side as well. Blu and Jerome couldn't have done as much as they did by themselves. They had their yes men, but there had to be another ringleader. Something told him he would be pulling up in a matter of minutes or even hours. If so, he and Carmen would be there to see him.

***

Victor could be labeled as a ringleader although he was far from it. Currently arriving home, after walking the city, his stench wouldn't allow him to go anywhere else. Not to mention, he was attracting the attention of the local police when he entered certain areas. His attire didn't present him as a bum yet his stench sent off warning signals. It had been hours since he'd lost Kristian or even heard from Blu or Jerome. No one had called him, which made him think something else had happened.

Now at Sola Estates, he looked at the entrance to his complex, wondering if he was making the right decision. If Blu was looking for him, he was sure enough about to find him. Just his luck, he would go to his apartment and find Kristian posted outside his door. From what he could see thus far, no one was there. He pulled his key out his pocket yet when he went to touch the doorknob; he remembered the door was unlocked. Blu and his men had broken in the night before damaging the doorframe as well as parts of his apartment. The damage wasn't bad from what his memory recalled, but what he was seeing now was on a totally different level.

Someone had been in his apartment, gone through all his things, leaving the evidence for him to find. He walked slowly inside, listening to see if someone was still there as he stepped on broken glasses and china plates. He didn't hear any sudden noises yet his guard was still up. He walked first to the guestroom where Kristian slept, seeing it had been ransacked as well.

When he came to his bedroom, it was no different; however, traces of his blood were still visible. Since calling the police wasn't an option, he decided to fix things himself.

He turned slightly at an angle to prepare to walk out the room, learning quickly he wasn't alone. An unidentifiable man was standing behind him. Without any words spoken, the man gave him a rabbit punch to the base of his skull. Once he was on his stomach, the man picked him up, carrying him over his shoulders and out the apartment.

24

Flight

San Juan, Puerto Rico

Jay took another glance at his watch. When he saw only five minutes had passed, he took another look at Roman whose eyes were planted on his phone. He had given him the assignment of finding and purchasing a plane, which Roman stated he'd done yet he hadn't laid his eyes on an aircraft.

Currently sitting in the middle of an abandon field, Roman promised a plane would be there as soon as they arrived. Somehow they showed up to see absolutely nothing. To add to his fury, he was now receiving tracking notifications of his package. About to release his frustration, it remained put when he heard the doors unlock. Immediately, his eyes faced forward, allowing him to see a white plane landing in the distance. Eventually, the plane stopped less than a quarter of a mile away from them.

"Stay here," Jay yelled. He got out the limousine without giving Roman the chance to respond. From what he could see thus far, the plane looked to be in decent condition. While it wouldn't be customized to his liking, the bare necessities needed to be there before he put his kids on it. Upon arrival, a man greeted him who appeared to be the only person on board.

"Roman Soliz?" the man questioned.

"Wrong guy," Jay replied. "I'm the one who bought the plane." Jay didn't give him his name, making his way past him as he headed up the steps. The pilot didn't block his entry and he immediately went to the cockpit starting to examine the space in detail. Jay went uninterrupted for several minutes until the pilot's patience started to wear thin.

"Is Roman here?" the man asked as Jay counted the number of fire extinguishers.

"He's at the limousine."

Jay continued inspecting the plane even as the pilot started a conversation on air safety. He tuned him out for the most part until he said something that caught his attention. "You're not flying the plane?" he asked, certain the pilot had asked if Roman was still taking over for him.

"That was never the deal," the pilot started to explain. "I oversaw the sale, I flew it here, and Roman agreed to have a car take me to the airport. He's flying the plane to New York. He's certified to fly or at least he sent over documentation saying he is."

Jay went to the exit and stuck his head out the doorway. Roman was still at the limousine, however, he was now joined by a taxi. He assumed it was the car sent to pick up the pilot until Linx stepped out the vehicle.

"Look, I can't be here all day. The plane is well equipped with everything you need. It has more than what is required. Roman made sure of it. The deal is done. I just want to know where the car is that is supposed to take me to the airport."

Jay quickly told him there was a taxi outside as he felt his phone vibrate from his pocket. He assumed it was Linx asking about Roman, but when he looked at his phone, it was a text message. The message was from an unknown number, but he knew the sender's identity. The words, *don't let me catch him before you do,* were said to him only a few hours earlier and now were being repeated. Jay didn't reply to the message, knowing it was time to get going. Blu was on his trail and his friend in Africa was aware of it.

It took only seconds for him to make his way off the plane and minutes to get to the limousine. Linx and Roman had been conversing heavily until he reached them. He didn't speak to either of them, starting to unbuckle Nyla's seatbelt. Once he had her free, he then unbuckled Rakim before grabbing his son in his arms.

"You want to explain who he is?" he heard behind him as he grabbed Nyla. Jay glanced behind him at Linx who had lowered his head into the backseat of the limousine. "If it wasn't for Silvas I wouldn't have known where to find you. I come here and there's some new guy talking about he's flying you to New York."

"His name is Roman," Jay replied, stepping out the limousine. He watched as Linx proceeded to grab his luggage. "He's Cesar's replacement. Get to know him."

Linx peered at Roman who was staring directly at him. Linx didn't say anything to him, but turned towards Jay to give him an update on his last assignment. "The contractors are already putting Flame back together. Carmen won't even know what happened."

Jay heard Linx loud and clear yet he didn't respond to him. He told Roman to grab the car seats while he carried Rakim and Nyla towards the plane. Behind them, the taxi was pulling off, the pilot inside, which meant it was time for them to leave, too.

"Talk to me, Jay," Linx pressed. "You knocked Cesar out the box; you bring this new guy in. I mean, you weren't in a rush to get to Brookstone this morning. What's the plan?"

Jay didn't respond to Linx not even when they stepped foot on the plane. Once inside, he studied the cabin area to determine the best place to put his kids. There was one long couch on the plane as well as four passenger seats, the latter seeming to be the most suitable. He directed Roman to put their car seats there and once in place, he sat them inside.

Once he started to buckle them in their seats, he decided to answer Linx's question, but was interrupted when he felt his phone vibrate. He pulled out his cell only to see another tracking update for his package. The notification made him move faster as he quickly buckled Rakim. It was then he felt his phone vibrate again.

"Start the plane," he ordered, glancing in Roman's direction. When he saw him nod his head, he took a peek at his phone only to see that Linx had texted his question. He rolled his eyes although he knew his right-hand deserved a response. When he heard the plane's engine come to life, he decided to stop stalling. "Brookstone then Georgia, that's the plan."

"What's in Brookstone that I couldn't handle while I was there?"

Jay shook his head as a sign to Linx he wasn't getting that information.

"Are you going to talk about Cesar?"

Jay stared at his kids who appeared to have fallen asleep. If Linx kept talking, they both would be awake, demanding attention from everyone. He decided to move the conversation to the cockpit, which is where he and Linx walked. "I'm tracking a FedEx truck," Jay announced, feeling the plane as it started to move. "The last notification I received has the truck in Miami. I want to visually track the truck. The airport isn't too far from Flame so I'm certain once we enter the city, we can land and get to the building around the same time the truck does."

Roman appeared uneasy. "You can't visually track a truck. I can't fly this thing that low."

"You don't have a choice."

Roman looked at Linx, hoping he would say something to convince Jay that what he wanted was dangerous. Linx didn't speak a word and even left the cockpit to go in the cabin. When he saw he wasn't getting help from him, Roman put his eyes on the field. "If you wanted to track something, I should've got a helicopter. A plane flying that low to the ground is going to track a lot of attention. You will have news crews, police, and everyone else on our ass."

"Exactly what I want," Jay admitted. He was now standing beside the co-pilot's seat as if he was going to sit down. "If the cops were at Blue Magic, they would've known I was being attacked. They refused to take my word for it until someone took a closer look at the surveillance tape. This time, things will be different. Blu is following the truck. It's not him, per se, but his men are. I don't have to put eyes on him to know that." Jay stood up straight starting to head out the cockpit. "Get us to Miami; I'll direct you from there."

After Roman gave a low okay, Jay returned to the cabin area. An open seat was next to Linx, which he claimed, since it was directly across from his kids. He hadn't forgotten his concern so he went ahead and addressed it. "What happened to Cesar was unfortunate. Don't worry about his family. They will be taken care of."

Linx turned his entire body around as Jay confirmed Cesar's death. He knew it was true yet a small part of him doubted Jay would murder a man who saved his life. Since he had, Linx knew he had to be on his p's and q's. One wrong move and he could have the same fate.

"You see that?" Jay asked, pointing at Nyla's face. He turned towards Linx to make sure he was looking at his daughter. "It's because of Cesar we get to see each other again. I will always be indebted to him. He did me a favor so I did him a favor." About to elaborate more, Jay was silenced when he felt the plane take off. The moment always silenced him. Even when the plane leveled off, he didn't speak. He simply sat there until Roman announced they were entering Florida.

***

While Jay had just arrived in the Sunshine State, Kane was already in Georgia, having secured another rental car. He had already called Jean to let her know he had landed as well as checked in with Akaila. His daughter was his main point of contact at home and from what she told him, things were good on the home front. It gave him one less worry, but he knew it would be short-lived when his phone rung from his pocket.

Not even out of the Enterprise parking lot, he pulled out his phone to see Harris calling him. Something told him not to answer yet he did out of respect for the lieutenant. A lot of commotion was in the background, which made him strain to hear the lieutenant's words.

"I need to put a tracker on you," Harris joked, not bothering to say hello. "I'm assuming you're in Georgia. Is that right?"

"That was the plan," Kane replied. "Did something change with Sanders?"

"He's good, slowly improving, but good. Actually, I'm calling because I got a call from the captain at the Triad about fifteen minutes ago. There may be a potential robbery in progress. He received a request for some extra help from the department in Dade County."

"Harris, don't do this…" Kane began.

"The potential robbery involves a FedEx truck and three black Benzes. If I remember correctly, it was a number of hours ago you were in my office talking about Benzes, Flame, and Blue Magic. You also mentioned a FedEx truck. Now, the Dade County office got the call, because the truck is on their interstate headed North. Oh and there's a plane flying above it. The police, FBI, and every other law enforcement agency in Florida and South Carolina believe this plane may try to land. We don't know when, but we have thousands of people on the interstate who need to evacuate before that bird drops from the sky."

Kane dropped his car keys in his lap at Harris' words. He was about to dismiss the whole thing until he mentioned a plane.

"The Triad shut us down, but the captain personally requested you. I don't know how you're going to go against a plane, three luxury cars, and a FedEx truck, but the Triad is going to back everything. The captain just needs to know what you need."

"Right now, nothing," Kane replied. "I don't need anything because this is Jay's issue. He's the one on the plane. He's also the one who's going to stop those Benzes from getting to the truck. Once he does that, then I'll need some help. I'm certain that truck is carrying black diamonds, which is what Blu is after. If he gets what he wants, he'll let Kristian go. The thing is, Jay doesn't want that to happen. Therefore, I have to make sure Blu gets what he wants."

Harris let out a deep sigh. "So what do you want me to tell the captain?"

"Tell him I'm headed to 85. I can't get to Florida because by the time I do, they'll be out of the state. Keep tracking 'em. Get the Triad, police, SWAT, whoever you can get. You're going to need the best of the best." Kane started up the car so he could check the fuel gauge. He only had half a tank, which meant he needed to get to a gas station.

"If you do this, Kane, the captain may take you back."

"That's not my concern, right now, Harris. I want my daughter back." The lieutenant didn't respond so Kane allowed the conversation to end there. He then pulled out the parking lot not knowing he would be driving for three hours before he saw the crisis.

As for Jay, he had watched the madness on the interstate since they had started trailing the FedEx truck and Benzes in Miami. It took less than ten minutes for their presence to be noticed by the general public and less than twenty minutes for them to notice the first squad car below them. Jay could see the nervousness on Roman's face when more squad cars appeared yet he didn't voice his concern. When the helicopters came, flying at the same altitude as them, Roman questioned his plan. Jay told him to keep flying, which he did, following his instruction.

For the longest, he watched as cars struggled to find a place to pull over. Some were abandoning their vehicles, while others were parked in the emergency lane or any place deemed safe. The FedEx truck and Benzes, however, remained moving. Since traffic was making room for the cars to come through, Roman had no choice but to keep flying.

"The FedEx truck isn't stopping," Roman shouted, looking at Jay, who was in the co-pilot's seat. "He doesn't see those bitches on his ass?"

"Would you stop if you had three cars trailing you?"

Roman didn't answer the question, choosing to place his eyes on the scene below. The question was rhetorical because he knew he wouldn't have. The second the truck stopped, the Benzes would attack. Then again, they could've attacked a long time ago. "Blu knows we're trailing 'em. What if we're following their plan?"

"Could be," Jay responded, keeping his eyes on the truck. "Or they're following ours."

"We need to do something, Jay. We need to do something fast. We have helicopters to the front, back, left, right, all the way up our fuckin' ass. You wanted a plane, I got you a plane, but I didn't sign up for World War fuckin' Three. What's the plan?"

Jay chuckled at Roman's antics because his nervousness was starting to show more than he expected. He turned around so he could meet eyes with Linx. His right-hand man wasn't smiling despite the grin plastered on his face. "Do you want to tell Roman what the plan is," he yelled.

The blank stare on Linx's face didn't change. At one point, he wasn't certain of the plan until he started to put two and two together. He also knew to think the worst before anything. When it called for it, Jay could be ruthless and heartless.

"Do you want to tell Roman what the plan is?" Jay repeated. When he didn't get an answer, he stood up and headed to the cabin area. He looked directly in Linx's face before peering at Rakim and Nyla. They both were awake so he planted kisses on their cheeks. While it wasn't his original plan to have them on the plane, they were there and he was going to make certain his feat didn't harm them. "I know what I'm doing, Linx."

"I didn't say anything. You're the boss. I work for you."

"Don't play that boss shit with me. You don't know what's in that truck."

"I've been begging your ass to fuckin' tell me," Linx barked. "You got two fuckin' kids on this plane. This is Roman's first day and you're putting him through this shit? You're leading him into this whole thing blind. Don't do this with these kids on the plane. Call Malik, let's land this thing, get them off, and then we can proceed."

Jay rolled his eyes because Linx's words made him remember his first assignment. He gave him the job of trailing Carmen and it wasn't even twenty minutes before he was pulling her out a moving limousine. "No one on this plane is going to get hurt."

"What's in that fuckin' truck, Jay?"

Jay didn't answer the question, ignoring Linx all-together. The bitch in Roman and Linx was starting to show and it was only because their own two feet weren't on the ground. They were high in the air and both of them feared a possible air strike or even plane crash. While it was a possibility, none of it had happened. "So you're not going to answer me?" Linx yelled as he walked away. Jay entered into the cockpit and stood over Roman who was still following the truck and Benzes. They were flying low enough for him to see they were about to hit Fort Mill.

"We're about to hit exit 85," he told him. "Once we do, I want you to land this thing."

Roman glared at him hard. "You...want me...to land...on the interstate?" His eyes focused on the road below him, staring at the numerous cars. Some of the vehicles were empty as evident from the people running to safety while others were struggling to get off the road. "You want me to land the plane on the interstate?"

"Yes and no," Jay replied. "I want you to land the plane *on* the interstate, but *on* them." He was speaking of the Benzes, which he hoped he caught wind of.

Roman felt his blood pressure rise yet he told himself to remain calm. He had been in a number of sticky situations, but none of them involved landing a plane on an interstate with his boss' children on board. It also didn't mean potentially killing innocent people in the process. He may have been a bounty hunter, but his job was to kill the target not the bystanders. There also was the chance of them crashing or the plane catching fire.

"I'm thinking clearly, Roman. The quicker we get rid of those Benzes, the quicker we can be done with this thing. We have to take 'em out."

Roman opened his mouth to speak, but before he could, he watched as two squad cars suddenly appeared alongside two of the black Benzes. Then, as quickly as the cars had come, more appeared, fighting their way through traffic. Seconds later, an exchange of fire began. The Benzes opened fire first, which the squad cars returned. At the sight of it, he accelerated the plane to a higher altitude.

Meanwhile, Jay kept his eyes on the war below as the Benzes took out the police. When he saw the last squad crash onto the side of the road, he felt his phone vibrate in his pocket. His first instinct was to ignore it, thinking it was another threat from his friend in Africa. However, as more squad cars appeared, his phone continued to vibrate. A look of annoyance was now on his face as he pulled out his phone. To his surprise, the person calling was Kane. The last person he expected to hear from, he wondered if he was below him. "Eh," he greeted.

"At what point in time are you coming down?"

Jay chuckled at the question as the plane continued to rise higher in the sky. He tapped Roman's shoulder as a way to tell him to go no further. "I'm coming down in a little bit," he replied. "Looks like y'all need some help. Here's a tip for you. Every single car heading towards the Arrowood exit needs to be abandoned. If I were you, I would get these people off the road."

"We got this, but here's a tip for you. They have some serious heat down here. You're going to need the works if you're trying to get inside that truck."

Jay rolled his eyes only because he knew the real reason Kane was calling. Kane wanted him to stop the Benzes. Since he was at Flame when Blu last hit, Jay knew Kane was trying to get his hands on his diamonds. If he did, the Narcotics department would be reinstated. To curve him, Jay replied with four simple words, "We only need God."

He hung up the phone as the Benzes continued to take out the squad cars. "Whatever we're going to do, we gotta do it fast." Jay looked behind him at the cabin area and watched as Linx carried his kids into the bathroom. The sight of it made him have second thoughts yet he knew he couldn't let up. Down below him, innocent men were dying and he had to put a stop to it. His mind made up, he tapped Roman's shoulder. When they met eyes, he gave him a look to let him know it was time.

Roman let out a deep breath before pulling the throttle back so he could land the plane. The nose of the plane dropped, the move catching Jay off guard. Still not at the altitude they were before, Roman took his time, trying to make sure he could land safely. When the wheels came out, there were squad cars underneath him still trailing the Benzes. Cars were driving off the road and a few accidents had occurred as a result of the gunfire. In addition, civilians were running from the spectacle as if they were being chased by zombies.

With the plane growing closer to the interstate, Roman became certain he wasn't going to be able to land without taking out a squad car or hitting one of the empty vehicles. "We're about to have a problem," he yelled. "At the speed I'm going, I'm not going to land on the Benzes. These cops gotta move or we're going to hit 'em. I can't go any slower." When he didn't get a response, he looked to the right of him.

"Tell your men to stand down," Jay was yelling, now on his phone again. He was speaking to Kane unbeknownst to Roman. "They don't see this fuckin' bird about to drop?" Jay continued. "Okay, okay, you think I'm playing."

Roman closed his eyes as the plane continued to fall to the ground. No longer hearing Jay's voice, he opened his eyes once he felt something hit him hard in the chest. When he opened his eyes, Jay was staring at him, angrily.

"Take the plane up," Jay yelled.

Roman moved quick trying to get the plane in the air. He knew it was a close call, but he wasn't quite sure what happened to create the change in plans. He thought to ask until he felt Jay's arm wrap tightly around his neck almost in a chokehold.

"You don't ever close your fuckin' eyes when you're landing a plane. That," he said in his ear, "is your fuckin' target." Jay was pointing directly at the Benzes, which were still moving at a steady pace behind the FedEx truck. "I didn't tell you to kill them," he stressed, pointing at the men and women below them. "You land this motherfucker without touching them. When it comes to the police, I gave Kane an order. If he doesn't have his men move, it's on him."

Jay let go of Roman's neck so he could pick his phone up. Kane's name was flashing on the screen and he knew it was because of his latest fiasco.

"That was a close one," Kane told him, trying to fight his way through traffic. "Your pilot almost took out twelve cars. You made bail, but for what, to get out and go back?" Kane chuckled until he watched the plane attempt to land again. "You don't want to do that, Jay. I promise you, you don't want to..." Kane's voice trailed off as he watched the plane land in front of him. A loud screeching sound erupted all around him as the wheels of the plane landed on top of a car. Unable to see who the plane hit, Kane slammed on his brakes only to hit the car in front of him. He cursed under his breath, but he didn't have time to let the accident faze him. Harris was calling, which meant Jay had disconnected the call.

"Yeah, I hit someone," he revealed to the lieutenant, turning off the engine. "I bet we all have." Kane stepped out the car, expecting to hear a response from Harris. When he didn't hear anything, he checked the scene double time. From what he could see, the chaos was still the same except for the ambulances that were driving through the traffic to attend to any potential victims. "Jay is fuckin' up big time," he said, walking towards the plane.

"We have to stand down."

Kane gave a side eye to Harris' words although the lieutenant couldn't see. "What do you mean we have to stand down? Jay just landed a plane on a fuckin' interstate. Officers are down."

"And according to the attorney general and Mr. President, himself, this case is beyond us. This is a private matter, and one we shouldn't be putting our noses in. From the way they see it, we're the ones in the way. The only thing they want us to do is clear the interstate."

Kane ignored Harris' words continuing to walk towards the plane. "He just caused thousands in damage and all you want me to do is clear the interstate?"

"I'm only giving you the information the captain of the Triad received along with the heads of the DEA, CIA, FBI, and every other three-letter agency we have in this country. This is not Jay's issue. This is the US government's issue."

Kane stopped in his tracks at Harris' last statement. He thought quickly about what he said, letting it sink in. "They let him out," he replied; his statement referencing Jay's initial release. "The government let him out, didn't they?"

"Those papers are sealed so the public won't ever know, but yes. Jay was released from his life sentence because the US government gave him a job to do. One that he is doing very well and one they want him to continue." Harris sighed as he said the words his friend didn't want to hear. "We can continue to arrest Jay, embarrass him, have him pay thousands for his freedom, but nothing will ever stick. His part of the deal is that he remains free for the rest of his life."

"He landed on innocent people."

Harris didn't speak because he wasn't in the area nor had he received word if any civilians were killed. "We don't know if he did. He probably did kill an officer or two, but that's our fault because we didn't stand down when he told us to. Or at least that is how your President sees it. Of course, he won't say that to the public. He's going to cover this up real good."

Kane stared at the scene in front of him, continuing to watch it unfold. The lieutenant had given him an order to clear the interstate, which he was seconds from declining. His entire trip to South Carolina was for nothing. Once again, work was getting in the way of what he should've been concentrating on—his daughter. "Harris," he called. Once the lieutenant answered, Kane told him his plans. "Send someone else to clear the interstate. I'm heading to Georgia."

The lieutenant tried to talk him down yet Kane only hung up the phone. He went to his vehicle only to see that the car he had hit had moved. He looked for it and spotted it on the side of the road, the driver no longer in the car. With people scattered everywhere, he figured the driver was more concerned about getting away from the gunfire than a little fender bender. He decided to put it behind him as well as he got in his car. As far as he was concerned, the incident on I-77 was no longer his problem.

The problem belonged to Jay whose plane had a Toyota Corolla stuck underneath its nose. Meanwhile, the FedEx truck maintained the same speed almost as if the driver was unaware of what was happening behind him.

"We've stopped," Roman announced, turning to look at Jay. He saw him fidgeting with something in his pocket, eventually pulling out a black object. Unsure of what it was, Roman decided to take matters into his own hands. It was time for them to go after the Benzes so he parked the plane and immediately went to the cabin. The plane was decked out in heat, which he knew Jay hadn't discovered. The guns were hidden in various compartments underneath the seats and Roman grabbed the first AK he found until the ground shook underneath him. He lost his footing for a bit, the gun dropping from his hands as he tried to get his balance. Once he was steady on his feet, he picked the gun up, retreating to the cockpit where Jay was sitting. It was then he noticed the smoke and debris in the air.

"One down," Jay said. He looked at Roman who was standing beside him wide-eyed. "Two more to go." He noticed the gun in Roman's hands before turning towards the front of the plane. "Flying low brings the attention. It scares the public, which alerts the police, or the circus as I call it, then," he continued, "you get them to work with you, clearing the interstate, getting the good people of the city out the way so eventually you can go boom."

Roman held the AK at his side as he tried to see through the intense smoke. The FedEx truck was barely visible, but he figured Jay knew that was going to happen before he set off the bomb. "You put a bomb on all the cars?" Despite his gruff voice, the words came out rather soft as he realized Jay had more men working for him. There was a responsible party in Miami who made sure the Benzes were well equipped with a death sentence.

"Take the plane up," Jay replied, not answering the question.

Roman dropped the AK at his feet in agitation. "You just set off a fuckin' bomb, I can't see shit, and we have a car underneath the nose wheels. I can't work like this. I need a fuckin' runway. A runway I can actually see. Look at that shit, Jay." Roman pointed towards the window to further prove his point. His words seem to go in one ear and out the other when he saw Jay move into the pilot's seat. "What are you doing?"

Jay didn't answer Roman's question as he started to do his job for him. They were on a time limit and the longer Roman bitched about a runway, the closer the Triad would be to finding their remains after the next bomb went off. It didn't take long for the plane to roar to life and when it did, he worked on getting the nose wheels out the Corolla.

"Move," Roman ordered, feeling the plane going in the wrong direction. "You're going to mess up the wheels that way. I got it." He knew not to force Jay out the seat so he waited until he moved before he grabbed the control wheel. He turned the plane in the opposite direction while Jay took the co-pilot's seat. Since he didn't know what was to come, he moved fast, steering the plane away from the Corolla until the right wing was able to slide over the car. He managed to take out a few cars with him, but the damage was minimal compared to what occurred moments before.

"We have five minutes," Jay announced, looking at his watch. "I need you to fly high so we won't catch this heat, but I still need to be able to put my eyes on that truck."

Roman gave him a side eye as the plane rolled forward. He gave it more speed until the plane was able to take off. The smoke, still very much thick, thinned out as the plane continued to rise. Once at a decent altitude, he looked below him. For the first time in the last few hours, he noticed the truck was no longer in the lead. One of the Benzes was in front, the distance growing between it and the truck. "Blu had a change in plans," he revealed. "They got the truck sandwiched." He thought his words would prompt a response, but Jay only said one minute.

Roman steadied the plane trying to control the speed so they could maintain visibility. Unsure of what was to happen aside from another bomb, he became skeptical of Jay's plan since the truck was still stuck in between the two cars. The position was short-lived as the Benz in front made a quick right. The second car remained in place until the FedEx truck overturned on the interstate. Moments later, the Benz blew up, engulfing the FedEx truck in its flames.

Curse words sounded out Roman's mouth just as Jay stood from his seat. About to voice his thoughts, he wasn't given the chance when Jay left the cockpit. Seconds later, he reappeared, as did Linx who was still holding Rakim and Nyla. When Jay sat down, Roman parted his lips yet Jay spoke before he could.

"Brookstone," Jay instructed. He wiped his face, removing the sweat that had formed as a result of his nerves. Slowly calming down, he gave Roman the information he knew he wanted. "Blu's men always drive cars with tinted windows. The cars are always identical except for the license plates, but even those can be duplicated. All they know is that their target is a truck. They don't even know if what they're looking for is actually in there."

Jay took a deep breath before he continued. "One of the Benzes was mine. What they were after was never in the truck. It's in the Benz that took the Arrowood exit. The truck overturned because the driver jumped out. Unlike the police, he wanted to live and knew to get out before the last car blew. My driver is going to switch cars and meet us in Brookstone."

A smile formed on Roman's mouth only because he had easily been fooled. "You fuckin' son of a bitch." Roman chuckled as Jay stood from his seat. Jay then held out his hand to him as a way to say thank you.

"Congratulations, Roman. You survived your first day."

25

Heavy Artillery

Copperton City, Georgia

Carmen stared outside the window, the sky growing darker by the hour. She had been in that position for the last two hours as Nicholas and Gully conversed behind her. Like her, they were both standing except their eyes were planted on the guns on the coffee table. They also had a glass of Jack Daniels in their hands. She was the only one not drinking as she constantly repeated their plan in her mind. Gully was to take the lead, the most experienced shooter out of the three, and Nicholas was to follow. Gully was set on her keeping watch, but Carmen argued against him. He then instructed her to stick close to Nicholas in case things got ugly.

So far, things had been peachy. The latter part of the day had been spent staking out Jerome's house until Nicholas telephoned, announcing his arrival in Copperton City. She suggested for him to meet them at Jerome's house, but Gully disagreed. He insisted on picking him up, which they did, only to return to Gully's house.

Carmen felt like time was being wasted until she heard Gully call her name. When she turned around, he was holding a pistol in his hands. "Are you ready?" He said the words almost as if he felt she wasn't. If he did, Carmen was prepared to change his mind. She walked up to him, grabbing the pistol from his hand as well as a few others which were on the coffee table.

"You know you don't have to do this, right?" Gully said.

Carmen eyed Gully suspiciously. Even after the heart to heart they shared, the hours they spent stuck in his car, he still wanted to give her an out. She thought that by now he would know her capabilities, but he obviously didn't. Too annoyed to entertain the question, she turned to Nicholas. In response, Nicholas lifted up his sweatshirt displaying the numerous weapons stuck in his waistband.

"Then, let's go," Gully ordered, grabbing a machine gun from the table. Carmen watched him as he left the living room, car keys in hand. Not the least bit surprised he was driving, Carmen followed him to the car, taking the passenger seat while Nicholas sat in the back. For most of the ride,

Carmen kept to herself yet every so often she would take a look at Nicholas through the rearview mirror. His face was blank, almost emotionless as they rode through the streets of Copperton City.

Since his father, Noc, once worked for Jay, she figured he was trigger happy yet he proved her wrong when they were behind Waffle House. He had told her then that King was solely responsible for the deaths at Blu's clubs. Now, she wondered how he was going to be once they were in front of Jerome or Blu. Carmen began to envision it until his gaze met hers.

"Kristian looks just like you."

Carmen blinked her eyes at the comment. She knew her daughter had her features, but she didn't expect Nicholas to speak on it considering their present situation. His words made her suspicious, which made her question his true intentions. "How well do you know Kristian?"

Nicholas parted his lips to respond yet Gully interrupted him, telling her to leave him alone. She gave him a side eye before looking at Nicholas again in the rearview mirror.

"We've had a few run-ins," he replied.

Carmen turned around because she knew what those words meant. "Did y'all have something going on?" She could hear Gully mumbling a few words under his breath, but she ignored him. "Did you?"

Nicholas didn't say anything, turning towards the window. The last thing he wanted to admit was they had a fling or even that he tried to take her virginity. He also didn't want to bring up the relationship he shared with her adopted daughter, Akaila, which resulted in several offsprings, all of which had been aborted.

"We're here." The agitation in Gully's voice forced the conversation to end. It also forced Carmen to turn around in her seat so she was facing Jerome's house. The house appeared even emptier, the image of it, making a loud sigh escape from her lips. "Not so quickly," she heard Gully say after Nicholas opened his door. He quickly closed it and Carmen looked at Gully to see what had caught his attention. He gave a head nod in the direction of the rearview mirror, which is where Carmen looked. A car was coming up from behind so she figured Gully wanted to see where it was headed.

"It's nothing," she whispered. Carmen watched as the car passed them and seconds later she realized she had spoken too soon. The car, a burgundy Mazda Protégé, pulled in Jerome's driveway before disappearing into the backyard. When she looked at Gully, his eyes were still on the house as if he was waiting for something to happen. He stayed in that position for a minute or so before she heard the doors unlocking again. Seconds later, he stepped out the vehicle. When she saw Nicholas do the same, she opened her own door, preparing to step out until an uncomfortable feeling came over her. She remained seated as Nicholas walked past her, following Gully's lead.

As usual, the neighborhood was quiet, which allowed Gully to hear even the slightest movement. When he heard the sound of doors opening, he knew to quicken his pace, but not to make too much noise. He looked behind him only to see Nicholas a few feet away. He motioned with his hand for him to stay put as he drew closer to Jerome's house. He crept into the yard, trying to stay in the shadows so he wouldn't be seen, but also so he could keep the same visual. It allowed him to see a man being pulled out the backseat of the car.

The man was unconscious, his face unrecognizable although Gully could tell he was dark-skinned. Other than that, he couldn't see much. He did notice the backdoor was left open, which meant the driver was coming back. When he did, Gully watched him as he returned holding a small bag. He then closed the back door before getting inside the vehicle. Gully went deeper into the shadows, crouching behind a bush as the man started the car.

Thankfully, the driver didn't turn on his headlights until he was in the street. Once the car passed his, he pulled out his pistol. Cars were coming from the opposite end of the street and based off their speed, the cars were headed to Jerome's house. Gully watched from the shadows as two cars pulled in the driveway. Four men emerged from the vehicles also heading towards the back of the house. Once he heard them go in, he followed them, Nicholas suddenly appearing. Carmen was nowhere to be seen, but Gully wasn't going to take the time to look for her. Instead, he whispered the words, "Let's go," and proceeded to move towards the backyard.

Now in the basement, Victor woke up shivering, a result of the cold water he was lying in. The temperature caused him to stir first, which allowed him to feel the water moving around him. He tried to open his eyes yet a throbbing headache prevented him from doing so. When he tried a second time, he blinked repeatedly, trying to adjust to the dim light. Once his eyes were somewhat comfortable, he raised his head so he could see more of his surroundings. A stairwell was about twelve feet away from him, which made him realize he was in Jerome's basement.

Automatically, he began to search the room. Only able to see things at eye level, he quickly realized he wasn't alone when he noticed two pairs of legs. He didn't have to meet eyes with anyone to know Blu and Kristian were in front of him. Blu sat in a chair while Kristian was on the floor beside him, her wrists handcuffed to the chair's legs.

"I'm glad you could join us," Blu said, finally speaking.

His head was still pounding from the blow so Victor fought through the pain as he raised his head. He managed to balance himself enough to take a look at Kristian. It was then he noticed her busted lip.

"You only had to do one thing," Blu told him, forcing Victor's eyes on his. "One," he reiterated. He didn't finish the statement, taking his hand out his jacket pocket so he could stick a cigar in his mouth. "You couldn't even do that." Blu paused to light the cigar. He took a small whiff before standing from his seat. The water covered his alligator shoes yet he didn't seem to mind. "Did you even try and look for her?"

Victor didn't speak, choosing to look at Kristian. The same scared expression he saw when she was in the basement of his restaurant was on her face. The only difference was, there was evidence she had been fighting. A lot had occurred while he was unconscious, which he was now learning from Blu. Apparently, Kristian had been hiding in the shed in the backyard the entire time he was gone. Victor assumed Blu found her since Jerome wasn't anywhere in the room. Instead of asking where he was, he turned to Kristian, asking her if she was okay. It earned him another blow to the head sending him onto his stomach yet he remained conscious.

"Do you think this is what I wanted?" Blu was now leaning over him, the scent from his cigar clouding his nostrils. "I take one step forward, you knock me three steps back. I took this bitch so I can get a shitload of diamonds. Thanks to you, I can't even keep her in my fuckin' hands." Blu spit his cigar out his mouth before grabbing a broken pipe, which was lying a few inches from Victor's legs. "Black diamonds, Victor, do you know what those stones are worth?" Feeling betrayed, he showed his disappointment by slamming the pipe down onto Victor's back.

The unexpected blow was followed by another, which made him black out. Not quite sure how long he was out, when he did finally come to, blood was trickling down the center of his face. It hurt to move his arms so he constantly tried to move parts of his face so he could maneuver the blood from his eyes. His vision was blurry yet he managed to see that Kristian was still handcuffed to the chair. However, she was now lying on her back, the sides of her face hidden by the water that had filled the room.

Loud footsteps sounded above them, but Victor tuned out the noise at the visual in front of him. Blu was directly on top of her, his pants at his kneecaps while his hips thrusted hard up against hers. Immediately, Victor tried to move to get to her, but his arms and legs both felt like bricks. The blow across his back made it impossible for him to get off the floor. He was practically numb, watching Blu as he raped Kristian in front of him.

An uncomfortable feeling settled over him, and once again, he struggled to move so he could stop what was taking place. He managed to raise his upper body off the floor, but he became stiff when he noticed Jerome lying face up a little more than a yard from him. The water had turned a bloody red underneath him due to the multiple gunshot wounds in his chest. Victor looked away in horror just as a round of gunfire forced him on his stomach.

The sound was enough to get Blu to stop, yet he didn't pull out. The thought crossed his mind; however, the intensity of a brewing orgasm forced him to continue. Kristian was untouched; something he learned when he dipped inside of her. The tightness and warmth of her love box made him push all his thickness inside her despite her cries of pain. He enjoyed her for several minutes in uninterrupted bliss until Jerome decided to make an appearance. He proved to be a threat so Blu took him out and then went to work.

Despite the gun battle above his head, he managed to explode, emptying his seed inside of her as planned. He acted as if the deed was consensual, whispering words of thanks for his brief period of ecstasy. Then, to leave her with some form of dignity, he fixed her clothes back.

At this point, the gunfire was ceasing, which meant there were several lifeless bodies upstairs. Blu grabbed his heat off the floor, not aware Victor was awake, and walked towards the stairwell. Victor, on the other hand, kept his eyes on Blu as he climbed the steps. When he saw him reach the top, the basement door opened and two men tumbled down. Blu fell down the steps with them, firing several shots in the air until he realized the men were dead.

The gunfire was moving into their vicinity, making Victor feel powerless. Physically incapable of protecting Kristian, he laid in the water, staring at her as she curled up in a ball. He tried to talk to her yet it was pointless. The noise in the room was escalating partly due to the brawl that was now occurring at the bottom of the steps. Two more men had entered the basement, one of them attacking Blu. The other, moved towards him, grabbing Victor's legs to pull him away from Kristian. Then, he was thrown against the wall.

Victor fell hard on his stomach, the pain in his back worsening. Still in immense pain, he raised his head to see a light-skinned man headed towards the opposite side of the room where Blu was being held in a chokehold. As if that wasn't enough, one of the men who he assumed was dead was now getting up from the floor. He charged at the light-skinned man, grabbing his gun from him only to be shot down. Victor watched as the man fell to the ground until another shot was fired.

Suddenly, the room became still. The man holding Blu was like stone as was the light-skinned man. Then, as if the silence was too much to bear, another gunshot sounded. It was then Victor noticed the woman in the room. She was standing at the bottom of the steps, the gun shaking in her right hand. He examined her carefully, noticing her disheveled appearance. Blood completely covered her pants and her face was filled with a mix of sweat and tears. She still had the gun pointed, but not for long. Seconds later, she collapsed on the floor as the room became filled with Triad agents.

26

Broken Silence

Kane sat in his seat quietly rubbing his hands together every so often as he stared at his daughter. After a thorough medical examination, Kristian was still in her hospital gown, now sitting there quietly as well. She had said plenty, which Kane was still taking in. After arriving in Copperton City, he made his way to the police department just in time for the call to come through of a reported shootout. The call was escalated to the Triad and he immediately went to work making sure he was a part of the raid on Jerome's house.

One of the first inside, he entered the basement to see two bullets in Blu's head, Kristian handcuffed to a chair, and his wife face down in a pool of water. Not to mention, her lower half was covered in blood. Not sure who to address first, he made the decision to see after Carmen who appeared unresponsive. Bullet-less and still breathing, it wasn't until the paramedics arrived he learned she had a miscarriage. All of the blood was coming from her vaginal area, which explained why her pants were bloody. She was immediately rushed to the hospital as the other paramedics started examining Kristian. It was then his daughter disclosed she had been raped.

The words did more than sting and he found himself beating Blu's corpse to a pulp. It took him an hour to calm down and once he did, Kristian was in an ambulance. He rode with her to the hospital, his hand in hers as he repeatedly apologized for not protecting her. He also made a promise that all precautions would be taken to ensure Blu's seed didn't grow inside her.

"How's Victor?" Kristian asked, interrupting his thoughts.

Kane was already staring at her, but he turned away at the question. He didn't know much about Victor aside from the fact he was badly injured and a business partner of Blu's who got caught up in the kidnapping. "I don't know," he told her, honestly. "He was in really bad shape. We got a few things from him, but they had to take him to surgery."

Kristian nodded her head understandingly. She looked at her hands, envisioning the handcuffs still around them, but quickly shook the image from her mind. "He didn't do it," she said, wanting to clear Victor's name. "Make sure you tell them that. I told them, but I don't think they believe me.

He didn't kidnap me. He tried to help me. Jerome tried to help me, too. He walked in the room when Blu was raping me and Blu shot him."

"Blu and Victor were partners. Whether or not Victor was in on the kidnapping, that's questionable, but they dealt with each other business-wise. As for Jerome, from what Victor managed to tell us, he kidnapped you. He's already gone, but Victor is a different story."

"I'm not lying," Kristian argued, her tone disturbed. "I know what he did for me."

Kane took his eyes off his daughter only because he didn't want to upset her. He also didn't want her to think he didn't believe her so he simply told her okay. She responded by saying she wanted to move in with him. "I think it'll be better for me," she was saying. "I know Mama is going to be dealing with a lot, losing a baby, me…" Kristian's voice trailed off for a few seconds. "I think the change in environment will be good for me. So can I?"

Thoughts of Jean were nowhere in Kane's mind so he quickly said yes. His daughter needed him and since he no longer had the duties of being a husband, he needed to put one hundred percent into being a father. "Your care is my main priority right now."

"So will you tell Mama?"

Kane rolled his eyes only because he didn't want to be the one to break the news. He hadn't said one word to Carmen since she had been admitted. Although he was aware she was awake and had given statements, he wasn't ready to face her. He still hadn't accepted the fact that Jay had impregnated his wife a fourth time. "Maybe, we should give her some time. Y'all both have been through a lot in the past couple of days." Kane grabbed his daughter's hand, something he had been doing on and off since he found her.

"So you're going to tell Mama my decision?"

Kane parted his lips yet he knew Kristian wasn't going to back down. As much as he wanted to tell her no, he decided to get out his feelings and do the deed. Instead of venting his frustration, he told her he would. Well aware Kristian was hours away from being discharged, he excused himself. Carmen's room was on the Maternity floor and once he reached it, he saw the privacy notice on her door. He ignored it, knocking only once before going inside.

He found her sitting in bed, cell phone in hand. She was completely alone, which made him wonder where Jay was. He was certain her fiancé would've been on the first thing smoking since she had lost their child. Since he wasn't there, Kane took a seat.

"Kristian is doing well," he told her. "All precautions were taken to prevent pregnancy."

Carmen laid her phone beside her at Kane's words. She had been informed by Gully of what happened, but unfortunately, her own issues kept her from being by her daughter's side. She tried to call her room so she could speak to her but neither Kristian nor Kane picked up.

"Once she's discharged, we're going home. She actually wants to move in with me. She thinks it'll be a better fit for her as she heals. You know, there's a lot going on at your house. She thinks she'll do better at mine. She wanted me to be the one to tell you."

Carmen narrowed her eyes yet she didn't speak. It wasn't a secret her daughter wasn't fond of her relationship with Jay, but the last thing she expected was for her daughter to move out. For one, Kane had lost his job and it would only be a matter of time before she would become his personal ATM. If Kristian was living there, she would have to support him.

Still not replying to his words, Carmen picked up her cell to see another message from Jay. He had been texting and calling nonstop but she didn't reply. She had discovered she was pregnant a day or so ago and didn't plan on telling anyone until the situation with Kristian was over. The first sign was the blood stain on Gully's sheets, which she thought was her period until she noticed her pad had remained stainless. It was then she got a pregnancy test and learned the truth. She had slept with Jay twice in the last couple of months so she knew they conceived the night Sanders raided his apartment. Barely even two months, she figured the stress of her daughter's kidnapping caused the miscarriage.

"I know you missed a lot being here so I wanted to let you know what happened with Jay. There was a FedEx truck on its way to New York. Blu's men tried to seize it and in true Jay fashion, he tried to stop it by landing his plane on I-77. He caused probably millions in damage, but—" Kane was interrupted when the door opened and Gully walked in. Despite the times they were in each other's presence, he never got to have a legit conversation with him. "Who are you?" he asked, standing on his feet.

Gully looked at Carmen and when they met eyes, he decided to introduce himself. "Guillermo Perez, but I go by Gully. I'm Jay's cousin. I work for him."

"Jay's cousin?" Kane questioned with a chuckle. "Well, that explains the resemblance. It also explains why you were following me. How long have you worked for him?"

"Stop," Carmen blurted. "You know who he is. Long story short, he followed you, crashed into your car, causing you to kill a girl. It's all said and done. There's no need to rehash and get all in your feelings. There are already enough feelings walking around here."

Kane took a step forward only because he wanted to give Carmen a piece of his mind. She was on ten, but if he gave her the same attitude, things would quickly escalate. Since he had spoken his piece, there wasn't much else to say or so he believed. About to exit the room, he got another thought, which he decided to share. "I saw the logo you plan on using for *Production* in your basement. If you decide to use my idea, I want a check."

Carmen didn't respond because she didn't know what he was talking about. She hadn't heard any reference to his fake clothing store in more than twenty years. If there was a logo in her basement, she knew Jay put it there.

When Kane realized he wasn't going to get a response, he decided to be the bigger person. "I'm sorry about what happened to you. I would never wish that on you, no matter how much I hate Jay," he began, grabbing the door handle. "But I'm going to make things easy on you. Whatever you want in the divorce, you got. Just state your demands."

The divorce was the last thing on Carmen's mind especially when she had just lost a child and had her eldest daughter be raped. Not something she wanted to deal with at the moment, she allowed Kane to leave the room without getting a response. Gully was still there so she looked at him with an expression, which read, *speak now, or get out.* He took the hint, but instead of sitting, he remained standing.

"It took a lot to keep Jay in Brookstone. You're not helping the situation either by dodging his calls. I know you don't want him to know about the baby, but he's going to find out. He's worried about you and Kristian. You need to talk to him."

"I just found out about the baby." Carmen huffed. "I learned what, two days ago, I was pregnant and then I have a miscarriage. I passed out from the shock. There's too much going on to put this on his plate as well."

Gully pulled out his cell phone only because he felt it vibrating. Well aware it was Jay, he ignored the call once he saw his cousin's name. "He's going to find out about the baby so you better tell him soon. If you don't, I am. I'm not keeping this from him."

Carmen knew she was going to have to come clean. Everything was still fresh so it was better for her to tell him when she got home instead of pretending it never happened.

"A lot of stuff happened while we were here," Gully continued. "Jay caused a lot of damage to one of the interstates, but he says it's being handled and not to worry. Whatever Blu was after, Jay made sure he didn't get. He says that whole part is settled. Whenever you're discharged, he has a private plane waiting for us."

"Kristian is going home with her father. She's going to move in with him."

Gully shrugged his shoulders. "Well, the plane will be ready. I've officially joined his team. He's going to let me have his penthouse until I can find something."

"Sounds good," Carmen expressed. She adjusted herself in the bed before grabbing her phone for the umpteenth time. Jay had left her another voicemail and she knew it was time to return his calls. "So why does he think I'm here?"

"Kristian," Gully replied. "He doesn't know you were admitted."

Carmen inhaled only because Jay was completely in the dark. She knew he didn't know about the baby, but she figured Gully had at least told him she was in the hospital. Since he hadn't, she told herself to get prepared. Gully was moving to Brookstone, which meant he would only give her a small window of time before he disclosed the miscarriage to Jay. "So, we're stuck with each other?" she joked. When Gully smiled, she couldn't help but to chuckle. Her smile started to fade as she looked back on the hard time they had given each other. Gully didn't think she was capable of handling Blu while she didn't like the idea of having to prove herself. Now, they were in a space where they both respected each other and knew each other's capabilities.

"I dig you, Carmen. In the beginning, I didn't know what Jay saw in you. I blamed you for what happened to him. These past few days taught me a lot, though. Now, I know why he loves you. I also want you to know that I accept you. I hope you accept me, too."

Although she knew he wasn't an affectionate person, Carmen still opened her arms for a hug. There was slight resistance on Gully's part, but eventually he leaned in to accept the gesture. He made it quick and once he pulled away, she grabbed her cell and told him she was calling Jay. He left the room shortly thereafter so she could have privacy.

Jay answered with a slew of curse words as he expressed his displeasure of being left out the loop. Carmen quickly apologized, but only the words, *I'm sorry*, were able to come out. He was trying to give her all the details of the last few days in a short amount of time and even confirmed many of the things Gully had told her. Then, he briefly mentioned how one of his men had gotten their things from the Ritz so they wouldn't have to go to the hotel. Carmen then informed him about her brief stay at the Super 8. She needed someone to get her things from there as well as her Honda, which was parked at Gully's. Their conversation lasted for over an hour and not once did Carmen mention the miscarriage. She never planned to tell him over the phone, only in person, which was set to happen quicker than she thought. Shortly after their talk, she was discharged.

She tried to visit Kristian only to be told by the nurses that her daughter requested privacy. Not surprised at the request, Carmen tried to reach out to Kane, but he never picked up. She waited for an hour with Gully before she became convinced her ex was ignoring her on purpose. It was then she agreed to leave without seeing her daughter.

Gully drove her to his house so they could gather their things and then as planned, they boarded a private plane, which took them to Brookstone. Upon landing, the first call she made was to Jay. He told her Rakim and Nyla were with Tiara since he was out handling business. Instead of questioning what he was doing, she called Tiara who confirmed her kids were there. Tiara sounded half asleep so she decided to wait until Jay brought them home to see them. After that call, she reached out to Akaila who informed her she had been staying at King's house.

Although Carmen didn't want to start the morning with bad news, she quickly updated her on her sister and even told her about the miscarriage. She could hear her daughter's pain loud and clear, which resulted in Carmen shedding tears of her own. Not much was said after they broke down, but Carmen promised to visit her later that evening. By the time she hung up, the limo was in front of her estate, allowing her to see the empty driveway. Well aware Jay wasn't there, Carmen was surprised her maid, Fiona, was also absent. Then again, no one was at home, aside from her mother, who could fend for herself.

Instead of checking in on her, Carmen used the time to her advantage. She showed Gully to one of the guestrooms before escaping into her bedroom. While she wanted to take a long hot bath, she resorted to a shower since the bleeding hadn't stopped. The heat helped to alleviate her cramps, which were slowly returning, an effect of the painkillers wearing off.

Little did she know, Jay was now standing in their bedroom. His eyes were focused on her luggage and the clothes strewn about yet he didn't bother to go near the bathroom. While he was anxious to see her, he couldn't at the moment. His phone was vibrating, a sign he needed privacy. He quickly left the room answering the call although he didn't speak until he was out of the house. The phone call was confirmation of Blu's remains. While Carmen had done the bulk of his job, a few finishing touches were needed. He gave the order for the remains to be taken from the hospital's morgue just as he walked in the pool house, a place he went for discretion.

He immediately drew his gun when he saw a shadow move inside. Soon followed by footsteps, he watched as Cesar emerged from the kitchen. He caught his breath only because his right-hand didn't know how close he had come to a bullet. "You almost made me kill you for real."

Cesar smirked at the comment before sitting on one of the sofas. "That lock was easy to mess with," he admitted. "I heard you were in town so I figured I would drop in so we could settle some unfinished business."

Jay rested himself against the wall only because he knew the real reason Cesar was there. His right-hand wasn't ready to say goodbye. He faked his death to protect him yet Cesar was still in America. "The longer you stay here, the worse it's going to get."

Cesar's eyes glanced downward before meeting again with Jay's. "This is hard for my family. All they know is Puerto Rico and now I'm forcing them to move. They don't understand why we can't just settle in Canada."

"This is hard for everyone," Jay replied. "I'm not saying that as an excuse, but as the truth. I didn't want this for you. I also didn't want you sitting in a cell for twenty years."

Cesar stood up from the sofa only because he was about to give a proposition. "With the life you live, you're going to have men coming and going all the time. Blu is dead. Who knows what's going to come because of that? You need men like me. We're ghosts who hide in the shadows. Maybe, we drive beside you like we're civilians. My last job for you was driving your package off the interstate. No one knew it was me."

Jay's eyes narrowed at Cesar's request. "I do need men like that, but hiring you as the first one means you'll be staying in this city. If you get caught—"

"Linx can remain your driver. Roman is now your right-hand, he replaced me, but eventually the police will pick up on him. They'll know he's in your inner circle. Not to mention, you just brought in your cousin. The Triad definitely knows your ties to Gully."

Jay rubbed his hands over his face as he felt himself being persuaded. "Right now, I have more money going out then coming in. I have two businesses down, Cesar. I pay you all very well and now you want me to add on more men in addition to Roman and Gully. The ink isn't even dry on the check I cut them. Shit, I may have to dip in Carmen's pocket." Jay took a moment to think the matter over. "I would pay and do anything to ensure my family's protection."

"Then, let's do it." Cesar stuck out his hand and waited for Jay to shake on it. It didn't happen as quickly as he would've liked, but once they shook hands, he got the confirmation he needed. He would move his family to Canada while he would commute back and forth between there and New York. He would find more men so they could work a rotation of two weeks on and two weeks off. "I'll get what you need. Six o'clock interviews always worked, didn't it?"

A small smirk flashed across Jay's face. "Sometimes it does, sometimes it doesn't," he said, thinking of Blu's initial interview. He ended the statement with a chuckle before giving Cesar a slight push. "Go ahead and get out of here. I better not see you again." He shook his hand a final time before Cesar left the pool house. He soon followed, heading in the house. His next stop was his bedroom until he saw Kristian's door open. Unaware she was there, he stepped in her doorway.

It didn't take long for her to notice him and once she did, she approached him. He thought she was going to slam the door in his face, but she didn't. Instead, she stood there waiting for him to speak. He began with, "I'm sorry," which seemed to do the trick because everything else poured right out. "Don't blame your mother for this. If you want to be angry at anyone, be angry at me. All of this happened because of me."

"I don't blame you," she said softly, still standing in front of him. "Blu's actions were his own. I blame you for ruining my parents' marriage. That's the only thing I blame you for. My parents would still be together if it wasn't for you."

Her words weren't a surprise especially when she had previously voiced her displeasure. She was always going to hold a grudge against him despite the history he shared with her mother. "You're young, Kristian, but one day, you're going to be in love. When that time comes, you'll understand. The love you have for a person will make you selfish. You no longer think about the feelings of others. You just think of being with that one person regardless of the hurdles you have to jump and the people you have to hurt."

Jay watched as Kristian walked away from him. Her attention went to packing as if he hadn't said a word. Certain he wasn't going to make her understand, he gave her another apology. She didn't respond to it so he simply left her doorway, heading to his bedroom. When he entered, Carmen was still in the bathroom. This time, the door was open. He could hear her moving inside so he immediately went to the doorway so he could see her.

He envisioned her standing at the sink, her hair freshly washed and face with no makeup. He also wanted to see her barelegged, which meant he had easy access for a rendezvous if she was up for it. The only downfall was the vision never came into fruition. Upon entering the doorway, he noticed the small trail of blood leading towards the shower, which told him something was wrong. Then, there was Carmen, seated on the toilet, bent over, as if she was in dire pain. Her panties were also at her ankles. He knew she sensed him when she raised her head. Her hair, no longer black, was now a light shade of brown and golden blonde at the ends.

The blood on the floor didn't bother him, which he proved when he ran in the bathroom. Automatically dropping to his knees, he pulled her off the toilet only to see the clog of blood in the commode. The blood, coming from her vaginal area, became smeared on his pants when he sat her on top of him. Certain her period didn't have her in tears, Jay realized he was witnessing a miscarriage. Despite her muffled voice, he heard her repeatedly apologizing. Then, the apologies turned to sobs. Naturally, he started to cry along with her.

Jay assumed they were on the floor for thirty minutes or so before Carmen pulled away. While he didn't want to let her out his arms, he allowed her to. She cleaned herself before grabbing a large pad from the bathroom closet and changing into a pair of clean underwear. He then started to clean up. His pants were completely stained; the toilet was a mess as well as the floor. He could tell Carmen had taken a shower so he prepared himself to see the worst when he looked inside the stall. Thankfully, she managed to clean it so it was the same spotless white he knew it to be. Jay stripped himself of his pants and started bleaching and cleaning the floor. By the time he was done, Carmen had finished scrubbing the commode. Words weren't exchanged between them until she tried to go in the bedroom. It was then he grabbed her arm, pulling her into him.

"I'm going to give you another one," he promised. "I swear."

Jay's words brought on another stream of tears. It reminded Carmen of what he'd seen, and how she was hoping to have everything spotless before he came home. Not wanting anyone else to see them, she pulled away so they could get decent. She went in the bedroom, not knowing the door was open until she saw her mother and Kristian. A wave of shock went over her only because it was her first time seeing her daughter since the kidnapping. Not to mention, she was clad in only her undergarments while Jay was in his boxers.

Without speaking, her mother quickly left the room. Not fazed by her behavior, Carmen closed the bathroom door. She then grabbed her bathrobe from the bed, covering herself. Kristian was still in the doorway, but she led her daughter to her room. It wasn't the ideal place to have a conversation since Kristian was packing to leave, but it was better than her bedroom.

"How far along were you," Kristian asked. It was a question Carmen didn't expect to hear or at least not so soon. If anything, she expected to be the one asking questions. She wanted to console her daughter and at the same time ask her why she banned her from her hospital room. However, Kristian was more concerned about her miscarriage than the rape.

"Almost two months," she answered, sitting on her bed. "It actually happened yesterday. The bleeding just hasn't stopped." Carmen didn't expect to see a look of disappointment, but that's exactly what she got. "I didn't want to talk about this with you," she continued. "I wanted to make sure you were okay. What happened wasn't your fault."

"I know it wasn't my fault," Kristian argued. "It was Blu's fault. I don't blame anyone but him. What? You think I blame Jay or something? Blu was the one who kept putting me in basements. He was the one who raped me. Jay didn't do it."

Carmen leaned back only because she wasn't expecting Kristian's demeanor to change as quickly as it had. "Sometimes underneath the pain and embarrassment, we blame someone. Jay isn't your favorite person by far, so can you blame me for thinking you had a grudge?"

"Jay didn't put a gun to Blu's head and tell him to rape me. He did it on his own. It was a terrible mistake, but he paid the price. You made sure he did."

Carmen ran her fingers through her daughter's hair as her tone became more tolerable. She wanted to hug her, however, she told herself to take baby steps. They weren't necessarily on good terms and although tragedy had struck, their relationship wasn't mended. "I did what any mother would do. My only regret is not getting there sooner."

Kristian didn't respond to her mother's comment simply laying her head on her shoulder. She knew her mother would've done anything to keep Blu from touching her. Anyone in her family would. Still, it happened and it was something she would have to live with. "Daddy told you about the move, didn't he?"

Carmen rolled her eyes although she knew Kristian couldn't see. "Yeah, he told me. I don't agree with it, but it's your decision. I don't want you to think you have to leave. There have been a lot of changes, but this is your home. We want you here. The only person who seems to be doing better not in this house is Malachi. Since he's moved in with King, he's been on the straight and narrow."

Kristian couldn't do anything but agree. Her little brother seemed to have made a vast improvement. He no longer got into fights and his attitude was more positive than it had been in months. Even Akaila, his biological sister, had noticed the change. "He wanted King's attention. Now that he lives with him, he gets it. King is practically his father."

"So was it your father's attention you wanted?"

Kristian mouthed the word no before saying it aloud. "He doesn't have anyone, Mama. You've started this brand new life and he's just over there in a condo by himself. I didn't want him to feel alone. I figured that since we're both healing, we might as well heal together." Kristian raised her head off her mother's shoulder as a new thought entered her mind. "I don't want you to testify against Victor."

Carmen raised her brow as she became confused. "Who's Victor," she questioned, now staring Kristian in the face. "And why would I testify against him?"

"He was in the basement with me. Daddy says he's a suspect, but he shouldn't be. When he goes to court, I'm going to testify for him. He didn't have to do what he did for me." Kristian took a deep breath only because she knew her mother was going to be shocked at her next statement. "I forgive Jerome, too. I know he kidnapped me, but the look on his face when he saw Blu raping me. I know that wasn't a part of the plan. It hurt him to see me like that. He tried to help me, too. I want King to know that."

"You shouldn't be concerned with that right now," Carmen whispered. "We'll handle it when it comes. I promise."

"I can't help but be concerned. Victor is fighting for his life and if he makes it, he might go to prison for something he didn't do." Kristian placed her head on her mother's shoulder once again before laying it in her lap. Seconds later, she felt her mother's hands in her hair. Her soft strokes calmed her, almost putting her to sleep, until the sound of footsteps forced her eyes open. She sat up straight only to see Akaila and Malachi running in her room. Before she could get off the bed, they were already on top of her. She became trapped underneath them as they held on to her for dear life.

Carmen, on the other hand, sat there quietly, not interrupting until Malachi and Akaila gave her the same embrace. That moment of having them in her arms reminded her of how things were going to change once Kristian moved out. Not wanting to be the one to tell them, after she had caught up with them, she excused herself from the room. Although it wouldn't affect Malachi, Akaila would most definitely feel alone. If she decided to move in with Kane, too, Carmen wouldn't take it personal. She knew Akaila wanted to be with her sister. One of many changes, Carmen told herself to tackle the issue once it came.

27

Daybreak

It was never Carmen's expectation for things to immediately go back to normal. However, the last thing she expected was to wake up alone. Typically, Jay would be asleep beside her until her movements caused him to stir. Somewhat surprised he wasn't there; she sat up in bed and listened for him. Not hearing any sounds, she grabbed her phone and checked for unread messages. A few were there, majority from Tiara and her receptionist, Cathy, but none from Jay. Unsure of where he had gone, she quickly texted him.

Jay, in fact, was only about fifteen minutes away, at Old Town Bistro. He saw Carmen's text less than a minute after she sent it, replying with a short message that he was meeting King for breakfast. A spur of the moment get-together, Jay left the house quietly, trying his best not to disturb her. His plan was to tell her once he got to the restaurant, but she beat him to the punch. Since she knew where he was, he changed his ringer to silent so there wouldn't be any interruptions. It wasn't every day his oldest son invited him to breakfast so it was his intention to use the time to mend their relationship.

Ready to put the plan in motion, he watched as King approached the table, a stack of papers in his hand. He was dressed to the nines while Jay was wearing a pair of old wrinkled maroon slacks and a dingy white button-up. Not his usual attire, he had plans after breakfast, which King would soon learn about. Before he shared any details, he had to question King about the papers. "I really didn't want to discuss business," he admitted once King sat down.

King moved the documents to his lap because he didn't want his father to see the papers. He also didn't greet him, immediately ordering a glass of orange juice and water from their waiter. Once the waiter was gone, he set an ink pen in front of his father. A confused look flew across Jay's face and when King saw it, he set the papers in the middle of the table. "Good morning," he greeted, finally addressing him. "You don't look good."

Jay looked at his clothes, but decided to ignore the comment. He was dressed in his worst for a reason. A reason he was going to soon share after he examined the papers sitting in front of him. "Well, you look like a king," he joked, admiring King's suit. "And like a king, you got something up your sleeve. What's this?" he asked.

"This," King began, "is an agreement, which needs your signature. For the past two years, you've given me full creative control over Sapphire and I've been managing the place. Now, I want full ownership. In fact, I deserve it. The majority of your focus has always been Blue Magic and Iceland so I'm asking for 100 percent of the club."

For the first time in days, Jay chuckled loudly. King's proposition wasn't exactly humorous, but the way he delivered it was. He sounded so sure of himself like he knew it was that easy to waltz in, sit down at a table, and demand a business. "You stopped smoking weed a while ago. What are you smoking now?"

"I'm not smoking anything. I'm breaking my ties to you, but I'm taking Sapphire with me. So instead of leaving with nothing, I'm leaving with something. Something I've worked hard for and deserve."

"Are you going to change your last name, too?"

King was taken aback at the question so he didn't respond.

"You made this same threat almost two weeks ago when I told you I didn't have anyone watching the girls in Georgia. You want to break ties with me, but you still want to walk these streets as a Santiago. Any son of mine who doesn't want to work for me, with me, or beside me, will not be wearing my name."

"You made me a Santiago."

"I did and from the looks of things, ten seconds of intense pleasure gave me twenty years of complete hell. Well, let's say three; I didn't meet you until you were seventeen."

Jay met eyes with King and automatically the guilt hit. While he was hurt by the reason his son wanted to meet with him, he didn't have to stoop to his level. "I didn't mean that," he quickly said. "I really didn't. Look, King, we have our differences, but this is taking it too far. I know you threatened to do this before, but we can work this out. Tell me what the problem is."

The waiter hadn't returned with his drinks, which was a good thing because they needed privacy. "I don't want to work for you anymore," King replied. "That is the problem. I also want Sapphire so I need you to sign these papers. Once you do, that will be the solution."

"Jayceon, I'm asking you…" Jay paused for a bit. He caught himself using King's first name, something he did whenever things got intense between them. "No, I'm begging you. Tell me what the problem is. Is it Rico? I can't bring back the dead. Is it Kristian? I take full responsibility for that and I've apologized to her personally. What is it?"

"You're selfish," King replied. "Everything you do and the choices you make revolve around two things—my mom and diamonds. Those are the only things you love. Everything else is a fuckin' bonus."

"Fuck you."

King smirked at the response. "Sign the papers so I can go on about my day. I will continue everything as normal as far as merging Blue Magic into the club. We will handle that move like business partners, contracts and all, but I need to officially own Sapphire."

"I do love your mother and I do love diamonds," Jay said, overlooking King's request. "I would never lie about that, but to say everything else is a bonus? You're not a bonus. You're my son. I love you more than you could *ever* hate me. Even now, as you sit up here and try to take your grandfather's business from me, I still love you. I love Rakim and Nyla, too. I love you all equally. I even love the baby your mama lost."

"Sign the papers."

"I have Blu's body," Jay announced, speaking low. "He's at Jimenez where we always conduct business. I'll give you some time with him. Just don't cut off his head. That's my job."

King's face scrunched up in disgust. "This is the shit I'm talking about. He's already dead. You don't need to chop off his limbs. Send his ass to Georgia and let his mama bury him."

"Too late," Jay replied, standing from his seat. He dropped his cloth napkin on top of the papers only for King to move it.

"Sign the papers," his son ordered.

Jay stared at his son hard before looking at the unsigned agreement. Instead of picking up the ink pen in front of him, he reached in his pocket, hoping his Swiss army knife was inside. He wanted to slash the papers right down the middle, but his hand was only wrapping around a cigar and lighter. An old pair of pants, he obviously hadn't washed, he pulled out the lighter and immediately lit the papers. The move caught King by surprise and he watched as his son jumped from the table. After the papers were destroyed, Jay tossed several hundred dollar bills on his chair for the damage he caused. His anger was building and he knew if he didn't leave, he was liable to do more.

A large part of him was embarrassed. He had come to the restaurant with the expectation to have a decent father and son breakfast. Something he now believed would never happen. He was also ready to have his entire will changed. King was set to inherit everything he had and now he no longer wanted him to. While he would always have money set aside for his children, King didn't have to own his empire.

"Unlock the doors," he yelled, startling Linx who was staring at his phone. He reached for the back door only to have it open for him. Roman stepped out, reminding him he had accompanied him to the restaurant. His presence made him think of Gully who was busy getting settled in his apartment. His cousin had expressed a desire to meet King, which Jay had originally planned on doing some time that day. Now, the idea was scrapped. At the moment, all he wanted to do was unleash. Remembering Blu, he ordered Linx to drive him to Jimenez Funeral Home.

No one spoke to him during the ride as if they knew something was wrong. Jay appreciated the silence even when he walked in the mortuary. Linx and Roman came inside with him, both remaining at the door while he walked to Blu's body. His remains were covered with a white sheet, which one of the morticians lifted off once he was in front of the corpse. Blu was completely naked, his body already changing colors and giving off a foul odor.

"Machete," Valdez, one of the morticians said, offering him his usual knife of choice.

Jay grabbed the knife from him, but he didn't strike Blu just yet. He allowed the weapon to hang at his side for a bit as he studied the man's face. In particular, he focused on the two bullet holes in his forehead. He tried to envision what it looked like when Carmen pulled the trigger. It played in his mind almost like a movie in slow motion. He assumed his fiancée felt the same form of relief he was about to feel when the first bullet struck him. "If only I had been witness," he whispered. He quickly raised the machete and brought it down hard onto Blu's neck. Once his head was severed, he felt someone near him.

"Cajas," Valdez whispered in his ear, dropping several boxes at his feet. "We have plenty more in the back. Just let me know if you need 'em."

Jay nodded his head. His plan was to deliver a box a day to Blu's mother until she had his whole body in her living room. It would take only days for someone to put him together, if that were her choice, while the rape would affect Kristian for a lifetime.

The whole process took almost two hours and he didn't leave the funeral home until the last box was loaded on a truck headed to Georgia. Once everything was squared away, he instructed Linx to head to his apartment so he could change clothes. Carmen had seen enough blood so he knew not to come home in his current state.

Thankfully, everything worked in his favor and when he returned home, the kids were still asleep and Carmen was in her bathrobe. Not wanting to start the conversation with news about Blu, he walked in the closet where she was standing and wrapped his arms around her. He hadn't forgotten about the miscarriage despite what had occurred that morning.

"How long do we have to wait until we can try again?" he whispered.

Carmen didn't mean to break Jay's grasp, but when she turned around, his arms naturally fell from her waist. "I have to go through another menstrual cycle," she replied. She faced him so she could see his reaction yet his facial expression didn't change. Since it didn't, she decided to change the topic of the conversation. "I got two phone calls while you were out."

Jay sucked his teeth only because he knew one of them was from King. "I set the table on fire," he admitted. "He made me look like a fool out there."

Carmen put both hands on her hips only because she hoped Jay had seen the error of his ways. His bluntness proved to her he didn't feel the least bit guilty. She believed King was wrong for what he did, but she also believed Jay was wrong in the way he retaliated. "You're not like most men, Jay. Most men would walk away, curse, maybe even tear up the papers, but you set the table on *fire*. That was a bit much."

"King asking me for Sapphire was a bit much. He can't inherit the club until I die. It's a tradition that started with my father that I plan on continuing."

"Well, this is my plan," Carmen began, dropping her arms at her side. "I'm setting up an appointment with you, King, and Dr. Stuart. All three of you need to sit down together and get this worked out. I can't be the mediator between you two anymore. I tried, it didn't work. Y'all need professional help. Setting tables on fire in public is not going to fix this relationship."

Jay rolled his eyes because for the last couple of months he had been skipping his appointments with Dr. Stuart. He had made tremendous progress so she had given him a pass. He wasn't against going back, but he knew King wouldn't be thrilled about the idea. However, if he agreed to it, he would be there.

"I also got a call from Clement. Kane's lawyer has been in contact with him. We're having mediation in a couple of days. It shouldn't take long because Kane already agreed to give me whatever I want. The reason I'm telling you, though, is because we need to start planning our wedding. It won't be until next year, but we need to get serious about it."

"Whatever you want," Jay replied, wrapping his arms around her again.

"Oh, and while we're on the subject of my ex, he found the logo for *Production* in my basement. Are you responsible for that?"

Jay snickered because his plan had worked. "It was a last minute idea so he would know you were working on something down there. It was just something to throw him off."

Carmen grunted because she didn't have time or even an interest to go through with the idea. The logo on her basement floor would be the farthest a *Production* collection would go.

"It was just something I did," Jay continued. "To tell you the truth, what I really want to discuss is this whole counseling thing. You're requiring me and King to go, but have you started setting up sessions for Kristian?"

Carmen placed both hands on Jay's chest to show him she needed support. "Well, I called her this morning. She said she wants Kane to handle it. I'm trying to be there for her, but every time I make a suggestion, she either says Kane is taking care of it or he will."

"She'll come around," Jay murmured. "Sometimes, she can be just like her brother. Maybe it's because they're getting older. They want to take charge of everything and think they have all the answers. We were probably like that at one point."

Carmen looked at Jay at the mention of the words, "getting older." The phrase made her think of Gully, which reminded her of something she had been meaning to ask him. "When I was with Gully," she began, changing the subject, "he told me you killed his bitch, his words, not mine. He said that was the reason he hadn't spoken to you in a number of years. Is it true?"

A sense of agitation came over Jay because he knew Gully had tricked Carmen. While the accusation wasn't a complete lie, Gully had withheld pertinent information. In a way, his cousin's word play was somewhat humorous.

"You think it's funny?" Carmen asked, noticing the grin.

Jay pulled Carmen closer to him so they were chest to chest. "I bet Gully has been telling that same story for the past thirty years." Jay shook his head as he started to correct Gully's lies. "One summer, Gully and I were at my house in San Juan. Our parents were away at an event so Silvas was watching us, but he was in the house and we were outside. Somehow we got a hold of one of my father's guns. We were taking turns shooting and long story short, I accidentally shot Gully's bulldog, Samantha, in the neck. She actually got shot trying to run from all the noise."

Carmen broke her hold only because she was confused. "You shot his dog?"

"Just like me, Gully, is an only child. Samantha was his best friend. After that day, I was the worst person known to man. I was his enemy. He held a grudge for a very long time. He probably still hates me because of it."

Jay smiled at the look of confusion on Carmen's face. "So that bitch he says I killed was his dog." A small chuckle escaped Jay's lips because Carmen's mouth was still wide open. "I already know why you're looking at me like that, Peaches. You thought I actually killed somebody. I didn't intentionally shoot the dog. I fired the gun and she ran in the bullet's direction. My father offered to get him a new one, a top breed, but he wanted Samantha."

Carmen wanted to laugh yet she felt it would show her insensitivity. She knew people were close to their pets and from the way Jay told the story, Gully was no different. It just surprised her to know the accident kept him away from his cousin for more than thirty years. "Well," she added, wrapping her arms around him, "at least you two are on speaking terms."

"We actually live together." Jay neared his face to hers wanting a kiss yet she quickly pulled away. Somewhat surprised, he looked at her strangely until he noticed she wasn't looking at him. When he turned around, he rolled his eyes to see her mother in their bedroom. A woman who was on his hit list, he was waiting for the day Carmen gave him permission to take her out.

"Oh, don't mind me," she said, walking closer to them. "Don't let me hold you up from making another bastard child."

Jay took a step forward only for Carmen to grab his arm. He knew she was advising him to stay put, but it would be hard to do the longer her mother was in his presence. Her comment was out of line considering they were still dealing with the miscarriage. Even if they weren't, she had no right to call her grandchildren bastards.

"I didn't even know you were expecting a baby."

Carmen remained quiet only because she didn't want to give her mother any fuel. She was already being disrespectful, which would further infuriate Jay and create an even bigger problem. By remaining silent, Carmen was hoping her mother would leave her room or better yet, her house. Now that her father was gone, her mother was more than capable of living on her own. She had inherited most of her father's estate, which was valued at millions.

"I guess I wasn't supposed to know," her mother continued.

Carmen tightened her grip on Jay's arm only because she didn't want him to move. If he stayed put and she did the talking, there was a greater chance of her mother leaving them alone. "It wasn't a secret. I found out I was pregnant the day before I had the miscarriage."

"Well, I'm sorry it happened. Even though the conception was wrong, it's still a child."

Carmen stepped in between Jay and her mother the second she felt resistance from him. Her mother appeared not to have noticed or maybe she didn't care because she simply turned around and left the room. Carmen breathed a sigh of relief only because she knew it was a close call. "I swear she's getting worse."

"She needs to get her own place," Jay blurted, walking past her so he could close their door. "She's a fuckin' millionaire. She needs to live in her own got damn house."

Carmen ran her fingers through her hair only because she knew she was going to have to give her mother an ultimatum. She couldn't stay in her house and be disrespectful. She also couldn't be in the house once she and Jay got married. If she was, Carmen swore she would build a new wing just so she wouldn't have to deal with her.

"There's something else I need to tell you about Gully."

Carmen raised her brow only because she thought their discussion on his cousin was over. Since Jay brought him up again, there was obviously something she needed to know. "Go ahead," she urged, noticing his silence.

"This is between me and you, okay?"

Carmen held up her pinky finger sarcastically only for Jay to walk towards her and link it with his. "Are we really doing this right now?" Carmen laughed until she saw how serious he was. "We are doing this right now. I'm not going to tell anyone. Just tell me what it is."

"My cousin is gay."

Carmen's eyes bulged only because she couldn't picture Gully, a tough as nails, rugged, stone cold killer as a gay male. Nothing about him screamed gay yet for Jay to say it, she knew it had to be true. She was practically speechless as she tried to recall every interaction she had with him. She could picture almost each one and nothing about Gully made her think he was gay.

"Yes, he's ruthless, a trained to go killer, but he's also gay. I figured it out when we were kids. I liked looking at ass and breasts, which bored him. Then, one day, he made a comment about a man he wouldn't have been making if he liked girls. One night, I overheard my uncle talking to my father about him. Gully had come out and he wasn't taking it too well. From what I heard, my uncle made Gully swear he wouldn't act on his feelings. Basically, he can be gay, he just can't act gay or do the things gays do."

"Are you okay with it?" Carmen asked, not sure if Jay was homophobic.

"I love my cousin. I want to see him happy. What I don't want is for Linx, Roman, or even Cesar to feel a certain type of way about him. You know how ignorant people can be."

Carmen walked up to Jay, staring directly into his hazel eyes. He had said a lot and she wondered if he even caught what he said. From the way he was looking at her, somewhat questionably, she knew he hadn't caught it. "Where is Cesar, Jay? Isn't he supposed to be dead?"

Jay parted his lips as he tried to remember his words.

"You said Cesar's name. I heard you. Where is he?" When Jay didn't respond, Carmen grabbed his chin only for him to pull her hand away from his face. "You led me to believe he was dead. Now you're telling me he's not? Where is he, Jay?"

It was never Jay's intention to tell her Cesar was still alive. Since he had slipped up, he now had to tell the truth. "He could be in several places. He even could be in the house."

Carmen felt a certain type of way because he lied yet she was also relieved because it was only a lie. What Cesar had done didn't warrant him losing his life. "I want to see him."

"You can't see him," Jay replied. "I made him a ghost. He came up with this idea for me to hire a new security team. It'll be a team of men who work for me that no one knows about. If you see Cesar then something happened we couldn't control. If he gets caught in this city, they'll arrest him. Luckily, right now, he's not their concern, I am. All I need right now is for Gomez to give me a court date. Then, once the trial is over, I'll go off their radar."

"We all need court dates," Carmen stressed, thinking of her own conspiracy charge. She separated herself from Jay, going in her closet again so she could pick out something to wear. Not yet ready to go to work, her plan was to stay at home until things settled down. She wouldn't put a timeframe on it, but she would know when she was ready. For now, she would focus on being a mother and fiancée.

28

Grand Opening

Four Months Later

Due to the change in seasons, the sky was extremely dark despite it being barely seven o'clock. However, the corner of 34th and Pendleton was well lit due to the numerous limousines, cameras, and ecstatic civilians. The grand opening of Blue Magic was the talk of the town. For the past ten minutes, Carmen had been watching the spectacle from the backseat of Jay's limo. Although the area was chaotic, security was able to control the crowd who were trying to fight their way inside. Seating was provided on a first come, first serve basis while the restaurant's private banquet hall was reserved for family, friends, and colleagues.

According to Gomez, the purpose of the grand opening was to help change the public's perception of Jay. He stressed the importance of people seeing him as a family man, one who was harmless, but lived to protect his own. Nevertheless, what had been shown to the world was a person who was the exact opposite. Now time to put it to the test, when Roman opened the back door, everything was taken to the next level. Voices were louder, lights were brighter, the combination of it all causing Carmen's adrenaline to increase. She stepped out the limo, hand in hand with Jay only to face the paparazzi who were snapping as many photos as they could.

She could feel the sweat in Jay's palm, a result of his nervousness, which led her to look at him. He was rather pokerfaced, not used to the cameras being directly in front of him although he was a staple on the local news. Carmen gave his hand a slight squeeze, which caught his attention. When they met eyes, she smiled, but instead of him returning the gesture, he placed a small kiss on her cheek. Only a peck, Carmen knew the move was a major photo-op. The show of support was what he needed because he immediately led the way to the red carpet.

Carmen replayed Gomez's words in her head as they passed several paps. He had asked her to keep all news regarding Flame at bay, instructing her to stand there and look pretty. As a fashion designer, the latter she could do easily. For the grand opening she had designed a dress completely made of carnelian lace, which stopped mid-thigh and was slightly see through.

Paired with a nude Christian Louboutin pump, Carmen knew she had the 'look pretty' part down pack.

When it came to Jay, she styled him in a classic black tuxedo, courtesy of the *King* collection. It was accentuated with a bright red bowtie and a handkerchief of the same color. On his feet was a pair of Christian Louboutin shoes as well, the Joey Flat design, which she handpicked specifically for him due to the fire red sole. Black diamond cufflinks were on his sleeves, a shameless plug for Iceland.

"Tonight is all about positivity," Jay had said while they were getting dressed. "Now that we're going to trial, everything with the shooting will be handled. Tonight, I want to celebrate this milestone. Then, in January, we'll celebrate Iceland."

Indeed, we will, Carmen thought as she stepped inside Blue Magic. The general dining room appeared to be filled to capacity. The private banquet room, located on the first floor, had been reserved specifically for them and VIP guests. Overly spacious, the majority of their friends and family were already seated inside except her mother who refused to come.

When Carmen walked in, the first person she noticed was Gully. Two empty seats were to the right of him, which were reserved for her and Jay. The heads of the table were also empty, marked specifically for Roman and Linx in the event anything popped off.

"The first three bottles are on me," Malik announced once they were seated. "This doesn't give y'all a pass, though," he added with a laugh, pointing at Kristian and Akaila who were across from him. "The last thing we want is to get shut down 'cuz of underage drinking."

His comment prompted Carmen to look in their direction. It was then she realized Kane hadn't showed. A seat was reserved for him, along with a plus one if needed, although it was against Jay's wishes. Kane's invitation was simply a compromise between them and Kristian to get her to come. As Gomez constantly reminded them, the plan was to show Jay in a positive light and for the world to see them as one big happy family. While they didn't have to speak to each other, they could at least appear cordial.

"Where's your father?" Carmen asked, looking in Kristian's direction.

Kristian shrugged her shoulders only because she hadn't seen her father since earlier that morning. She had spent the majority of her time away from home with Akaila as they got glammed up for the event. "He said he was coming. I thought he was sitting with Coco's parents, but that end of the table is full." Kristian pointed in the direction of her best friend's parents who were seated across from King and Coco.

Naturally, Carmen's eyes went in that direction. A waiter was standing there, collecting drink orders, so she turned her attention to Kristian. When she did, she noticed Kane, who was walking towards their table. He wasn't alone, having used the plus one he was given. This was only the second time she had actually seen him with another woman so her heart dropped. She tried not to let it show on her face, but it was hard. Automatically, she sized up his date, becoming envious. She even resented her dress, a strapless green fishtail gown designed by the late Oscar de la Renta.

Continuing to stare at her, Carmen studied her flawless makeup and plump lips until she felt Jay's hand on her thigh. Before he could say anything, she felt the temperature increase to two hundred degrees as she recognized Kane's date. She pushed her chair back, preparing to get up, only for Jay to grab her arm.

"Not right now," he told her as their eyes met. "Tonight is too important."

Carmen glared at him as she tried to come to grips with what Kane was doing. His date, Monifah Harris, was a woman who she and Tiara both had history with. They were close friends in college until Monifah's boyfriend, Rakim, died in her arms. Monifah hated Carmen for having that moment, left town, and was never heard from again. Somehow, Kane had linked up with her and brought her as his date to the opening of her restaurant.

"Did you know about this?" Carmen asked the question because of Jay's calm nature. She was certain he would've been just as shocked as she was since no one had heard from Monifah in more than twenty years. When he didn't answer, Carmen knew Monifah's appearance was of no surprise to him. "You did, didn't you?"

"We're not going to do this right now, Peaches," he whispered. "We have a restaurant filled with spectators who want us to fail. They want to see us fighting. We also have the first course about to come out. We're supposed to be focusing on positivity, remember?"

Carmen's face tightened only because Jay was intentionally withholding information. "Tell me," she begged. "Did you know? Don't lie to me."

Jay let out a small sigh only because he knew Carmen wasn't going to let up. "She came to San Juan. She's a psychiatrist in Dr. Stuart's office. According to Silvas, she wants to take me on as a client. I never got in touch with her because of all the stuff that happened with Kristian. To be honest, I forgot about her. And, just so you know, I never planned on talking to her."

Carmen rested her arms on the table as her anger intensified. Monifah and Kane were now at the table, her ex pulling out Monifah's chair like a true gentleman. Monifah's presence automatically caused commotion as Malik and Tiara recognized who she was. Now the main topic of the table, Carmen turned to Jay. In the process, she met eyes with Kane. She expected to see an evil grin on his face; however, he had the opposite. In fact, his face was the same as hers, hurt and confused. He looked at her for only a second or two before turning to Monifah.

"I don't think he knew," she heard Jay say.

Carmen couldn't hear the conversation, but Kane's facial expression told her something was wrong. When she saw him cover his face, she knew he had been tricked. Monifah was rubbing his shoulder as she explained things, but Kane wasn't buying it. In a way, Carmen felt sorry for him. Aside from that, she also felt guilty. *How can I cause a scene when I'm sitting here engaged? I've always encouraged Kane to move on with his life. Whether he's with Monifah or Vivica A. Fox, it doesn't matter. I'm not going to break up with Jay to be with him.* At that moment, Carmen started to come to grips with the situation. Nevertheless, when Kane left the table, she got up as well so she could speak to him.

The entire restaurant was packed so there was little to no privacy. Carmen could tell Kane was looking for a quiet place to vent when he opened the door to the concierge closet. "We need to talk," she told him.

"Do I look like I want to talk right now?" he shot back. He closed the door to the closet, not bothering to go inside.

"I didn't do this to you," Carmen replied, seeing his anger. "I didn't bring her here."

"Oh, so this is my fault?" Kane yelled. "Just my luck, I meet a girl at a bar, start dating her, only to find out she's been lying to me from day one. This shit is crazy, Carm. I didn't bring her here so I could find out some shit like this. All I wanted was to introduce y'all to the woman I'm falling in love with. Now, I look like a damn fool." Kane paced the floor as he talked, their discussion starting to attract attention. "She told me her name was Jean Monet," he explained, "She was from Florida, new to the area, and trying to get a job. She didn't say shit about being your best friend."

"I'm sorry this happened to you." Carmen took a deep breath only because she could see how bothered he was. Monifah had lied to him on purpose because she knew he wouldn't have dated her if he knew their connection. "Look, Kane," she began, grabbing his arm. "We're going to have to make the best of this sit—"

"Carmen," a voice said from behind.

Without even turning around, Carmen knew Monifah was behind her. Ready to deal with her in a civil manner, she slowly faced her. "Welcome to Brookstone," she greeted, warmly. "I see you've made yourself at home … again." When Monifah parted her lips, Carmen interrupted her. "I think we all can agree that this is not the time or the place for this. We will deal with this later, much later. For now, let's enjoy dinner. I mean, it is your first time eating at one of Brookstone's finest establishments, right?"

Deep down, Monifah was wearing a scowl, which she didn't allow Carmen to see. Instead, she gave her the same warm smile she received. When Carmen's expression didn't change, she turned to Kane. She could tell he was still upset from the way he looked at her. He had every right to be even though she apologized. Not to mention, she tried to throw the blame on him by saying he never gave her the chance to tell him. The truth of the matter was she never planned on telling him until a moment like such occurred. Now, the moment was here, and everything was out in the open.

"I think we're done here," Carmen said, interrupting Monifah's thoughts. She looked at Kane who appeared to still be seething. "Take the time you need. These things aren't easy."

To Kane, time wasn't something he felt he needed. If anything, he wanted a brick. A brick he could use to smash Jean's face in. *Shit, that's not even her name,* he remembered. *Her name is Monifah, Monifah Harris, the bitch lied about everything.* He stared at her, not wanting to even be associated with her. However, he only had two options. He could deal with her and stay at the event or he could go home. If he chose the second option, he would've wasted the money he spent on his suit and the car service.

"Can we just make the best of it?"

Kane didn't reply to Monifah although he had made his decision. He simply headed to his seat without a word to her. Monifah joined him shortly thereafter just as the first course was being served. He didn't look at her, turning his attention to Malik and Tiara who appeared uneasy. For all Kane knew, the whole table was probably uncomfortable.

Carmen returned to the table only to be faced with questions from Kristian and Akaila. Both her daughters were curious to know who their father's date was, claiming they never met her. Not wanting to get in a full blown discussion, Carmen quickly told them she was an old family friend. They accepted the answer although they started to talk amongst themselves about their father's girlfriend. Carmen didn't want any parts of the conversation so she drowned them out hoping they would dead the subject.

Eventually they did, but it wasn't until two waiters approached the table with the evening's appetizers. Two large bowls of Blue Magic's classic seven-layer house salad were set at each end of the table along with baskets of honey biscuits. Seconds later, two more waiters appeared, each carrying a tray of vegetable soup. With food on the table, it helped to ease the tension as everyone's mind went to eating. Nevertheless, the silence was only short-lived.

Although their table was nearly full, Carmen didn't notice Nicholas was missing until he walked in the room. He was styled in a grey Sean John Pindot suit, his attire almost identical to King's. He wore a suit well, having his own unique swag, which gave her the idea of having him model for the *King* collection. Unfortunately, the thought left her when he approached the table. As a result, Akaila excused herself. Nicholas tried to say something to her, but she only brushed him off. He tried a second time, his words inaudible until he finally gave up.

Carmen tapped the table to get Kristian's attention until she saw Nicholas sit in Akaila's seat. She wanted Kristian to check on her sister yet Nicholas spoke before she could get a word out.

"Victor Fontaine made bail an hour ago," he announced, speaking directly to Kristian. "I came to share the news. I know you have a soft spot for him." When he didn't get a response, he thought for a moment she was offended. He knew she had feelings for Victor even if she had never told him personally. "So you're not speaking to me either?"

"How are things at Sapphire?" Jay asked, trying to steer his attention.

"Good," Nicholas responded. He looked at Jay for a brief second before turning to Kristian. "I see Dijuan's parents are here. He didn't come?" More seconds of silence passed. "Well, are y'all still together?" he asked, speaking of Kristian's boyfriend. He watched as Kristian continued to ignore him. "Okay," he continued. "I see how you're going to be. I guess it's your lucky night. You don't want to talk and I need to get to the club."

"Don't let me hold you up," Kristian said, finally speaking.

Nicholas was taken aback, but he didn't say anything. Well, at least not to Kristian. He turned to Jay and told him everything was set to go with Sapphire. "The bar is well stocked, DJs are on deck, security is in place," he told him. "It's going to be a packed house."

"That's what I want to hear," Jay replied. "Make sure the money is right, too."

Nicholas held out his hand to Jay as a sign they were on the same page. They shook hands only once before Nicholas excused himself. Akaila still hadn't returned so Carmen sent Kristian after her. Her daughter was barely out the room before Jay voiced his thoughts.

"They've messed around," he said, picking up a bottle of Rosé.

"I don't want to believe that," Carmen began. While she didn't want to accept that Blu had taken her daughter's virginity, medical evidence said he had. If Kristian had been with Nicholas, her body didn't show any signs of it. "Maybe they kissed or something," she added. Carmen inhaled as she picked up her own empty wine glass. She handed it to Jay who poured her a glass of the tequila-flavored liqueur. "If he's supposed to be working at Sapphire, why did he come all the way over here to talk about Victor?"

"He wanted to know if she was going to give him a chance," Gully stated. "Kristian has been whining about Victor ever since she got out that basement. It got worse when he was released from the hospital. Shit, only to go straight to jail." Gully had been listening to the entire conversation although he was quiet while Nicholas was there. "You were right all along," he told Carmen, "Something happened between them, which he wants to rekindle. Kristian doesn't want any parts of him, though."

"Some things we don't need to discuss," King blurted. He knew he could end the speculation if he simply told them they had a fling. Since it was something that happened years ago, he felt it needed to stay in the past. He wanted to sweep the whole thing under the rug because he would never let Nicholas get close to his sisters again. "Let it go and let's enjoy the night. We did all that talk about Blu and Victor months ago. We're moving past that. We're healing from it. Right now, we're back on top. Let's celebrate that."

Jay raised his glass at his son's words. His spiel seemed to get everyone's mind where it needed to be. Even when Akaila and Kristian returned, right when the main course was being served, no mention was made of Nicholas or Victor. So much was weighing on the night; they didn't need to let anything shift the focus. For one, negative attention impacted more than the business since Blue Magic was heavily connected to his trial. While he did have an agreement in place to ensure his freedom, it didn't automatically give him a not guilty verdict. He still had to cut through the red tape before he could walk the streets as a free man.

Certain everything was going to work in his favor, he decided to voice it. Dessert was now being served, but he didn't let it stop him from speaking his mind. With the bottles steadily flowing, he asked everyone to grab a glass.

"Some of y'all weren't even born when I relit the match on the Santiago name," he began. "Most people don't know, but when I first started, all I had was a little bit of ambition and a butler. My father's businesses weren't in my control because I was too young to handle it. Once I graduated high school, I started educating myself on entrepreneurship and took control of what was rightfully mine. Then, I conquered the drug game. I was the King of New York and no one even knew I existed. I stayed in the shadows despite the moves I made.

"Then, all hell broke loose." He paused for a bit only because it was the first time he was publicly addressing his imprisonment. "Everything was stripped of me. I lost my best friend, my girl, my businesses went down, and I lost my son. I lost my faith in that cell. Then one day, I got the opportunity to regain it. That day is just like today. We're sitting here eating the best food and drinking some of the best wine this country has to offer. We're with the people we love and even some we hate. Life isn't always going to be like this. I know because it wasn't. Sometimes we have to remember where we were so we can stay focused on where we're going."

Jay peered at Carmen whose eyes were on him. Her right hand was around her glass, which he grabbed, wanting her to stand by his side. "Reopening Blue Magic is all about rebirth. That is what we're celebrating. I think we all can agree that this has been a long time coming. So tonight, I want to propose a toast to success, love, and the start of a new life. It's something we all can drink to."

Jay raised his glass with his right hand and in true fashion, the others followed. He took a long sip of his drink and once he was done, he set the glass on the table. His left hand was still intertwined with Carmen's, an embrace he didn't want to let go. Deep down, Jay knew the grand opening of Blue Magic was the start of something bigger. Once Carmen took his last name, everything she touched would have Santiago on it. Their success would prove to the naysayers that they were more powerful together than apart. He already knew Carmen believed it, and in due time, the rest of the world would believe it, too.

Next: Diamonds N' Roses

www.ingramcontent.com/pod-product-compliance
Lightning Source LLC
Chambersburg PA
CBHW031411250626
47155CB00004B/1492

9780988800441